CW00765896

Murmurations

An Anthology of Uncanny Stories About Birds

EDITED BY

NICHOLAS ROYLE

TWO RAVENS PRESS

Published by Two Ravens Press Ltd.
Taigh nam Fitheach
26 Breanish, Uig
Isle of Lewis HS2 9HB
United Kingdom

www.tworavenspress.com

ISBN: 978-1-906120-59-7

British Library Cataloguing in Publication Data: a CIP record for this book can be obtained from the British Library.

Designed and typeset in Sabon by Two Ravens Press.

Cover image 'Starling *Sturnus vulgaris* flock or "murmuration" above Ham Wall RSPB Reserve, Somerset UK, winter'
© Mark Bretherton I Alamy.
Cover design by Two Ravens Press.

Frontispiece: image of ravens © Sally Titterington
(http://sallytitterington.blogspot.com)

Printed in Poland on
Forest Stewardship Council-accredited paper.

About the editor

Nicholas Royle is the author of a short story collection – *Mortality* – as well as two novellas and six novels. He has edited fourteen previous anthologies including the British Fantasy Award-winning *Darklands*, the bestselling *A Book of Two Halves* and *The Best British Short Stories 2011*. A fiction reviewer for the *Independent* and the *Warwick Review*, and a senior lecturer in creative writing at Manchester Metropolitan University, he also runs Nightjar Press, publishing original short stories as signed, limited-edition chapbooks. Forthcoming from No Exit Press is a second collection of his short stories, *London Labyrinth*.

Thanks

The editor wishes to thank Kate Ryan; Rosie Harvey, Sharon Ring and Lynn Townsend; Adam Marek and Clare Wigfall; John Fanshawe of BirdLife International; Doug Christie, Paul Lewis and Bryan Bland of the RSPB; Angelica Michelis of Manchester Metropolitan University; Sharon Blackie and David Knowles of Two Ravens Press; John Oakey of johnoakeydesign.co.uk; Sarah Lewis of Curtis Brown; Simon Smith of Peter Owen Ltd; Mike Harding of Touch; Michael Moorcock; Deborah Kermode and Sally Titterington.

Sally Titterington wishes to thank the Booth Museum of Natural History.

Contents

For my sisters, Julie and Joanna,
birdwatchers both

Foreword
Angelica Michelis

In ETA Hoffmann's tale 'The Sand-Man' (1816) the main character, Nathaniel, is introduced to the reader via his childhood memories, which centre on the fantastic figure of the Sand-Man, used as a threat by his mother to get the children to go to bed. Intrigued by the mysterious Sand-Man, Nathaniel presses his mother in vain for more information. Eventually, his sister's old nurse divulges further details:

> *'Oh! he's a wicked man, who comes to little children when they won't go to bed and throws handfuls of sand in their eyes, so that they jump out of their heads all bloody; and he puts them into a bag and takes them to the half-moon as food for his little ones; and they sit there in the nest and have hooked beaks like owls, and they pick naughty little boys' and girls' eyes out with them.'*

This gruesome little story marks the beginning of a trauma that will haunt Nathaniel throughout his life and will eventually lead to his suicide. The compelling image of the Sand-Man's children feasting on the eyes of naughty little boys and girls with their 'hooked beaks like owls' indicates the only appearance of birds in a tale that would re-emerge famously a century later at the centre of Sigmund Freud's essay on the aesthetic concept of the uncanny. Written in 1919, 'The Uncanny' explores and attempts to explain why certain images, things, events and situations arouse dread and horror, and a feeling of the uncanny (*unheimlich*, in German). In order to produce a psychoanalytically sound explanation Freud takes his readers on a journey through the German dictionary to uncover the various meanings of the word *heimlich*. In a truly intellectual *tour de force* Freud shows that the word is shot through by ambivalence, meaning originally: 'of the house', familiar, intimate and friendly and, at the same time, its opposite: secretive, hidden – *unheimlich*: 'Thus *heimlich* is a word the meaning of which develops in the direction of ambivalence, until it finally coincides with its opposite, *unheimlich*.' Trawling through the dictionary, Freud produces amongst many others the following entry:

> *'Of animals: tame, companionable to man. As opposed to wild, eg, 'Animals which are neither wild nor heimlich', etc. 'Wild animals … that are trained to be heimlich and accustomed to men.' 'If these young creatures are brought up from early days among men they become quite heimlich, friendly' etc – So also: 'It (the lamb) is so heimlich and eats out of my hand.' 'Nevertheless, the stork is a beautiful heimelich bird.'*

Once more, as in Hoffmann's story, the text introduces the image of a bird to provide an explanation and, again, as in the fictional tale, the bird features literally only at the margin of the essay's central meaning. However, being in the sphere of the uncanny it feels slightly unnerving that two narratives so intricately linked with each other should both ever so fleetingly and randomly refer to birds. Considering Freud's argument that *heimlich* is inhabited by its opposite, *unheimlich*, the image of the stork, used as an example for the familiar and known, might slowly but surely tip over into the dark side, teasing the reader's mind like an optical illusion. The ephemeral appearance of birds in the shape of the cruel owl-like offspring of 'The Sand-Man' and the *heimlich/unheimlich* stork (which, uncannily, is in folklore the bringer of babies) in Freud's essay hovers at the margins of these texts and by doing so contributes to the sense of uncertainty and eeriness at their centre.

Birds are everywhere. Their song greets us first thing in the morning, their arrival in spring lifts our heart and they are an integral part of the way in which we experience life on a daily basis. Often, they are so familiar that we don't notice them at all: birdsong can become nature's 'muzak' when we are wandering through the woods, and in our cities it is not unusual to see pigeons walking urban streets. And yet, for every innocent little feathered friend there is the dark presence of its menacing opposite. The dead body of a bird run over by a car and half-eaten by maggots turns into a modern-day *memento mori*. The sinister cackling of magpies and the haunting cry of a bird of prey at dusk lift the species out of their ordinariness and confront us with a fleeting flash of mystery in the middle of our mundane existence. Paintings, poems and literary texts often exploit the way in which birds inhabit the border between the mundane and the extraordinary when they use them to create feelings of fear and a sense of strangeness. Visual art provides many examples of the way in which birds can conjure up a ghost-like and haunting atmosphere that is difficult for the viewer to shrug off. *An Owl on a Bare Tree, Landscape with Grave, Coffin and Owl*, and *Owl in a Gothic Window*, all paintings by Caspar David Friedrich from the 1830s, confront the spectator with the majestic stillness of owls which, like exclamation marks, punctuate and accentuate the eerie atmosphere of the empty landscape which they inhabit. Francisco Goya's gothic and haunting paintings exhibit the predatory violence of vultures feasting on flesh, and present a human figure literally shrouded by owls in full flight in *The Sleep of Reason Produces Monsters*. In the painting *In Your Dreams*, Goya depicts ghostly human figures who like Icarus in the Greek myth can fly with the help of artificial wings. Whereas the figure at the centre of the painting clearly shows a human supported by a flying contraption, further away towards the margins of the image we see some monstrous creatures, neither human nor bird, a metamorphosis that indicates that the dream has turned into a nightmare. Although very different in style and theme, Friedrich's as well as Goya's paintings seem to sense something intrinsically uncanny in the very shape of the birds they depict. The perfect death-like stillness of Friedrich's owls and Goya's ghostly winged creatures draw the viewer into a world where every movement is frozen but, one feels, at any minute a terrifying storm could break loose.

This moment of tangible suspense also defines the terror at the centre of the most famous film about birds, Alfred Hitchcock's adaptation of Daphne du Maurier's short story 'The Birds', which is probably one of the most shocking visual examples of this strange metamorphosis of birds from the familiar to the terrifying. One minute we see birds sitting on a wire, a ubiquitous visual background foil of everyday life, and the next frame turns this image into an omen of horror and dread. What makes this scene so uncanny is the fact that one cannot really explain the change in mood, but the audience instinctively knows *something* definitely has changed, is different. What we see is the same but what we feel is different.

Not knowing the exact source of fear and not being able to recognise the precise moment when the familiar dissolves into its opposite are the two most potent contributing factors to an atmosphere of the uncanny. Bruce Gilbert in 'Sliding Off the World' captures this perfectly when the call of the cuckoo turns the innocent world of the little boy into a nightmare scenario:

his house (home/*heim*) transforms into a place that is foreign and strange to him and, worst of all, his mother, his saviour, sides with the force of evil, the cuckoo. The reader does not know *why* the cuckoo should have this uncanny effect on the boy, and it is precisely this absence of explanations and reasons that opens up the cornucopia of the unconscious and the world of the imagination. Furthermore, by linking the terrifying call of the cuckoo with the figure of the mother, the story emphasises what Freud regarded as one of the most central aspects of the uncanny: it 'constitutes that class of the frightening which leads back to what is known of old and long familiar'.

By turning the familiar into its opposite, locating the terror at the heart of the home and uncovering what is hidden in and by the fabric of the mundane, the effect of the uncanny questions the parameters of the very world we live in and take for granted. In Edgar Allan Poe's 'The Raven' (1845), the eponymous bird serves as a chilling reminder of the fact that there is – literally – no place like home. The raven, silently and menacingly, invades the narrator's study and refuses to confirm that there is such a thing as meaning by answering every question with an enigmatic 'Nevermore'. However, although the bird can be read as a symbol of despair, its refusal to provide an affirmative answer to the narrator's enquiries encourages the latter to question the very idea that there might be a given answer 'out there'. Meaning, the stoic presence of the bird seems to suggest, rather than residing in a positive and reassuring answer, comes into being via questions and doubts. It can only be understood as the process of attempting to make sense of the unknown and of re-viewing the seemingly familiar as something strange and unexpected. The earliest recorded use of 'uncanny' in the Oxford English Dictionary goes back to 1773 and defines the term as meaning 'not quite safe to trust to'. Birds, as the stories collected in this volume will remind the reader, can inexplicably turn from innocent songbirds to haunting creatures of darkness; they are our feathered friends and harbingers of doom. Can we trust them? Nevermore!

And the raven, never flitting, still is sitting, still is sitting
On the pallid bust of Pallas just above my chamber door;
And his eyes have all the seeming of a demon's that
is dreaming,
And the lamp-light o'er him streaming throws his shadow on
the floor;
And my soul from out that shadow that lies floating on
the floor
Shall be lifted – nevermore!

Swallows Sleep in Winter
Adam Marek

Sam cut a thick wedge from the loaf, taking care to stop before the curved teeth of the bread knife gnawed the edge of the plate.

'You'll not get your mouth round that,' Ted said.

'I've never been able to cut bread straight,' Sam said. 'One of my many disabilities.'

Ted batted away a wasp investigating the rim of the jam jar. 'It's because you were brought up with sliced bread. From packets.'

'You might be right. But then, how come Emma can't do it either?'

'Well, she used to be able to do it.'

'I guess that would be my influence then,' Sam laughed.

Ted halved a current bun with his thumbs, and with impressive dexterity spread an even slick of butter across each piece with one sweep of his knife.

'So anyway,' Sam said, 'that's why. A one in thirty-four chance is too high for us to make a decision and be confident that we've done the right thing.'

'One in thirty-four sounds like small odds.'

'Not when you're talking about a kid.'

'But Charlie's such a good boy. If you didn't know ... you'd hardly know.'

'I don't think we can take that risk. *We* don't think we can. We're terrified, it could be worse next time, and then we'd never be able to forgive ourselves.'

1

'One of the hardest things in the world,' Ted said. 'To decide without knowing the outcome.'

'Yes,' Sam said. He cut crumbly chunks of Stilton from the round and tessellated them on the slope of his bread. 'You take your picnicking pretty seriously,' Sam said, waving one hand around in a circle over the spread, the proper crockery and cutlery, the real glasses, and in a most monstrous casserole dish, a slab of yesterday's lasagne. A feast of cold ham, apples, cheeses and preserves lay unpacked on the tartan blanket beside the River Dart in an order so fine that all the wasps and horseflies had come to marvel at it.

'Apparently I take everything seriously,' Ted said, the butter in his throat quickly turning his laugh into a throaty cough. 'But what's the point in doing anything if it's not with your best effort?'

'True,' Sam said, tilting chutney jars to read the labels. 'Well, thanks for inviting me. This might be the best picnic I ever had.'

Ted posted the remainder of the bun through his lips, sending it home with his knuckle, nodding and blinking gratefully at this deference. His right cheek bulged at full capacity.

Overhead, the first swallow zipped past, its wings folded back to swoop low and fast through a cloud of gnats celebrating above the bank-side nettles.

'There's one,' Sam said.

'There'll be lots more.' Ted swallowed. 'Give it time.'

The men stared at the river, mesmerised by the sound of it jostling ten thousand pebbles awake.

'Is that a tank?' Sam said. On the opposite side of the river, the top of a rusted iron turret poked its crown up through the tall sedges.

'It's a Churchill tank, from the last war,' Ted said. 'There used to be a big heath behind that line of trees. They trained the troops there before both wars. Driving tanks. Digging trenches. Target practice. I used to come and help out. They got us local boys to hide behind the rifle butts. After they fired, we'd pop up and point with sticks at where they'd hit so they could see.'

'You hid behind the targets? How did you manage not to get shot?'

'The targets were on big mounds of earth. They called out when it was safe to pop up.'

'I can't believe they let kids on a firing range.'

'Things were different then.'

'So, is the whole tank buried underneath there?' Sam had sat up straighter, lengthening his neck to get a better view. His excitement levered his mouth open. Already he was looking at the water, wondering how deep it was, whether he could cross in the wellington boots Ted had asked him to bring.

'It's just the turret,' Ted said.

'So can you climb into it?'

Ted nodded. 'You should bring Charlie down here one day. Now you know the way.'

A squeaky twittering sound from above alerted them to a party of swallows, about twenty, flashing their white bellies, their coat tails streaming out behind them.

'Here they come,' Ted said. From his picnic hamper – an army surplus holdall – he took out two long cotton bags, like giant socks.

'What are those for?' Sam asked.

'You'll see in a moment,' Ted said. 'An old Croxford family secret.' He tapped the red bulb of his nose with his forefinger.

Sam poured more apple juice into his glass and swirled the cloudy green liquid round. He took small sips because it was sharp.

More swallows arrived. And more. Hundreds and hundreds of them. A relentless procession of smart little bodies, dart-like, their pell-mell aerial battle soon coalescing into a clockwise funnel. Amongst the willow branches, the swallows fanned open their spotted tails, struggling to hover, searching for a space to grasp. Tens of them clung to each dangling rope, swinging up and down like bell-ringers as they pecked bugs from the backs of leaves. Sam set both hands on the blanket, and shuffled back to a safe distance. So exuberant was the whirlwind that it buffeted his face with puffs of air. Ted handed him one of the bags.

'What's this for?' Sam asked.

'You're the first non-blood relative to see this.' Ted had to slow his speech, and shout above the accumulated wingbeats, because now there were thousands of swallows, a solid swirl of them, filling the air from the open sky above the treetops, right down low, close to the river, where they dipped down, beaks agape, to sip water and drowned flies from the surface.

Sam lowered his head, and raised his hand to protect it. Each of these tiny missiles was scorching past, barely an arm's length from him.

'Keep watching,' Ted yelled. 'Any second now.'

To Sam's eyes, the flock was a dense ball of flickering static. And then, suddenly, the birds at the top dived down, the ball widening out into a donut shape, and all together the swallows dropped, taking Sam's breath with them. They made a sound, a perfectly choreographed one-clap applause as their bodies hit the water.

There was stillness.

Now the only sound was the river. The big empty sky rang with their absence.

'Oh my God,' Sam said. 'What just happened?'

'I thought you'd enjoy that,' Ted said. Already he was up and walking towards the edge of the bank.

'Where are they though? I mean, what …?'

'We'll give them a second and then we'll go in. Get your boots on.'

All of Sam's fingers were in his hair, interlocking, driving it up into antennae. 'But that's incredible! Surely they don't stay down there?'

'Yep. That's them for the winter now. They won't come out till next spring, after dark on the first warm day after the full moon in April. Not all at once like that. They slip out a few at a time as they wake up. I always come down here with a flask of chocolate and a big old torch to shine across the water.'

Sam stood at the edge of the river and looked out. 'I can't see them,' he said.

'The camouflage is spot-on. Their backs are the exact colour of the dark ripples reflecting the sky. It makes you wonder how many thousands of years it took them to evolve like that, slowing changing colour. Even the way they arrange themselves on the river bed perfectly matches the pattern on the surface of the water. If they were to move you'd see them, but they won't now for months. Now they sleep. Come on, get your boots on.'

Ted waited at the edge for him, scratching the pink skin that showed through his messy white hair, and scratching at the back of his neck, which was almost reptilian where it wrinkled.

'What are we...?' Sam said, sitting on the blanket, pulling at the lip of the cold wellingtons to get his heel through the pinch of the ankle.

'Gathering,' Ted said. 'Just a few. Just enough.'

'Pick them up? With our hands? But why? What for?'

'For an answer. This is for you and Emma. So you can know your outcome.'

'What do you mean?'

'They know things. Their heads fill up with secrets, whizzing about all day in the ether.'

'You're disturbing me, Ted.' Sam laughed, hoping that Ted would laugh too, admit now that he was pulling Sam's leg.

'Just put your boots on. Pick up your bag. Come in with me. You do want to know, don't you?'

'Know what?'

'How your second child will come out.' The weathered topography of Ted's face and his watery stare gave huge gravity to this notion, which from anyone else's mouth, in any other location, would be ludicrous. Sam felt compelled to believe. To show excitement at this proposal, even if only fake, just to show appropriate respect for Ted. 'Charlie needs a brother or sister,' Ted continued. 'Kids grow up better in pairs. And I want another grandchild. I've got a good feeling about this. You just need to get some faith that it will be all right. You only get to ask one question a year, and I want you and Emma to have it.'

Sam stared at him, poking an embarrassed thank-you over the hurdle of his teeth with the tip of his tongue.

'Back at the house we'll cook up the old Croxford recipe, and tonight you'll dream like you never dreamt before. When you wake up in the morning, you'll have your answer.'

Ted beckoned him into the water with a rare smile. Sam could not decline without causing offence. He stood and scrunched his toes up, away from the tight end of the boots. 'I've done something stupid,' he said. 'I've brought Emma's boots by mistake.' The boots made him move like he was walking on stilts. He could not roll from heel to toe, but had to plant each reluctant step flat and with bent knees.

'It won't take long,' Ted said. 'We only need about twenty. The water's cold. It'll soon numb ya. Come on.'

Ted was in the river, crouching, peering down, wading slow, like a heron, stretched neck projecting his head out. Sam stepped down from the bank. The water was indeed cold.

Ted rolled up his sleeves, took off his watch and put it in his pocket. 'Remember to take yours off,' he said.

'It's a diving watch,' Sam said, looking at its face, though he'd never actually taken it underwater. It was five-thirty. Right now, Emma would be picking up Charlie. Sam felt a pang of loneliness as he inched across the river bed. Beneath his feet, the pebbles ground against each other. Just by thinking about Emma and Charlie, Sam could imagine himself right there, smell the chemical freshness of their new car's interior, hear the squeegee sound of Charlie's spit-covered fingertip drawing on the windows, see Emma pushing out breaths through the tight letterbox of her mouth. Sam longed for the safety of familiarity and routine.

He remembered Emma's goadings from this morning, her disbelief of his headache, her insistence that 'Dad never does this', that this was an invitation he could not refuse without permanently damaging his relationship with her dad. A part of him imagined with glee the satisfaction he would feel when he got home and described for her this picnic with its most insane purpose. But then, for something which Ted suggested was so secret, so generous, why had he not invited Emma, rather than him? Had she known her father's intention? Was this some wonky method of hers to persuade him? Sam knew that she was less conflicted about the question of a second child and the potential risks than he was, given to greater optimism – a symptom of her faith that everything happened for a reason, that even Charlie was meant to be the way he is, *meant* implying some cosmic intention, exactly the opposite of how they'd felt at the moment of his birth, when it felt like they had been the despicable perpetrators of some irreversible accident.

There had been times in the past when he'd been able to convince himself with certainty that he and Emma had been chosen because their love was strong enough, their desire for a child great enough, to care for a boy whose needs would break lesser parents. Sometimes this delusion was comforting. But if they had a second child, and if it went wrong again, it would prove that the universe had not interfered at all, and that rather, Charlie was evidence that at the level of their genetics, he and

Emma were incompatible. And then how much keener would the guilt be? What if it did happen again, and the pattern of their baby's construction slipped even further askew on a second iteration? The regret they would feel then would be so much more terrible than the regret they'd feel about not taking the risk in the first place. To Sam there was no ideal solution, there were only probabilities, and the idea of acting without certainty terrified him. To Emma though, there was only longing and fear, irrational opposing forces, causing her to swing unpredictably from one pole of decisiveness to the other. Was today just one of those swings? Was she to blame for putting him here? So much was unknowable.

Ted slipped his hand into the water and out again in an unhurried second. His closed fist went straight into the bag.

'Did you get one?' Sam asked. Ted held up the bag. Something small inside struggled at the bottom, causing the bag to bulge here and there, to twist back and forth.

'They're right here. You've got to do it with confidence. See your bird, see yourself grabbing it neatly, then straight down and up again and into the bag. Don't spook it. Don't grab any pebbles or you'll cloud up the river.'

Sam came up close to Ted, each footstep further deforming his toes. Ted pointed. 'See them?'

At first, Sam could see nothing, but as he shifted the depth of his focus, the swallows appeared, smaller than they'd looked in the air, curled up tight, all pointing in the same direction, upstream, not huddled close together for warmth, but evenly spaced.

'Well, come on,' Ted said. 'What you waiting for?'

'I'm not quite …'

'Just grab it.'

'Just grab it?'

Ted mimed the action, and Sam mimicked it in the air, the

thrust and the grasp. He had never held a bird in his hand. In his mind it would be brittle, vicious. He didn't want to grip so limply that it had enough freedom in his fist to scratch and peck him, but at the same time, he didn't want his grip to be too forceful, to break it. What if he startled the others? Woke up the whole flock, sent them flaying their wet wings all about him and Ted? Made them angry? That many birds together would have weight. Be dangerous even.

And what after they were caught? To pick even one up would be to concede to whatever else Ted had planned for later.

'Go on now,' Ted said. 'Nothing to be afraid of.'

Sam practised several more times, mumbling aloud the movements which he'd named for comfort. Thrust, grasp, pluck. He crouched low, singled out one of the swallows with his gaze, sucked in a final fortifying breath, plunged his hand into the icy water.

For the True Anatomy
Claire Massey

S arah claimed the downstairs room. Bare except for a single bed and a chest of drawers, it had the luxury of being next to the bathroom, and of being a flight of stairs away from the living/kitchen/dining area and the other two bedrooms. She could hear the clatter of doors as her mum rooted through the kitchen cupboards above, checking they had everything they needed, and the familiar buzz of a telly, her dad probably searching for football to watch.

'Annie wants you to sleep up here with her,' her mum called down. 'There are two single beds in the room, you should share.'

She didn't reply.

There was a cold draught coming in from around the poorly sealed window panes. It carried the smell of manure with it. She unzipped her suitcase and pulled out a cardigan.

She didn't open the top drawer in order to start unpacking, but to see if there was anything in it. The drawer was stiff and creaked on its runners. The interior was packed with feathers. She slipped her fingers into the soft plumes. They were all shades and variations of grey and white. A few were black, ribboned with white edges. Others were white and mottled with brown. Some were tiny; they lifted into the air as she stirred the contents of the drawer. Others were larger; thick, with fibrous rods and sharp points. It was almost a shock when her palms touched the cold paper that lined the bottom of the drawer. She lifted them slightly, stood with her hands still submerged and looked out of the window. There was a farmhouse opposite. The moor rose behind, leaving just a sliver of grey sky visible along its dark edge. On the windowsill, which was deep enough to sit in, there was a pen. Ink had welled from the nib and made a black smear on the paintwork.

'Sarah, you need to come and get something to eat.'

Later, in the harsh light of the unshaded bulb, she found that the lower three drawers were also full of feathers. She took up handfuls and let them fall, watching them drift and settle into new patterns. Night was at the window. A pane of too-quiet black. She heard her parents' and sister's footsteps trace the path down to the bathroom and then back up the stairs, one by one, followed by the clicks of everything being switched off above. She left the drawers open and turned off the light. When she wriggled beneath the layers of thin sheets and blankets she didn't think she'd sleep and was surprised when she woke to a sliver of bright blue sky, muffled footsteps, the banging of cupboard doors, the hum of the telly. They'd shout her soon.

'Sarah, breakfast. Now.'

Her dad had a rucksack with a pocket for everything, but he'd forgotten to bring the map. He didn't tell them until they were out on the moor. Annie was running round in circles, jumping over sheep muck, and screeching and flapping her arms like wings.

'Will you stop it?'

'Scrawk.'

'Stop it.'

'Sarah, leave Annie alone.' Her mum had stopped to unwrap a bar of Chocolate-Covered Kendal Mint Cake.

'I'm sure it's definitely this way.' Her dad pointed to a path that stretched on through more unremarkable grass before dipping out of sight.

A sharp wind hit her in the face as she turned to follow. Annie hurtled ahead, arms still outstretched.

The first skeleton was right beside the path. Annie stuck her trainer into the ribcage. 'What is it, Dad?'

'A bird, I think.'

'But there's no beak, Dad.' Annie was still prodding at it with a scuffed toe.

She yanked on Annie's cagoule, pulling her backwards, away from the bones. 'How could there be a beak? There's no skull, stupid.'

The second skeleton was more fragmented. A solitary rib arched from the grass. After that, skeletons seemed to litter their path like markers – even when they'd left the dirt track to cross a field, taking what was supposed to be a shortcut. Each one was stripped of its flesh and feathers. Some had bones that looked like old leather, twisted and pliant. Others were bleached and riven with fine cracks like porcelain. None had skulls.

The bubbles looked like strange growths on her feet. She plunged her heels back into the water and let her head slip beneath the surface, tangled her fingers in her hair. When she emerged she heard a creaking sound: the top drawer in her room being opened. She jumped up into the steam-misted air and wrapped herself in a towel.

Her mum was pulling handfuls of feathers from the top drawer and stuffing them into a Sainsbury's carrier bag.

'Mum.' Water dripped from her skin and made small thuds on the rough carpet.

'Sarah, this is ridiculous. Why didn't you tell me?'

'Mum, don't.'

'We're here for a week. You need to unpack.'

'It's OK. I'm not bothered about –'

'I'm going to have to complain. I know they said they hadn't had much time to clean up between the last guest leaving and us arriving but this is ridiculous.' Her agitated hands were downy, tiny white plumes stuck in the creases of her palms. 'And why would someone do this? Why would they?'

'It's OK, Mum. I'll empty it.'

'Fine.' She wiped her hands on her jeans, freeing feathers to the air. 'Fine. Just make sure you do. And put the bag straight in the bin outside.'

The carrier bag was half-full but it felt like it had nothing in it. She pushed the door to and waited till she could hear her mum's voice raised over the sound of the telly upstairs. There was now a bare patch in one corner of the top drawer, revealing a fragment of a drawing on the paper at the bottom. She put the carrier bag down and pressed more feathers aside, uncovering a diagram of a small bird skeleton. She shifted the feathers around: there were numerous diagrams and illustrations laid out. They looked like photocopies from textbooks. There were skeletons with wings outstretched. Disembodied wings. Small lizards with wings. There were pictures of fossils that showed wings with claws and feathers etched into stone. One image showed a crouched human skeleton with a bird's skull. Another showed a bird skeleton with a human skull. There was a note handwritten underneath it: 'For the True Anatomy – Early Bird. Barry Cleavin, 1976.' The human skull was perfectly aligned with the bird's neck. The white bones of the body looked like they were in motion on the inky background, about to take off.

She tipped the contents of the carrier bag back into the drawer, obscuring the pictures. Then she sank to her knees to pick every stray feather from the carpet.

The play area, where her mum had demanded she take Annie, turned out to be a swing and a sandpit behind the barn. She sat on the swing and dug her heels into the ground. It was freezing.

Stark blue sky rose above the barn's red corrugated roof. She watched her breath make clouds as Annie plunged her hands into the old earthenware sink that had been commandeered for sand.

'I wish I had a bucket.'

'Shut up.'

Annie whimpered and pulled her hands from the sand.

'What is it now?'

'There's something sharp near the bottom.'

'Well, don't put your hands in there, then.'

Annie pushed her hands back beneath the surface.

'Why are you doing that?'

'Because I want to know what it is.'

'No, let me do it.' She jumped from the swing and pulled her gloves off.

The sand was damp. She ground her fingers into it until she touched something hard and smooth – a shell, perhaps, but the contours weren't right. She prodded and tugged, the weight of sand making every movement arduous. Finally, she dragged the skull free by its beak.

'I'm telling Mum.' Annie ran in the direction of the cottage. 'Mum! Mum!'

The skull was yellowed, the colour of old paper. Sand tumbled from its crevices and pooled in the dirt between her boots. She looked into the eyeless sockets and prised the beak apart to extract its crumpled, ink-stained secret.

'This way, Mum.' Annie's voice bounced ahead of her through the cold air.

'Sarah? Sarah, what is that you've got there?'

The paper softened on her tongue. As it disintegrated she felt her arms lift a little at her sides.

Sliding Off the World
Bruce Gilbert

The young boy was playing alone on the green in front of the house. His mother called him and told him to go to the shops with her. He did not want to. She said he would have to stay indoors. He did not want to. He cried until he got his own way. Reluctantly, his mother left him playing alone on the green. He was absorbed in his play until he heard a strange sound. He had never heard a cuckoo before. He looked around. It was early afternoon. There were no other sounds. It was quiet except for the cuckoo. The call of the cuckoo terrified him. He could not imagine what could make such a noise. He ran to the house. In a blind panic, he slammed the knocker as hard as he could. He kept throwing the brass handle down and screaming for his mother through the letter-box. He could not grasp that his mother would not be there if he was frightened. He ran to the back door but it was locked. The cuckoo rang through his young body. It seemed to know him. The house was now unfamiliar. He ran back to the green. Back to where he'd been playing. He threw himself on the ground. He clung to the grass as if he were in danger of sliding off the world. His mother found him sobbing on the grass. As she comforted him, she asked him if he could hear the cuckoo.

The Gannets
Anna Kavan

It was springtime, a windy day. I had walked a long way on the cliffs by a path that I did not know. Gannets were diving like snow falling into the sea, pursuing a shoal of fish that kept parallel with the shore. I'm not certain now whether I walked so far in order to watch the gannets or to explore the coast, or simply because it was a bright afternoon.

After winding for a long time between low bushes and rocks, the path suddenly began to climb steeply over a headland. Seeing the difficult track ahead made me realise that I was tired, and that I had already come much further than I had intended. From the position of the sun I knew that it must be getting late. The sensible thing would have been to turn back then: especially as the gannets, which I had perhaps been following unconsciously, were vanishing round the rocky point shaped like the snout of a huge saurian. But instead of starting the long walk home I kept on, telling myself that I might as well see what lay beyond the head since I had come so far. It was quite a stiff climb, the path was slippery with pine needles and loose stones, and I was breathless by the time I got to the top. There was nothing about the view from the crest, either, to justify the effort of getting there. However far I looked I could see only a vista of the same yellowish rocky cliffs topped with pine trees and scrub which had been in front of my eyes the whole afternoon.

A few yards away, in a hollow of the downward slope, was a dilapidated wooden shack. At first I thought it must be some old boat-shed or deserted fisherman's hut. The half-ruined place, apparently only held together by roughly nailed boards and wire and patched with beaten-out tins, seemed much too ramshackle to be inhabited. But then I saw signs of occupancy: a heap of fresh potato peelings thrown outside the door, a few indescribably sordid rags hanging from the crazy posts of what had once been a fence.

I stood there in the wind for a minute, resting and getting my breath after the climb. And as I was wondering how any human being could be so unfortunate or so degraded as to live in such squalor, five or six children appeared and clustered together staring out to sea: they were, like the hovel, indescribably squalid, almost naked, hideous with neglect. They pointed towards the sea where the gannets on this side of the point were diving much closer in, with folded wings hurtling like bolts through the air, to strike the water one after the other in jets of spray. I could not hear much of what the children were saying, but it seemed from certain words and from their gestures that they expected the birds to come near. I waited to see what would happen. We all gazed at the gannets which were no longer diving or searching the waves but planing portentously towards us with infrequent wing strokes. And sure enough I was presently half-deafened by a storm of harsh cries immediately overhead. Long black-tipped wings hid the sun, shadowing everything; only the cold round eyes and the fierce beaks glittered. And hardly had the flock sighted the children than they seemed to be menacing them, screaming headlong towards them in horrid haste. I shouted some sort of warning, urging the children to run into the house. They took no notice. I saw their looks full of excitement and anticipation, but without any amazement. They seemed to be taking part in a procedure well known to them. Already the gannets were swooping upon one of them, the smallest of the group, whom two of the others dragged along by her stick-like arms. And it was beyond all possibility of doubt that this miserable little creature was the victim among them, already dedicated to the birds. Not terror alone gave such a shocking blankness to her lifted face, darkened by two great holes, bloodied pits from which the eyes had already been torn. I shouted again and began running with an idea of beating the gannets off with my hands; but then I must have stumbled and fallen heavily. I must have been stunned by the fall on the jagged rock, for when I got up the cliff was silent and lonely, the wind had died down, and the sun was sinking behind sullen bars of cloud edged with fire.

How did all this atrocious cruelty ever get into the world, that's what I often wonder. No one created it, no one invoked it: and no saint, no genius, no dictator, no millionaire, no, not God's son himself, is able to drive it out.

Fight or Flight
Emma Jane Unsworth

Every Saturday Laura went to her father's house. The journey took just over an hour as the bus wound its way through the northern streets of the city and then out on the Oldham Road towards east Manchester. The blurry estates that appeared on the way to Miles Platting seemed half-familiar and half-strange to Laura, like the faces of the kids from her old school. When it rained, flocks of umbrellas covered the pavements and the bus windows darkened so that Laura could see her own reflection in the glass. Whenever she caught sight of herself, slouched down in her seat, her jacket puffed up around her chin, Laura reminded herself of a baby bird sheltering on a branch.

Laura's father's house was on an orange-brick estate that backed onto a fishing lake. The living room was decorated with striped green wallpaper that her father hadn't chosen; he had just left it there when he moved in, along with a hulking blue sofa that sagged at the back and, in the narrow galley kitchen, a gas cooker with blotches of rust on the front. Laura wondered why her father hadn't painted the walls but she didn't like to ask because her father still seemed fragile, two years after the divorce. He seemed uncomfortable whenever she put him on the spot, even if it was just to ask him where she should put her coat.

'Cream soda? Cherryade?'

These were always his first questions. He stocked up on the things she wasn't allowed at home: sugary drinks, processed cheese, novelty-shaped crisps. Laura knew it was love, coming out in a funny way, since her father had never been able to say he loved her directly. She had also learned from the times she sat hunched on the stairs in her pyjamas, straining to hear her parents' voices over the hum of the TV, that not saying things directly was one of his main problems.

When the weather was dry, her father would suggest that they go out into the garden, which smelled like the salad drawer in her mother's fridge: green and safe, with a base note of sweet rottenness. Her father was proud of his garden. He grew marrows and sunflowers. Whenever he had a cup of tea or an egg, he put the used tea bags and egg shells into a special bin for compost. When he moved out of the family home, the day after her mother had put her fist through the smoked glass coffee table, her father had said he was heading for the 'quiet life'. In Miles Platting it was so quiet that Laura could hear the blood in her ears at night – a world away from the rowdy southern suburb where she had moved with her mother. There, teenaged boys shouted at her from outside the corner shop as she passed, the same boys who raced motorbikes over the back croft. Laura had often thought about running away herself. Sometimes she thought about how easy it would be to just not get off the bus in Miles Platting; she could stay on until Oldham, and from there catch another bus up to the moors, and never come back. She told herself she'd do it the day of her twelfth birthday, or the first Saturday after.

A variety of birds visited her father's garden: robins, dunnocks, greenfinches, goldfinches, thrushes, blackbirds. The goldfinches were Laura's favourite. She liked their bright red, yellow and black plumage and the way they chattered away to each other. When it was cold outside, she climbed onto the work surface in the kitchen and sat by the microwave, watching the birds land on the feeders her father had hung from the gutter. When the light from outside caught the glass at the right angle she was invisible to them, and so was able to get very close. As they approached the feeders the goldfinches whooped and bickered, knocking each other off the perches. When they eventually settled they emitted little short, quiet whistling sounds as they fed – 'small-talk', as her mother would have called it, the *hello how are you*s, the *move up a bit*s, the *excuse me*s. The goldfinches were messy eaters, stripping off seed husks, which floated around in the air like little ghosts of seeds, and knocking smaller seeds onto the floor, which the dunnocks and robins skittered over to gobble up.

During mating season the finches' behaviour became more elaborate. They squeezed out long notes across the garden, then released a series of clipped squeaks – *chihuchihip* – as they approached the feeders. They dived at each other, open-beaked, to secure a perch. If Laura was really lucky, they showcased their entire range of calls, from a cackling sound to an angry rattle, ending in a barrage of electronic *pows* like a Martian ray gun. But if they caught so much as a glimpse of her, if she moved even slightly, then they were off – zipping away over the trees like bullets.

Laura's father made fat balls for the birds in the wintertime with leftover bacon fat. She liked to watch him stirring the ingredients in a bowl, his nose bowing and dipping until the consistency of the mixture was right. When everything was combined she would help him shape the balls and they would become spiked with stickiness in her palms. She and her father would slap them onto greaseproof paper and put them in the fridge to set.

'You like feeding things, don't you, Dad?' she had said once, trying to start a conversation about something other than birds and plants.

'No more than I like being fed.'

Laura wondered whether her mother had ever seen her father

cry. The most emotional Laura had seen her father was when she found his stash of pornos in the airing cupboard. She was looking for string to thread through the cold fat balls and had instead found a pile of magazines.

'Get out of there!' her father yelled, pulling her backwards by the neck of her jumper, but not before Laura had glimpsed a patch of dark hair clawing out of a pair of zipped-down jeans on the cover of something called *Hot Chicks*. Laura glanced at her father before she ran into the kitchen. His face was bright pink and twisted into an expression that Laura hadn't seen before. It made her want to laugh out loud and she didn't know why.

Laura wondered what the birds had seen of her father's life, through the window, when he was alone. She wondered what he might have told them that he couldn't tell anyone else.

Later that same day she was sitting by the microwave while her father did a crossword in the other room. A goldfinch came and sat on the kitchen windowsill, less than a metre away.

'Hello, birdy,' Laura said. 'Are you watching me, too?'

The goldfinch cocked its head this way and that. It seemed to be staring straight at her.

'I've ruined everything,' Laura whispered to the bird.

The bird continued to stare. Then after a few moments it flapped, lunged forward and struck itself against the glass. Laura gasped with fright.

'Dad!' she shouted.

Her father came rushing through from the living room.

'What is it?'

'A bird just tried to get me.'

The goldfinch struck the window again. Her father tutted.

'He's not trying to get you,' he said. 'He can see his own reflection, except he doesn't know it's his own reflection. He thinks it's a rival.'

Laura sat uncomfortably with her father for the rest of the

afternoon, flinching every time she heard the telltale knock from the kitchen that told her a tiny skull had struck the pane.

Laura made an excuse not to go to her father's the following week. When she did go the week after that, her father had bought even more cakes and biscuits than usual. She felt guilty. It was obvious that he had missed her. After they'd had their dinner he took her out into the garden and lifted her up on his shoulders to show her an empty nest in the old apple tree beyond the back fence.

'Will they come back?' Laura asked as she surveyed the bare nest with dismay. Her armpits hurt, pinched as they were in her father's tense, unaccustomed grip.

'Not likely,' her father replied. 'They'll build a new one for next year.'

But the birds did return. A couple of months later, Laura and her father found a fledgling on the grass by the fence. It was barely alive, moving only when touched.

'It's in shock,' her father said, looking up at the tree. He picked up the bird. The baby goldfinch shivered in his palm. 'We have to put it back.'

'Shall I get it some bread?' said Laura, anxious to help.

'No,' said her father. 'It's a baby one. It doesn't eat bread.'

'Milk, then?'

'No, nothing like that.'

Her father had to climb onto the fence to reach the nest. Laura watched him navigate his way upwards, holding the bird steady, like a full cup of tea. As he deposited the bird in the nest, there was a chorus of tweeting, and then an angry *churring* sound, almost a growl, as the mother goldfinch appeared on a far branch of the tree.

'Okay,' said Laura's father to the female finch. 'I'm getting down now.'

He jumped down off the fence, agile as a boy, his shoes

hitting the ground with a thud. Laura had never felt so proud that her father was her father.

Twenty years later, Laura thought about her father and the birds as she stood in the foyer of the newly rebuilt St Mary's Hospital in Manchester. The courtyard was bright and airy, mostly open-plan, divided up with curvaceous partitions and low seating. Pure white light belted down through the glass roof. It felt like being in the middle of the sky.

Laura was holding a pharmacy carrier bag in one hand and her mobile phone in the other. She stared around the huge room. A colourful mural stretched upwards on the lift shaft. As Laura's eyes followed the abstract pattern, she caught sight of her friend Karen waving from a window on the far side of the courtyard. Laura waved back. She noticed that patients were visible in many of the windows, their hands clasped as they sat hunched in their chairs, waiting.

Karen's baby wasn't with her in the room because he was so premature: twenty-five weeks, almost three months early. He weighed less than three pounds. Laura was half-afraid to see him.

'I brought you some of those things you wanted,' Laura said, shaking the carrier bag. 'I didn't even know breast pads existed. They look like sanitary towels.'

Laura didn't have any kids.

'Cheers,' said Karen, peering into the bag. Karen was wearing a white vest and loose trousers. She held her mobile phone in her right hand. As she moved in for a hug, Laura felt a hard tube near Karen's stomach. She tensed.

'Oh that's just the catheter,' said Karen. 'They put it up my Franklin.'

It took Laura a moment, and then she laughed.

'There are some other things I should warn you about,' said Karen. 'Arthur's skin isn't the same colour as that of full-term babies. He's sort of purple. There are also a lot of tubes and machines, and the alarms are constantly going off, but it's usually nothing to worry about.'

'Okay.'

'And you mustn't look at the other babies on the ward.'

'Why not?'

'It's just not the done thing. Intensive care etiquette.'

Laura felt in complete awe of her friend. The biggest events that had happened in her own life so far were, in descending order of importance: her parents' divorce, getting her heart broken by an American singer-songwriter, and not making the rent for six months so that the bailiffs took away her TV. As she followed Karen to the neonatal intensive care unit, she noticed how the supple juts of her friend's shoulder blades rose and fell like clipped wings as she walked.

The girls washed their hands with antibacterial gel at the tiny sink by the door of the ward. There were no pockets in her trousers so Karen placed her mobile on her collarbone and trapped it there, her chin against her chest in a pose of devotion. Laura copied the way Karen rubbed the suds between her knuckles and for a moment it looked as though they were doing some kind of '60s dance together. Karen looked at Laura and opened her mouth, miming laughter.

Arthur's incubator was at the far end of the ward, next to the window. As they walked across the ward, Laura heard machines whirring and beeping on either side. She tried not to make eye contact with the other parents as she passed. Arthur's incubator was half-covered with a pink and blue quilt. When she was a few feet away Laura saw the baby's small shape through the incubator's thick plastic wall. He was about the same size as one of her father's hands. As he breathed, aided by the tiny ventilator covering his mouth and nose, his plum-coloured ribcage quickly rose and fell. His entire body was bruised and wrinkled but, on a minuscule scale, everything looked to be in place: eyelashes, fingernails, even tufts of black hair poking out from beneath his knitted hat.

'He's a proper trouper,' said Karen, opening one of the little doors in the side of the incubator.

'He's perfect,' Laura said. She felt tears prick the backs of her eyes.

Karen slid her hand inside the incubator and stroked Arthur's arm. The baby twitched.

'Does he know you're there?' Laura asked.

'Well, I think so,' said Karen. 'I tell him everything anyway. It's about all that's keeping me sane.'

Karen stroked all of Arthur's limbs in turn and Laura watched the baby respond to her touch, stretching and flinching and screwing up his face. When Arthur had been born, Laura had – against everyone's advice – immediately done some reading on the internet. She discovered that Arthur's chances of survival were good because his birth weight was more than two pounds. Laura had also read that premature babies preferred being tightly swaddled because otherwise they felt as though they might fall apart. They're in the air too soon, Laura thought. As she looked at Arthur she felt grown up and guilty; as though she was glimpsing a world that wasn't meant to be seen, someone else's secret.

'I have to express some milk now,' said Karen, retrieving her hand and closing the incubator door. 'Do you want to stay here for five minutes?'

Laura looked around, suddenly embarrassed. Nurses flitted across the room from side to side, adjusting the machines. Screens flickered with coloured graphs and numbers. Parents were staring at their babies. No one was looking at her.

'All right,' she said. She pulled a chair up to the side of the incubator and sat down.

Once Karen had left the ward, Laura brought her face close to the side of the incubator.

'I'm very proud to know your mother,' she whispered, and the baby slowly opened and closed his hand.

Birds of Prey
Joel Lane

When I was a child, we lived on the second floor of an old-fashioned apartment block that had balconies and railings with black steel roses. Across the road – a long tree-lined avenue – was a park with a small museum at one end. My favourite exhibit was the long glass case of *raptors* or birds of prey. They were perched on branches and rocks or suspended from wires in still flight: eagles, falcons, hawks, buzzards and owls. However long I watched them, I never lost the sense that they would come to life the moment I turned away.

My first year at music college was rather lonely. The other students all seemed to have a lot of money and be very sure of their place in the world. I'd been quite isolated as a teenager, and moving to a small town where I had even more studying to do reinforced that. I used to work though the evenings in my room, then go for nocturnal walks through the narrow back streets and tree-lined avenues of the student area, blind to any sense of danger.

One night a revving of engines sounded in the distance, like a single machine copied or echoed. Then I could feel a vibration though the pavement. Suddenly motorcycles were gliding past, the stink of their exhaust burning in the night air. The silhouetted image of a dozen or so boys in leather jackets, sitting upright in their saddles, imprinted itself on my vision. Then they were gone.

On Friday nights, I sometimes dropped into the college bar for a pint. One night I saw Robert, another first-year student I'd worked with in violin classes. He was sitting on his own, a hunched silhouette with a crest of dark hair. We said hello and chatted for a while. Unlike me, he was a local boy – 'Never found the way out,' he said. 'Might as well not belong here as anywhere else.'

He asked me what I thought of the music we were studying. 'If you can't give yourself to it, let it speak through you, what's the point?' I made some vacuous comment about the importance of technique. He said: 'Technique is just the vehicle. What drives the vehicle is the spirit in the music.'

Having some company encouraged me to drink more than usual, and I was swaying as we walked out into the narrow street. It was February; our breath left frail scars on the air. A few students cycled past us under the bridge, and I said something about the motorcycle gang I'd seen a few nights before. Robert pulled his coat tighter around his shoulders. 'I used to know them,' he said.

We walked on in silence to the main road, where the pavement glittered with broken glass. Robert told me he was playing a gig at a pub near the college in three nights' time. 'I play the fiddle with a band called Birds of Prey. Come and see us if you like.' His thin hand brushed my arm.

The pub had no real stage, just a raised area at the back away from the tables. Birds of Prey turned out to be three music students playing a mixture of what I vaguely recognised as folk and blues standards, with no drums or amplifiers. The singer-guitarist and bass player were sound enough, but Robert's fiddle was what gave the band its edge. He played as if the music was something he had to drive out of his head. It was the same violin I'd heard him play Tchaikovsky on at the college.

In the break after the first set, Robert went to the bar. I suddenly felt nervous about talking to him, as if I might get an electric shock from being too close. Given the age of the sound equipment, that might have been a realistic fear. He saw me on his way back to the band's table, and smiled. I sat holding a glass of strong cider. My hands were trembling.

The second set included a couple of long, fatalistic ballads about betrayal and murder. Robert was playing with his eyes shut, drawn into the chilly world of the songs. The wild energy of the first set didn't return; even the band's instrumental finale was subdued. The audience were getting restless. The end of the gig coincided with last orders, and there was no encore.

As the band were packing up their instruments, I walked up to the stage area and looked at Robert through the wooden railings. His dark hair was out of shape; his face was glossy with sweat. 'That was fantastic,' I said. 'Want a drink?'

'Thanks! Whisky, please. Think we've been better. It's hard when you've been working all day.'

I joined the band at a table where more drinks were already waiting. Robert told me a little about the songs. Most were traditional – from the West Country or the Scottish border – but a few were recent. 'I'll make you a compilation tape,' he said. The singer and bass player exchanged glances. Last orders were renewed, and Robert got another round in.

We left the pub as they were cleaning the tables. Robert was quite drunk; he put his hand on my arm to steady himself. A motorcycle revved up in a nearby street and he glanced around apprehensively. 'Were they here?' he asked.

'Who?' The other two band members had faded away into the mist. The street was nearly empty.

'Doesn't matter.' Robert's face was blank. 'I'm glad you came, Paul. Look, I've got some brandy in my room, would you like to come back for a drink?'

I tried to remember what was happening the next day. 'Sorry, I've got an early lecture tomorrow. Maybe at the weekend, if you like?'

He stared at me for a moment, as if not sure what I'd said. 'That'd be good,' he said. 'I'll make you a tape. See you in college.' His hand reached towards my arm, rose a few inches, fell slowly. 'Take care.'

That night, I dreamt I was back in the museum. Wings were beating and claws scraping at the inside of the glass case. Suddenly the front shattered and the air was filled with birds of prey, flying upwards in the dim electric light, circling and swooping. I could see tawny, gold and steel feathers, hard blue eyes, and from something a streak of blood that trailed across the polished floor. I stepped onto broken glass, almost dancing, as hungry birds flapped around my head and sharp talons caught in my hair. The smell in the air wasn't formaldehyde: it was acrid, warm, the mingled scents of feathers and blood.

Despite the electric heater the room was cold; the paper shade trembled from a ceiling draught. The walls were decorated with prints of stark Expressionist paintings. The only light in the room was the red bedside lamp. Robert and I lay side by side on the bed, exploring each other with hands and mouths. Then he slipped over me and I felt his hard penis rubbing against my stomach. I bit his nipples and ran my fingernails down his back. He turned me over, and I gripped the pillow as his arms locked around me and his legs spread inside my own. I felt his fingers applying lubricant, and then his cock thrusting into me. He reached up and ruffled my hair with one hand. Then he was moving inside me, a deep steady rhythm; his bony hands trembled on my shoulders like vestigial wings. I heard him cry out, felt him kiss the back of my neck. He reached under me and stroked me gently until I came over the white cotton sheet. We lay together, kissing in a dazed way, our eyes out of focus, until our breathing returned to normal. Then Robert pulled the duvet over us and we drifted into sleep. I bled afterwards, but not much.

Winter brightened into spring. Robert and I met two or three times a week, usually sleeping together at the weekend, but trying not to look like a couple in public. After all, it was the 1980s and we were only nineteen: anyone could have made trouble for us. I saw him playing with Birds of Prey a few more times that term, and got to know the other two musicians. They both had girlfriends, but seemed glad that Robert had found someone.

Having a lover seemed to take me into a different life: I remember walking home from Robert's bedsit a few times, late at night or early in the morning, and feeling open to every trace of sound or movement – but at the same time strangely invulnerable, as if nothing could touch me. I was also getting used to alcohol, which was already a part of Robert's life. I didn't know then that drink has a jealousy of its own: it always wants you for itself.

As neither of us had a phone in our lodgings, we only spoke when we met. Perhaps that increased my sense of a loneliness in Robert that I couldn't touch. He made love to me as if I was an instrument: something that deserved care and respect, but was still only a way to realise his vision. I used to watch him moving over me, his eyes shut, flying. In some ways I felt closer to him when he was playing the violin. I was a capable musician, a potential teacher perhaps, but I had little of his talent. They never invited me to join the band.

Robert didn't talk much about his past, and I had none to talk about. But one night, after a few drinks, he sat up in bed staring at the curtained window – his head tilted, as if he was listening for something. Cars drove past on the narrow road; in the stillness I could feel their faint vibration, see their lights flicker on the curtains. He turned his head and saw me watching him. A confused smile twisted in his mouth. He looked back at the window and began to speak quietly.

'When I was fifteen there was this boy in my school, Danny. He used to pick on me. Tell other boys I was watching them in the showers, that kind of thing. One time after games he followed me out of school and started asking me questions ... what I thought about boys, if I did anything. He persuaded me to go to the reservoir with him and suck him off. It was the first time I'd been with anyone.

'After that, we carried on for more than a year. He left school and started a job, but he used to wait around for me and we'd go somewhere quiet. I let him do what he wanted. Sometimes it was good. But he wouldn't talk to me, wouldn't be seen with me anywhere. And sometimes he was brutal. But I never said no.

'Then Danny started seeing a girl. I didn't see him for a few months. And then, one night, he was waiting for me in an alley near where I lived. He took me to the reservoir again. Made me kneel down, then hit me across the face. He said I'd corrupted him, he couldn't do it with women, if I ever came near him again he'd kill me. Then he knocked me unconscious. When I woke up it was dark. He'd broken three of my ribs, I had to go to hospital. But the first thing I realised when I came round was that he'd come in my face.

'The last time I saw him, he was with some motorcycle gang. They were all speeding down the road together, and I was on the pavement. He swerved to try and hit me. I jumped aside, only just avoided his front wheel. Three years and he's still looking for someone to blame. How much longer?'

I thought about it. 'If you keep on playing the same record, does the tune change?' That made him laugh. I kissed him and we lay down, too tired to do more than hold each other. Robert lay very still, but I knew he was awake. The next day we cycled to a village a few miles out of town, drank cold beer in a sunlit pub garden, then went back through a forest that was bright with growth and warm with decay. Neither of us mentioned what he'd said the night before.

At the end of the spring term, I went home for Easter. Robert came round the night I was packing and gave me a tape that Birds of Prey had just finished recording. I wanted to play it while we were in bed, but Robert asked me to put something else on: 'Don't want to soundtrack my own orgasms.' He left after midnight, and I didn't get to bed until nearly two in the morning. My train was at nine a.m. Still, I could catch up on sleep – and work – when I got home.

I was hardly aware of closing my eyes before we were back in the forest. Robert was running between the trees, trying to dodge the birds that swooped and tore at him from the low branches. Falcons and owls were circling overhead, and a white eagle dropped from the sky to grip Robert's head and smash him into a tree. As he dropped, beaks and talons sprayed his blood over the new leaves. The cries of the raptors were like a motorcycle racing past, fading into the distance.

The room was dark. I rubbed my eyes and tried to focus on the alarm clock. It was half past four. Still confused, I dragged my clothes on and stumbled out of my flat and into the street. If I could warn Robert, maybe it wouldn't happen. There were a few people around: beggars and drunks in their closed orbits, the odd early riser on the way to a morning shift. I ran as fast as I could, but went the wrong way a couple of times and had to retrace my steps. The night sky was overcast, wrapping the town in a cocoon of blurred artificial light.

There was a park quite near the tenement house where Robert lived. We'd walked through it one recent morning, our hangovers exposing us to its poorly maintained state. Running past in the night, I saw a wrecked bicycle caught between its railings. A few yards further on, a figure in a green overcoat was slumped on the ground. Blood was smeared over the pavement around his head. For a moment I let myself imagine his sleep was natural. His hair was clotted with blood, his lips split and bruised. But I could feel his breath on my fingers.

I had to leave him to call an ambulance, but when I came back he was still breathing. While waiting I noticed the muddy tracks on the pavement where narrow wheels had run off the road to trap him. As the ambulance drew into the hospital bay, Robert opened his eyes and looked at me. His lips moved silently. I gripped his hand and he cried out with pain.

An hour later, a nurse told me Robert had been badly knocked about, but he was in no danger; the only fracture was in his right arm. Robert told the police he had no memory of the attack. I didn't catch my train, but the hospital discharged him in the evening and I went home early the next day. Before I left, he told me it was too dangerous to accuse a gang. 'You can stop one, but the rest will get you.'

Robert's arm healed, but his playing was less confident after that. We saw less of each other in the summer term – partly, of course, because we were preparing for the first-year exams. The Bird of Prey gigs were less frequent and more low-key. So was our lovemaking. In the week of exams I felt desperate to be with him, to feel the wings of his desire beating at my back. We finished on the same day, and I left my other fellow-students drinking in the college bar and went to see him.

He was tired, understandably, and didn't return my kiss with his usual hunger. We drank some whisky and dissected the exam papers, agreeing that only a concerted effort by all the lecturers could have been so effective in systematically eradicating fair questions. Then I moved closer to Robert and started to unbutton his shirt. He gently stopped me. 'Paul, I don't feel very well.'

'Then let me make you feel better.' Alcohol, lust and sleep deprivation combined to make me impatient. I brushed his nipple and he gasped with pain. His face was suddenly pale. I waited for him to look at me, but he avoided my eyes. Without quite knowing why I was angry, I gripped his shirt and tore it open, scattering buttons on the faded carpet. His chest and belly were marked with ugly weals and bruises, no more than a day old.

'Robert, what the fuck is…?' I stared at him. 'What's going on?' My mind twisted with sudden rage. 'Who?'

Shivering, he stepped forward and held me against him. Then he put his mouth to my ear and whispered: *Kill me.*

The museum was still pretty much as I remembered it from twelve years before: the dim lighting, the black steel frames around the glass cases. I recognised the Egyptian mummy, the cavern of reptiles, the scorpions in the wall. But the raptors had gone. I walked from end to end of the natural history section, but there was no sign of them and no gap where they might be restored in place. I walked back down the stairs and asked at the reception desk: 'Where are the birds of prey?'

'They haven't been here for years,' the attendant said. 'These exhibits don't last for ever. I think they're still in the basement.'

'Can I see them? Please? It's important.'

She thought for a few seconds. 'Are you doing research?' I showed her my college library card. 'Maybe then. I'll ask a colleague.'

Ten minutes later, an older woman led me to the back of

the museum and unlocked a door in the wall. She reached up to switch on the light, which made little difference. 'This way.' Our footsteps echoed in the narrow passage. I glimpsed dark shapes on pedestals or hanging from wires on either side.

We went down a flight of steps, along a further passage, then down again to another door, which she pushed open. Beyond was a dimly lit hall that smelt of formaldehyde and decay. She pointed towards some narrow shapes that I could barely make out. 'Come back when you've found them.' Then she turned and walked back through the doorway, leaving me alone.

The air was cold. As I walked through the hall, I realised the thin standing objects were trees. I felt dead leaves crack beneath my feet. There was a half-moon overhead, and a few stars. I walked on for some time. Then I glimpsed a hawk on a low branch, just above my head. An owl was waiting in the hollow of a trunk. I could just make out a kestrel silhouetted against the midnight blue of the cloudless sky. There was no breath of wind. I stopped.

The raptors gathered around me. They perched on branches, stood on the hard ground, hovered in the air close by. I waited for them to strike. A network of black twigs stood out against the moon. I saw wings outstretched, beaks raised, but no movement. I stripped off my clothes and stood naked.

The birds didn't move. Neither did the moon.

It didn't matter.

The Egg
Alison Moore

William stands at the window, looking out through the snow-speckled glass. There was no summer to speak of, and now, already, it is winter. The first frost arrived overnight, and now the snow. In the small garden, and over the wall in the sprawling park, on the heath and the paths and the frozen lake, it is starting to settle.

Water drips from his damp hair, the greyed remains of it, trickling down the neck of his dressing gown. He looks down at his bare feet, at the blue veins in his winter-pale and water-softened skin; at his bloated ankles, their waxy appearance. They do not look like his; they look like somebody else's.

In the bathroom, his wet footprints are already evaporating from the tiled floor.

The boy was in the park, standing in the wet grass, when William went into the garden to fill the bird table. He watched the boy bending and picking up a stone, holding it in both hands and inspecting it, and then dropping it back into the long grass.

William, standing on his lawn with his hands full of leftovers, said, 'Have you lost something?'

The boy looked up at him, came closer and stood near the gate, resting his hands on the low wall, on the damp stones. His canvas shoes were soaked and his trousers were wet around the ankles as if the water were climbing his legs. Under the gate, by the boy's feet, there was a puddle full of dead leaves.

*

Downstairs, William makes breakfast, cutting the rind from the bacon and cracking an egg into a bowl, finding a blood spot in the yolk. His bare feet chill on the kitchen's cold stone floor. The snow is falling densely now, settling on the windowsill, pressing up against the windowpane. There is no traffic on the road behind the cottage, and nobody in the park. It is almost silent; any sound is muffled. William whisks his egg.

On the table, there is a shard of rock. He looks at it while he drinks his coffee.

He takes the rinds and crusts out to the bird table, gazing out at the trees, at their cold, bare limbs, and up at the empty sky, looking for the birds.

There are pigeons on the roof. He hears them in the night, the scrabbling and scratching of their claws on the slate. There are geese and swans in the park. There is bird mess spattered and encrusted on the sandstone; there is dark green slime on the grass.

Not much has changed about the sandstone cottage since he was a boy. The garden is just the same, the grass a little long, the shrubs a little overgrown. On the front door there is a lion's head knocker. When William was little he liked to touch it, tracing the cold curves of the lion's face. In the hallway, by the door, are his mother's shoes with mud still on the heel, as if she has just stepped out of them, as if they would still be warm inside. In the living room, her vinyl is stacked by the record player, a favourite on the turntable. Her clothes, hanging in the wardrobe in the master bedroom, smell of mothballs.

The boy moved his hands from the cold coping stones into the deep pockets of his duffel coat. The coat was the colour of holly berries and made William think of winter.

'How old are you?' asked the boy.

William, turning to drop the bacon rind and the toast crusts onto the bird table, said, 'Shouldn't you be in school?'

'It's the holidays,' said the boy.

William spread the birds' breakfast more evenly over the table.

'I'm going to find a fossil,' said the boy.

'You'll be lucky,' said William.

'I bet I can,' said the boy. He took his hands back out of his pockets, lifted the flap of the satchel he wore across his chest and reached inside. He took out a shard of rock and showed it to William. 'I found this,' he said.

William moved towards the boy to look at the rock, the suggestion of a body in the stone. 'You collect fossils?' he said.

'I've only got that one,' said the boy, returning it carefully to his otherwise empty satchel.

William turned and began his careful walk back up the wet path towards his front door.

'You're older than my granddad,' said the boy, 'and he's dead.'

William, slowly stopping, turning back, said to the boy, 'I've got a collection.'

He had wanted to be a natural historian. He had imagined working in a museum, sitting in a back room, labelling acquisitions. He had not got on at school though. He was bullied, and often his mother had said he did not have to go. 'We'll say you're sick,' she had said, settling him at the kitchen table to draw his birds.

He had missed a lot of school. He never even applied for a museum job, has never even been to the Natural History Museum, but he has his annotated sketches of birds pinned to his bedroom walls, and he has the skeleton of a bird in a jar beside his bed, and he has his collection.

As a boy, William climbed trees, climbed up to the roof of

the house, looked in tree stumps and under bushes and in the reeds around the lake, finding nests and taking eggs, just one from each nest, just one of any type: a sparrow's brown and blotchy egg, a blackbird's pale turquoise and brown-speckled egg, a pigeon's white egg.

In William's hands, a warm egg turned cold. Beneath the thin, crackable shell, an immature bird, with embryonic eyes closed, grew still, trapped in its watery environment, suspended like an insect in amber.

In his bottom drawer, underneath his jumpers, there was a large shoebox, and it was full of birds' eggs: a starling's pale blue egg, a thrush's bright blue and black-spotted egg, a robin's white and red-spotted egg.

One day, he came in from the garden, into the kitchen, and found his mother sitting at the table with his shoebox out, the lid off, his stolen eggs in her hands: a yellowhammer's white and purple-scribbled egg, a skylark's greyish and brown-freckled egg, a reed bunting's pale lilac and black-blotched egg.

'What's all this?' she asked him.

William looked at the box, picked out an egg and began to tell her the name of the bird which had laid it, where he had found the nest, how many eggs had been in it.

'These are not yours, William,' she said, taking the egg from his hand, putting it back in the shoebox and taking the shoebox away.

He stood at the window, watching her standing outside, unable to put the eggs in the bin. In the end she pushed them gently under the bush beneath the kitchen window, as if, in the right habitat, they might still hatch.

Later, when he crept down from his bedroom to take the eggs back out from under the bush, his mother was watching. In the garden, on his knees, his head down while his hand groped, he turned and saw her coming towards him. He had not had time to get to his feet before her soft hand flew out and smacked the side of his head so hard he lost his balance, and before he had regained it another blow landed. It all happened so quietly, but he can still feel the smarting and flushing of his skin; he can still see the glare of her small, dark eyes.

When he looked again, she had moved the eggs and he had to start his collection from scratch, with a new hiding place.

William knelt down and retrieved the shoebox from under his bed. He lifted the lid and showed the boy the eggs nestling inside, amongst the balls of cotton wool: a kingfisher's roundish white egg, a coot's buff and brown-spotted egg, a tufted duck's olive-coloured egg. Each was one labelled in a child's handwriting on a small strip of paper pinned to a cotton wool ball.

The boy was impressed. He said, 'There can't be any you haven't got.'

'I haven't got a swan's egg,' said William.

'Why not?' asked the boy.

William had always wanted one, but he was scared of swans. He was afraid of their big, heavy bodies, their powerful wings, their serpentine necks, the hard snap of their beaks, their hissing and biting. And he was especially afraid of nesting swans, which were ferociously protective of their eggs. He had seen their huge nests on the shore of the lake and on the island, but he had never got close to one. There was one on the island which had been there since the spring, abandoned with an unhatched egg inside it. He had watched it through his binoculars.

'They're not easy to come by,' said William, looking down at the boy, at the small, dark head bent over the shoebox. 'You'd be lucky to get one.'

He imagines the first chilly moment of clambering into the lake, the cold water perhaps only up to the knees at first, or up to the tops of the thighs or just above the waist. He imagines the struggle through the reeds, the effort, half-wading, half-swimming and then actually swimming through the icy water to the island. He imagines the swans, which have not left the lake, which have remained into the winter, witnessing the taking of the egg from the nest. He imagines the plunge back into the lake, the body already numb with cold and exhaustion, encumbered by waterlogged clothing and by the bag in which the egg has been stowed; and again the almost-swimming, the struggling in the reeds.

The shoebox is on William's pillow with the lid off. He sits down beside it, holding a tiny rectangle of white paper and a pin. He touches the smooth, cool shells of the eggs: the pale green egg of a mallard; the creamy egg of a goose; a large, light-grey egg beneath which he positions his label, pushing the pin through the paper and through the cotton wool. The tip slides into the soft pad of his thumb, and the blood is slow coming to the surface. The handwriting is scratchier, shakier, than on the other labels. The still-wet ink says, *Mute swan.*

He replaces the lid on the shoebox and pushes it back under his bed.

He had imagined a wife, but it never happened. The master bedroom is vacant now, but his single room suits him fine; he has never used the double bed.

He rarely leaves the house. His shopping is delivered by a Tesco van and brought into his kitchen in a plastic crate which is then taken away again, empty.

But every morning, before his bath, before his breakfast, before feeding the birds, William walks around the lake. He goes early, when it is barely light, so that he will have it all to himself. It is three miles all the way around, and these days it takes him a while. Often he walks the whole way just looking at his shoes and he doesn't even notice the changing seasons. Other times he sees things.

This morning he saw the frost.

He saw the puddle by the garden gate frozen over, the dead leaves trapped, the ice cracking under his heel as he walked out.

He saw the emptiness of the park beneath the blank dome of the sky, and the snow beginning to fall.

He saw the overwintering swans in amongst the reeds, and the empty nest on the island.

He saw something in the water, near the bank, holly berry red under the snow-mottled ice, and the frosted grass beside the lake crushed beneath his feet.

The Raven
Russell Hoban

One says 'a black time', but actually the black of things is all kinds of colours. Sometimes it's the grey rainlight in an empty room; sometimes it's the sound of one's own footsteps under yellow streetlamps; sometimes it's an unaccompanied cello from a long time ago. It was difficult to understand the reality of my days, that this was now my life that would last until my death, that I had closed a door and gone, that there was no going back, that no one was there any more. No one was there because you don't just leave people, you leave a time. And the time wasn't there any more.

I wanted to talk to somebody about the black so I went down into the underground, came up out of it on the long and windy escalator at Camden Town, walked up Parkway to Regent's Park, followed a footpath through green distances and the autumnal shouts of football players, and turned into a road in which a squad of trotting men in red T-shirts and green shorts came towards me, their leader chanting words to which they responded. The words were indistinct, probably not:

> There was a man, his name was Jack,
> he tried to swim across the black.
> THE BLACK WAS DEEP, THE BLACK WAS WIDE,
> HE NEVER REACHED THE OTHER SIDE.

The road took me to the Zoo entrance, where I entered,

went past the apes and a little white clock tower and found the ravens. There were two of them perching on a sawed-off dead tree in their cage. When I took some grapes out of a bag one of the ravens opened its wings and the whole outspread blackness of the bird suddenly appeared in front of me. Standing on well-worn and polished black feet, it folded its wings and stuck its bill through the chain-link mesh of the cage. It was a large black bill of clerical aspect, the upper mandible hooked over the lower with a long curving point that was like a fingernail that needed trimming. A little yellow sign on the cage showed the silhouette of a hand with a large piece bitten out, so I sidled away from the raven and dropped a grape through the wire mesh.

The raven picked up the grape neatly between its upper and lower mandibles, walked a little way off with an old-man walk, placed the grape on the concrete floor, tore it into three pieces, and ate them one at a time. Then it went to its bath, a circular concavity in the floor; it sipped some water, lifted its head and stretched out its neck as it swallowed, and came back to the wire mesh. Its wet throat-feathers were like a beard, its purple-blue blackness was as precise as an engraving, its shining black eye when it blinked showed a clear bluish-white disc like a little round mirror of scepticism.

How's it going? I said to it, not speaking aloud, but with my mind.

Well, you know, said the raven, also not speaking aloud, there's not a lot happening here.

The cage was small, with neighbours on both sides. I think there was some kind of vulture in the cage to the left, some exotic corvid to the right. From time to time the vulture flapped its wings and lifted itself off its branch, then settled down again. The October day was warm and humid, people carried their coats and jackets over their arms. Someone stood next to me and pointed to the raven and said to a child, 'See how tame it is.' I looked down at the child, a boy of three or four. His face was pale and sticky like a bun that had been standing in the sun. His expression was doubtful, his eyes wild. The sky was grey, dead leaves rattled on the paving, in the distance something screamed.

How can you live without flying? I said to the raven. How do you get through the days? How do you not go crazy?

The raven looked at me for a while, the little round eye-mirror blinked like a camera shutter. Lots of people live without flying, it said.

But you used to have the whole sky to move around in.

Wait a minute, said the raven.

What?

How do I know I'm not talking to myself? Maybe I'm just imagining this conversation.

I've been thinking that very same thought, I said. Tell me what to do to show that I'm receiving you.

Hold out your arms and flap them up and down.

I held out my arms and flapped them up and down.

'What's that man doing?' said a passing child to its mother.

'Perhaps he's trying to get above himself,' she said.

I've given you a sign, I said to the raven. How about you?

Walk in a circle round your bath if it's really you speaking to me.

With its old-man walk the raven slowly walked around the bath. Then it came back to where I stood. You were saying, it said. Its voice in my mind had changed: it was all around me in vast and reverberant diapason, as if rebounding from the face of a black escarpment that ringed the horizon under a grey and primordial sky. It was a giant voice of supernatural power, and a thrill of fear went through me as the raven grew before my eyes. The cage and the zoo seemed to have faded away; the raven loomed over me like a black cliff walking towards me on well-worn and polished black feet in the grey October afternoon. How could I ever have been such a fool as to speak to it as if I were its equal?

The immense raven flashed its eye-mirror in which I saw only blankness. Its voice filled the sky. You were saying, it said.

How do you not go crazy? I whispered in my mind.

I have a lot to do, I'm busy all the time, chorused the massed echoes from the black escarpment.

What is it that you do?

I do the black.

Of course, the black. I'd come for the express purpose of talking to the raven about that very thing and I'd forgotten all about it. When you say 'the black', I said, you mean ...?

Different things at different times.

And when you do the black, how do you do it?

I just go with it.

How do you do that, how do you just go with it?

All kinds of ways and very, very far sometimes.

How far? I was looking into the raven's left eye when I said that. Then the mirror flashed and I was in that eye looking out. Around me the vast blackness of the bird opened and lifted and the earth fell away below us, all the feeble constructions of humankind and the smoke of its engines blurring into dimness and distance as we rose above the grey sky and into the brilliant clarity of the blue dome in which the present curved endlessly upon itself to compass past and future.

Up we flew, high, high into the blue dome, then whistling down in a dizzying black-winged rush we shot the long, long curve past faces huge and tiny on the flickering screen of memory, faces in the shadows, in the light, lips shaping words remembered and forgotten in the moving gleams of time, the wavering of candlelight, the whispering of gold watches, the boom of tower clocks, the fading ink of letters tied with faded ribbons; faces wheeling with horsemen and battles and cannon, marching with armies, screaming in burning cities, drowning in shipwrecks and the thunder of the wild black ocean; palimpsested voices, distant figures and the changing colours of processions, plagues, migrations, ruins, standing stones, cave drawings, jungles, deserts, dust, meteorites, dinosaurs, giant ferns, volcanoes, floods, blue-green algae, silence, the grey rainlight in an empty room, the sound of my footsteps under yellow streetlamps, and an unaccompanied cello from a long time ago.

That's rather a long way to come for not very much, I said to the raven.

With this kind of thing it's always trial and error, said the raven. We can go a little further if you want to.

We might as well give it a try.

All right, then, here we go.

Down, down we arrowed blackly through the silence and the rainlight and the footsteps and the streetlamps and the unaccompanied cello to a dim and smoking red that seethed and cracked and bubbled and was veined with golden rivulets of lava. Down, down through that red to a dimmer red, a deeper silence, an older stillness.

Where are we? I said.

In the black.

This isn't black, it's red.

Sometimes the black is red. We have to walk from here.

I looked down at the raven's worn and polished black feet. They seemed far, far away. I imagined the raven sitting down on the edge of its bed and lacing them up every morning. Far below me in the dim, dim red the raven's left foot moved and then its right. Is it very far? I said.

It's where we are when we come to it.

The raven's old-man walk made its head lurch from side to side so that I swung like a pendulum in a black clock. We didn't talk, there wasn't anything to say. Sometimes the red was smooth, sometimes it was gritty underfoot. Some kind of music would have been suitable for the gait of the raven but there was no music. Do you come here often? I said.

It isn't always here when I come.

Well, yes, I could understand that. There were no landmarks at all and the densities and textures of the red were probably unreliable. Time and silence receded before us steadily until they became the same as they were before. We were in a cavern dimly lit by the red and flickering light of our mind, the raven's and mine.

Here, we said.

What?

Here, here, here. Our voice had become many voices, voices without number, tiny and great. The raven was no longer a raven, raven, raven, raven. Nor was I what I had been; we were without form, we were not yet alive: tiny, tiny, dancing giants looming greatly in uncertain shapes and dwindling in the shadows; fast asleep and dancing in the dim red caverns of sleep.

Through agelong dimness of red we danced and sang incessantly the long song of our sorting: yes and no we sang in silence, grouping and dispersing and regrouping in the circles and the spirals of the sleep-dance. Many, many, sang the many of us, all of everything the same.

We danced the red until it became red-orange; then we danced red-orange in the sameness of our unbeing; in the caverns of sleep we danced orange and orange-yellow while the mountains cooled under the long rains and the deeps filled up with oceans. When the yellow came and the yellow-green it seemed that green and blue-green were only a matter of time.

Same, same, sang we tiny, tiny dancing giants through all the colours of the years: all of us the same.

What us? said some.

All of us, said others.

All of us what?

All of us the same.

Same what?

Same us.

What us?

All of us.

And so on through revolving repetitions over hundreds of thousands of millions of years. From time to time there were attempts to move the discussion on to new ground but always it reverted to the same revolving repetitions. Little by little we were losing energy, and although I had at that time no identity I was becoming more and more impatient with the apparent unwillingness of my fellow tiny, tiny dancing giants to pull themselves together so that we could make something of ourselves. My particles were beginning to scatter when, with a tremendous effort, I said, Un…

Un what? said the others.

Un the same, I said. Unsame.

Same, insisted many.

Unsame, said more and more. Over the next hundreds of thousands of millions of years this alternating challenge and response slowly developed in us a forward motion; we could feel ourselves moving out of unbeing into a new state. SAME, UNSAME, we chanted all together as we surged forward through shallow seas and primordial salts into the blue-green algae of our beginning.

Having begun, we pressed forward through floods, volcanoes, giant ferns, dinosaurs, meteorites, dust, deserts, jungles, cave drawings, standing stones, ruins, migrations, plagues, the changing colours of processions and distant figures, palimpsested voices, faces huge and tiny on the flickering screen of memory, faces drowning in shipwrecks and the thunder of the wild black ocean, screaming in burning cities, marching with armies, wheeling with horsemen and battles and cannon; faces in the shadows, in the light, lips shaping words remembered and forgotten in the moving gleams of time, the whispering of gold watches, the boom of tower clocks, the fading ink of letters tied with faded ribbons. Nothing stopped us, and in time we arrived at the grey rainlight in the empty room, the sound of my footsteps under yellow streetlamps, and the unaccompanied cello from long ago where the raven stood on its well-worn and polished black feet looking at me through the chain-link mesh of the cage.

I wanted, said the raven, speaking to me with its mind, to ask you about the black.

What can I tell you? I said. It's different things at different times but it's more or less the same.

I left the Zoo and walked back the way I'd come. When I turned into the road where the trotting men had chanted I saw them coming towards me again. Again their words were indistinct, probably not:

> There is a thing, it has no name,
> this thing is everywhere the same.
> THIS THING IS DEEP, THIS THING IS WIDE,
> IT HASN'T GOT A FARTHER SIDE.

I walked down Parkway, went down the long and windy escalator at Camden Town, came up out of the underground at my desk but didn't sit down at it. I lay down on the couch, fell asleep, dreamed that I was writing, and woke up unable to remember what I'd written.

The Rhododendron Canopy
Elizabeth Stott

Wren writes furiously with her fountain pen, covering two pages of heavy vellum with large, erratic strokes. She folds the paper crookedly, so it won't fit into the envelope, and she has to fold it all over again. The envelope looks over-stuffed, but she smooths down the gaping flap with her fist. If she leaves the house now, she will just manage to catch the post.

She does not wear her coat, but it is warm enough to go without it; one of those mild October days when you can almost believe that it is still late summer, and only something in the smell of the air tells you that the year has made its irrevocable turn towards winter. Her shoes are the sensible countrywoman's sort, and she walks briskly along the rough surface of the single-track road from her cottage. There is little traffic here and grass has pushed its way through the thin tarmac. Small bronze leaves have collected around the tussocks like confetti.

Wren looks upwards. There is a bare tree outlined in sunlit water with birds dotted along the branches. The water is like glass, and the branches almost invisible, giving the water the appearance of crystal filaments. It shimmers momentarily as an unseen startlement causes the birds to fly off, and a shower of water sparkles to the ground, leaving the tree in darkness.

She reaches the post box slightly out of breath, drops her letter into it and walks more slowly home. The glass tree is now dull and still. Birds fidget secretly in the undergrowth. Wren is aware that the wind is changing and leaves peel off in shoals from the tall trees flanking the road, each leaf returned summarily to the soil at the end of the year. So many individual departures. None escapes the shedding.

On the slate path to her doorway, Wren finds a dead mouse. She hadn't noticed it before. It will be the cat again, she mutters to a weathered stone figure of Aphrodite. The cat is always around – you have to be careful.

She removes the small body of the mouse with a shovel and places it under the dark, sterile canopy of a *rhododendron ponticum* at the back of her garden. There are other small bundles here, desiccated clumps of feather, skin and bone. The cat is always at work. Wren knows the rhododendron poisons the soil, so that nothing else can grow around it. But even the cat does not come here.

Afterwards Wren makes tea in a small silver pot with teabags she bought from the supermarket. The porcelain cup she always uses has a small chip on the rim, and she holds it up to the light to check for cracks. Her tea is strong; she knows it stains her teeth, but she'll polish them later. The china cup she cleans with special care, leaving no blemish. It goes into the cupboard, with a matching sugar bowl and jug – the last items of her mother's favourite tea service. Out of the kitchen window she sees the cat and taps the glass, rattling the pane. The cat looks up lazily and saunters into the hedge. It hasn't really gone away and Wren sees him watching through the cage of bare twigs. She remembers the spring – the hedge budding new green – and the blackbird's nest, so carefully built, hidden within it. The young male blackbird had been attentive, gathering food for his mate. One morning, Wren had woken to find the nest dislodged, blue eggs scattered on the lawn, broken, with three scrawny chicks exposed. By the next day, all that had remained of the clutch were fragments of sky blue shell on the grass.

*

On the last Friday in October the phone rings. Wren answers in her best voice then, after the call, lowers the receiver carefully, but it slips from her fingers and clatters onto the rest.

For the remainder of the morning, she cleans the little house. There is much dust, and when she is finished Wren decides that she must bathe and wash her hair. Then she puts on a good dress. It's an old one, and it still fits. Wren wonders if the green silk crêpe, with its low neckline, suits her now, but it will have to do. She puts her hands to her throat, pulling the skin taut, stretching her jaw forward.

There were once shoes to match the dress, but they have long since fallen apart and Wren wears what she has. She brushes her hair back and examines the strands of grey, frowning. There is nothing to be done about that right now, but from her dressing-table drawer, she takes some make-up she has had for years, and applies the caked foundation with a damp sponge, pleased that she can still do it. The iridescent green eye shadow reminds her of peacock feathers. She is careful not to use too much. Water loosens the dried-out mascara, but it clogs her lashes, and Wren wipes some of it away with a damp cotton bud, leaving her eyes slightly bloodshot.

In the bathroom, Wren scrubs her teeth with abrasive paste. They look translucent, slightly blue, like egg white. Finding a stub of lipstick, she paints a careful outline with a straggly brush and fills in her lips with colour, but the lipstick has become granular, and bits flake off, making it difficult to apply. But with much dabbing and blending, the result is passable, although the colour is rather too bright for her now.

Wren does not eat lunch and sits on her sofa, her hands clenched in her lap. By half past two, when there is a knock at the door, she feels composed. Standing in the porch is a tall, thin man, damp and windblown. She can see his car outside in the lane. It looks reasonably new. Not large, maybe, but a good model.

The man extends his hand and Wren shakes it, finding it cold. 'I am sorry that I gave you so little notice,' he says.

'It is no problem, do come in,' she replies, holding open the low front door. The man steps over the threshold into the small parlour. He is too tall for it and his head brushes the lampshade, catching his fine strands of grey hair.

'I hope that I haven't inconvenienced you, but I have a business appointment in the area. I thought I'd kill two birds with one stone, as it were...'

'So you said. You have not inconvenienced me. I had nothing arranged.'

Wren takes his wet raincoat and hangs it on a peg near the door. She sees a wisp of dusty cobweb on the peg, but covers it with the coat.

'Would you like some tea?' she asks. He replies that he would, looking down at Wren's small sofa, its shabby cushions and the tassel fringe trimming that is coming away from the bottom. He bends his knees and sits down on the edge of the seat, his long legs collapsed like a frame and his arms resting awkwardly on his thighs.

Wren gets the tea things but she has only one cup, the one she always uses – he can have that. For herself she gets a pottery mug she keeps for measuring bird food. There is only one tea bag left and she hopes that it will stretch to both of them. She sets it out on a wooden tray and carries it through to her guest, putting it down on the low table in front of him. She sits in the armchair opposite. They both begin to speak. Just pleasantries, but their voices jar against one another's and they fall immediately into silence. Wren pours the tea too soon, and it is very weak. The man clears his throat, and mutters thanks as she hands him the cup and saucer.

'This china is very old.'

'It's Victorian, it belonged to my mother.'

'Ah. I shall take extra care then.' His voice is reedy, lacking resonance.

He sips, pursing his lips and dipping his hooked nose into the small cup. He makes some show of relishing it. Wren notices her lipstick has left a curved mark on the thick pottery of her mug that reminds her of a marigold seed.

'I would have come sooner, but I have been unwell,' he says, looking at her over the cup.

'I am sorry to hear that. I hope that you are quite well again.' Wren places the heavy mug on the table.

'Your name is unusual, were you always called *Wren*?'

'My mother named me *Irène*. It is the French pronunciation, after a distant relative I never knew. As a little girl I called myself Wren and it stuck.'

'This is your house?' the man asks. He looks around at the small open hearth with its smoky fire spitting from damp wood, the faded chintz curtains and the worn rug.

'Yes, I have been here for some years. If you like, I can show you around.'

'I don't wish to intrude…' But Wren stands and gestures towards the kitchen. The man puts down the cup and saucer. He follows her hesitantly, ducking his head under the low doorway. Bunches of dry lavender hang from the beams and the man has to dodge around them.

'Here is my little kitchen. It has a good view out into the garden, don't you think?'

The man stoops to look out of the window. There is a line of mould around the frames and Wren hopes that he does not notice it.

'Is that your cat?'

Wren sees the cat, sitting by a molehill on the mossy lawn.

'No, he just likes to visit; I'm not fond of cats.'

'But I see that you're fond of geraniums.' He gestures to the row of plants in algae-coated terracotta pots on the windowsill.

'Pelargoniums, those. I'm over-wintering them. Geraniums are the garden kind.'

'Oh, you are an expert then.'

'Never an expert.' Wren wrinkles her nose. 'I have no such pretensions.'

'Have you ever been married?'

He does not take his eyes from the window.

'Yes, a long time ago. Let me show you the garden.'

'Divorced?'

'No, my husband died. Shortly after we were married.' She looks at the man. 'My garden is not elaborate, but I take some pride in it.'

'I'm sorry, it must be painful for you to talk of your husband.'

'I have been alone for many years now; I have come to terms with the facts. See, the rain has stopped.'

She tugs the door, which has swollen with the damp, and it judders open. In the garden, the stone paths are shiny with water. They go outside without coats. Although it is not actually raining, there is a mizzle and their clothes are soon felted with fine droplets. He remarks on several molehills in the lawn.

Wren replies, 'Moles are common in this area. I've learned to live with them.'

'You did not mention that you were a widow in your letter.'

'It all happened a long time ago, an accident. It is almost as if none of it ever happened.' She points to a large shrub. 'Most of my flower beds are empty now, but I have some winter colour with the holly.'

'That is very sad, I am sorry.'

'I hope that you are not cold without your coat.'

Wren shows the man her perennial border. 'Asters,' she says, pointing to a clump of purple star-shaped flowers. 'Prone to mildew, but they survive.' In the hedge behind, Wren is aware the cat is hiding.

'That's a thorny hedge.'

'It's a mixed hedge of blackthorn, bramble and dog rose – *rosa canina*. Some elder. I make elderberry jelly.' They walk between a pair of gnarled and lichened apple trees, to where the *rhododendron ponticum* spreads its broad canopy. The rain comes on more heavily. Wren knows that under the canopy the little bodies stay dry.

'We had better get back inside,' she says. 'I'll show you the rest of my house. There is just the upstairs you have not seen.'

They quickly walk back, and Wren leads them into the kitchen, her dress clinging awkwardly. Her hair sticks to her face and her make-up is running. She offers to take the man's jacket and brings out a wooden clotheshorse from a corner and sets it in front of the fire in the living room. Without the jacket he is scrawny, and his shirt falls in vertical folds over his chest. Up close Wren can see a small tear above the pocket of his shirt. It has been mended with tiny, cleverly worked stitches. She sees his breath rise and fall and the shallowness of it. He wheezes slightly, looking cold and miserable. She sits him by her meagre fire.

'I'll make us some more tea,' she says, remembering then that she has none to offer. The used tea bag does not look promising, but she covers it with boiling water and snaps the lid onto the teapot. Through the kitchen door, Wren can see the man is shivering. She hastily dries her hair with a hand towel.

She carries in the tray and sets it on the coffee table. 'I can see that you are cold. I am afraid that this is not a warm house. I have no heating apart from the fire.' She puts on a log, but it does not catch straightaway.

'Whilst the tea brews, I'll show you the upstairs.'

The man rises slowly, and eases his damp trousers away from his legs.

59

Wren indicates the narrow staircase that leads from the living room and the man has to lower his head at the top. They stand close together on the small landing.

'There are only two rooms up here. The bathroom, see…' She opens the door. 'It was a bedroom once; the bathroom is not original, of course.'

The man glances at the room. Wren is aware that it is shabby.

'And I suppose the other room is yours.' The man looks uncomfortable. 'Please don't trouble yourself…'

'It is no trouble. Here, let me show you.' She opens the door wide, but the man scarcely looks.

'It is small, but adequate. I don't generally entertain.'

For a moment, Wren looks at the man. He towers over her in the confined space but without his jacket, there is no substance to him. It is as if his strength is diminished by his height. Wren finds that this inclines her to despise him. He looks disconcerted at her expression; Wren is aware she has a habit of rubbing her teeth over her bottom lip. She allows the man to walk downstairs and quickly checks her appearance in the bathroom mirror. Mascara streaks her pale face and her top incisors are smeared with the red lipstick. She tries to repair the damage, but her eyes remain smudged and the lipstick has marked the thin enamel of her teeth with a faint tinge of red that she cannot remove. Her hair hangs about her face in tatters.

Wren hears the man cough from her living room and runs downstairs.

The tea comes out almost colourless.

'I hope that you do not like it strong,' she says.

The man does not reply to this, staring into the fire, which shifts and drops ash through the grate. He speaks without looking at her.

'My mother likes an open fire. She says that there is nothing like tea with homemade cake in front of a good blaze.'

'Indeed,' Wren replies. 'I'm afraid that I do not have any cake.'

'I did not expect that you had, I mean to say…'

Wren interrupts. 'Your mother is still independent then, living in her own house?'

'Yes, she is remarkable for her age.'

'Does she live far from you?'

The man fidgets uncomfortably. 'Not at all, in fact we share her house. I am away so often that it makes good sense. My father died over thirty years ago.'

'You have never had your own home, a wife?'

'No. But my mother has left me her house, which is substantial, although she could outlive me if she carries on like she is.'

He forces a smile. Wren can see that his teeth are crowded and discoloured.

'What a sad thought,' Wren says, looking over the man's shoulder out of the window. It is raining quite hard now.

'I must leave shortly,' he says.

They stand in the porch; the man holds out his hand and Wren sees how pale his nails are – fine, like seashells. His coat is still wet, and she notices the musty smell of it, the smell of old age.

After the man is gone, Wren paces the kitchen, still in the green dress, which is now creased and limp. She catches sight of a fluttering in the hedge and runs out into the back garden, but the cat already has a bird in its jaws and runs off to the neighbouring garden. Wren throws a stone after it, but misses, hitting a paving slab and raising a chip. It is starting to get dark.

The next day, Wren finds the brown-feathered remains of a bird on her doorstep. With her shovel, she carries the dead creature to the back of the garden and places it under the rhododendron.

A week or so later, at the local shop, she buys a set of crockery in a nondescript pale pink, with a suggestion of a rose shape on the cups and the edges of tea-plates. She also buys a rich fruit cake and a packet of inexpensive brown hair dye in a shade called 'Copper Fire'. Wren asks for some rat poison, which comes in a small cardboard box with a black silhouette of a dead rat and skull and crossbones. She is careful to keep it separate from the food.

Wren combs the dye to the tips of her hair and, after the specified time, rinses it out over the bath, staining the tub with rust-coloured streaks, which she has to scrub with scouring powder. Wren thinks that the dye is much darker than the shade on the packet. It has made her hair wiry and matted and gives it the appearance of tattered feathers.

The rat poison Wren puts into a dessert bowl that came with the crockery. She mixes it with some raw minced beef and leaves it outside covered with a large colander. In the morning, she notices that the colander has been displaced and the food eaten. Wren considers it wise to dispose of both bowl and colander.

It is now late November; there have been no calls. She doubts if the man will visit again.

The night is freezing, and Wren feels the cold, iron-hard through the thin soles of her boots. All smells are frozen into the air, which warms in Wren's nostrils telling her the sad truth of the year's ending. Only her feet make a sound, a soft grinding on the frosted blades of meadow-grass. The moon is almost full and Wren can see the leafless trees outlined in pallid gold. It is bright enough to see by, like stealing fire to light the dark, she thinks.

She stumbles over the uneven ground to the churchyard, carrying two heavy plastic bags and a small border spade. The wrought-iron gate is stuck and she has to push hard to open it. Through her flimsy boots she can feel the stones of the gravel path like lumps on her numb feet. Wren knows that there is a bare patch of soil near the yew hedge in the furthest corner of the graveyard.

It is very hard work, but Wren eventually manages to loosen the solid surface of the soil with the spade. Underneath it is still workable, although, by now, her feet and hands hurt with the cold. When she has dug a sufficient hole she lifts a wrapped bundle from one of her bags. It is stiff and awkward, but Wren manages to force it into the hole she has dug and cover it with chunks of frozen earth. Before she covers it completely, she opens the other bag and takes out a clump of hellebore dug from her own garden: *Helleborus niger* – Christmas Rose – and lowers it into the hole. It is pretty, but poisonous in all its parts. She has brought planting compost to bed it in. When she has finished, she tramples over the lumps, leaving a small mound she hopes will not be obtrusive. As she walks home, flakes of snow melt in her eyes.

Wren sits by the embers of her fire at midnight, drinking tea and eating a large slice of the fruit cake. Her hands and feet burn. In the spring, the blackbirds will nest again.

Huginn and Muninn
Tom Fletcher

'Icelandic horses were never kept or bred for work or racing,' said the trek leader. 'They were all wild for hundreds of years when in other countries they were being bred. This is why they are unique. Out of all the horses of the world they are the closest to their ancestors.'

It was difficult not to think of the Icelandic horses as ponies. They were pony-sized. Really, they looked like ponies. One thing that the trek leader had made clear, though, was that these were Icelandic horses – *not* ponies of any description. 'We do not like it when people call them ponies,' she had explained, her Icelandic accent clipped and yet also fey. The accent, with its plentiful rolled 'r's and short vowels, gave the impression of a constant, child-like curiosity, or a kind of subtle, thoughtful excitement. Or both. 'Calling our horses ponies is ignorant,' she had said.

Every Icelandic person we had met since arriving in Iceland had been friendly and kind, but by no means indirect.

We were wearing bulky red boilersuits that were greasy and stained from years of constant wear. They each bore the navy-blue badge of the horse-trekking centre on the left breast. As the trek leader told me and Doug about the horses I ran my hand down the neck of the one I'd be riding; his name was Krabí. Doug was riding Gretl. They were beautiful creatures. They were small, with long, thick manes and tails, and huge expressive eyes. They were charmingly rotund; barrels on legs.

They had been chosen for us – especially placid specimens, given that we were beginners.

'What are your names?' the trek leader asked.

'Doug,' said Doug.

'Lisa,' I said.

'Doug and Lisa,' the trek leader said. 'Hello. I am Hulda.' She smiled and stepped forward and shook our hands. We were all wearing thick gloves but even so her hand felt strong. 'Are you married? Boyfriend and girlfriend?'

'No!' I said. 'No, but everybody thinks that!' I saw Doug squirm a little bit but pretended that I hadn't.

'You are on holiday together but you are not a couple?' Hulda asked, frowning slightly. 'You are with friends?'

'No,' I said. 'All our friends wanted to go somewhere hot. But we do that every year.'

Hulda gazed at both of us for a moment longer, her eyes lingering a little on Doug, and then she nodded once, briskly. 'Nobody else is coming on this trek today,' she said. 'It is quiet here at the end of the season, and the Lava Field Trek is more popular.'

We had chosen the Hidden People Trek. A slightly longer trek than the lava fields one. It would lead us round a few locations that, allegedly, had some folkloric significance, hence the name of it. According to Icelandic folklore, an ancient race of people lived unseen amongst the rocks and rivers and earth and ice. Sometimes they revealed themselves to modern human beings. Sometimes they just caused trouble. Sometimes they laid charms or curses or gave warning. They were wild yet proud, mischievous yet fiercely dignified. They were – if you subscribed to the general consensus amongst other holidaymakers – completely fictional. 'We're not falling for that,' the other tourists laughed. 'Those stories are just for tourists.'

The October sky was pale grey and there were thin, icy

patches of snow tucked away beneath rocks and under thick, knotty grass. We'd been bussed from Reykjavik by the trekking centre and the bus had passed over some mountains. There had been three or four feet of snow pillowing the ground up there. And that was just next to the road – it was probably a lot deeper, further away. Coming over that landscape at that time of day, before the sun came up – it was about eight o' clock, and the sun wasn't really rising until about nine – had been fantastic in itself. Plumes of steam had been jetting up from the smooth, blue hills of snow, but otherwise everything had been totally still. That steam had lit up in the moonlight like some kind of liquid mother-of-pearl fountaining out.

We rode slowly along the edges of iron-hard, scrubby fields. Thin bands of ice rested in ruts and reflected the golden light of the giant sky. The land was flat from the sea in the south as far as a range of low mountains in the north, and endlessly flat to the east and the west. Those mountains in the north were the ones that we'd passed over on our way to the trekking centre. There were no trees; only black rock, sparse grass, the occasional low building made out of metal. The sky was streaked with hazy clouds that diffused the sunlight and made it all yellow.

'This was all water once,' Hulda said. 'This was all the sea. All that we are riding on now. You see those mountains?' She pointed in the direction in which we were headed. 'Those mountains used to form the coastline of this country.'

I twisted round in the saddle to look behind us, in the opposite direction. The coastline was a long, long way away.

'What happened?' Doug asked.

'One of those mountains is a volcano. It has been dormant for many years now. But it erupted. It erupted and all of the lava made this land here.' She gestured broadly with her arm. 'It destroyed a lot too. Farms and villages on the other side.

It erupted in the same year that Iceland became a Christian country.' She turned around and smiled sheepishly at us. 'People said – you know – it was the old gods showing their anger.'

She sounded and looked friendly when she spoke but it was difficult to know how to respond to a lot of things that she said. It was difficult not to conform to the roles of teacher and student even though things could barely be any less formal, and even though there were only three of us. Maybe it was that Hulda was used to larger groups who spoke amongst themselves, or was used to tourists who asked more questions than we did.

'Are you OK on the horses?' Hulda asked, looking from one of us to the other.

'Yes, thank you,' I said, and smiled.

'Should we try moving a little faster?' Hulda asked. 'We could move to a trot.'

I looked at Doug and we nodded at each other.

'Yeah, I think that would be OK,' I said.

Krabí would trot for a little while and then just stop, whereas Gretl seemed to do whatever Doug wanted her to. Once Krabí stopped, it was difficult to get him going – frequently I dug in too hard with my heels and he took off at speed, careering off to the left or right and then just stopping again. Hulda would move up alongside me and coax Krabí along. 'He is being a silly boy,' she would say to me, tucking stray blonde hairs back up over her ears and under her helmet. Then she would address the horse. 'What has got into you today, Krabí?'

The peace was incredible. There was so little movement, so little sound. Occasionally in the distance you would see steam escaping from some natural vent in slow, chaotic curves, or hear the bleating of a faraway sheep, but that was about it.

'We will soon pass that building,' Hulda said after a little while, pointing to a low, beige structure in the near distance.

'It is a hostel. They have trouble with the Hidden People.'

She spoke about the Hidden People and the old gods in the same tone that she spoke about the horses. It was difficult to tell what was folklore and what wasn't. Maybe none of it was, to her. That was the impression I had, anyway.

We stopped on a path that passed the closed-looking hostel, and Hulda turned her horse around to face us. 'They built an extra room here, without asking the Hidden People for permission,' she said, 'and the lights and the heating in the extra room keep turning on and off on their own. Things move around in there or disappear. In Iceland, if you want to build anything, you have to ask permission from the Hidden People. Only certain humans can talk to the Hidden People so you have to find one of those humans who will communicate for you. It is especially important if you have to move any stones or rocks to do your building. The Icelandic Government has a special person who communicates with the Hidden People whenever a big building project is going on. Roads or big buildings, for example. If this is not done then the Hidden People will be angry and upset and the structure will have bad luck.'

'Who's that?' Doug said, pointing towards the building. I followed Doug's finger and Hulda turned and looked too.

'Standing by the fence at the back,' Doug said. 'All in black.'

I jumped when I saw it, and beneath me Krabí bucked just slightly. There was a person there, standing completely motionless.

'Oh,' Hulda said, turning back. 'That is not a person. That is a raven standing on a fencepost.'

'No,' Doug said, 'it's too big to be a raven!'

'That is how big they really are in Iceland,' Hulda said. 'Here. Look.' She stood up in her stirrups and cried out in Icelandic.

The raven – because she was right, it was a raven – spread its huge wings and flapped clumsily a few times in rapid succession, and then lifted itself into the air and flew upwards, graceful now, the size of a small person. It flew away from us, and then dipped down low to the ground and disappeared against a stretch of black rock.

'Oh my God,' I said. 'Doug, that was nearly as big as me.'

'I know,' Doug said. 'Jesus Christ.'

'Don't worry,' Hulda said, grinning. 'Ravens are wise birds.'

'I wasn't worried that it was stupid,' Doug said.

'Sorry?' Hulda said, wrinkling her forehead. 'I do not understand.'

'Oh, it was nothing,' I said, answering for Doug, who looked embarrassed, angry.

'The God Odin had two ravens,' Hulda said, swinging her horse around and setting off without waiting for Doug or me. 'Huginn and Muninn. Thought and Memory. They flew out all over the world and then went back to him and – you know – reported.'

I felt on edge. I think Doug did too. I had been enjoying the trek thoroughly – the landscape was dramatic, the horses were lovely, the things that Hulda was telling us were fascinating – but something had changed with the appearance of the raven. The air was cold – it had been cold all along – but suddenly I felt it deeply. The day, even though it was only noon, was dim. That was natural, of course, it being Iceland at that time of year, and on other days, even earlier on that day, the low light had felt exciting and exotic and unusual, but then, right then, it just felt slightly gloomy.

At one point, when there was a bit of distance between Hulda and us, Doug turned and spoke to me in a low voice.

'I told you it would be weird,' he said.

'It's not weird,' I said. 'Friends go on holiday all the time.'

'In pairs?'

'Yeah, in pairs,' I said. 'And yes, before you ask, in mixed-gender pairs too. Why wouldn't they?'

'Other people think it's weird,' Doug said. 'Hulda thinks it's weird.'

'I think she was just clarifying the situation, Doug. Because actually I think she likes you.'

'Well,' Doug said, 'nothing'll be happening *there*.'

'Why not?' I asked. 'She's gorgeous!'

But Doug just shrugged, and fell silent.

Not for the first time, I wondered if Doug had got the wrong idea about this whole holiday. It would be understandable, but I'd checked with him, I'd made it clear to him – just friends. That's all.

We continued northwards, towards the mountains. After about ten more minutes of silence, Hulda twisted round in her saddle again.

'Icelandic horses have a fifth gait,' she said. 'Would you like to try it?'

'A what?' I said.

'A fifth gait. In between a trot and a canter. It is called a *tölt*. Would you like to try it?'

'Come on then,' Doug said. I couldn't see his face – we were in single file, and he was in front of me, with Hulda in front of him – but he sounded chirpier than I felt. That was Doug though. His moods would come and go like shadows. They were grey clouds that swept stealthily between the intricate landscape of his brain and the inside of his skull. Sometimes these clouds passed behind his eyes, and you knew, when you looked into his eyes and could see the clouds, that the inside of his head was dark right then.

Hulda explained how to instigate the *tölt* – squeezing the horse's barrel-belly with your knees and shifting your weight a certain way – and we began to *tölt*.

'The fifth gait is a mystery,' Hulda shouted back over her shoulder, all of us having to raise our voices now that we were moving faster and the horses' little hooves were louder. 'Really nobody knows why Icelandic horses can do this and no other horses can.'

Neither Doug nor I knew enough about riding to know how different the *tölt* was to a trot or a canter, but it was a pleasant speed to be travelling at – it was faster than my walking speed, but it was not too fast to maintain control or to take in the views. It tired the legs out though. They would ache the next day.

The sky and the iron-hard landscape retained their slightly golden cast. Our breath was forming clear, hard-edged cones of white mist every time we exhaled. Other than ourselves, everything was completely still and silent.

It was probably the silence, really, that made the voice of the raven so shocking the next time it rang out. It was like a serrated blade ripping through the sky. It was like a hammer striking the metal Earth. It was something we all heard inside of our own skulls, I am pretty sure – I mean, not through our ears, but just there, inside our heads. Even the horses faltered in their *tölt*. Hulda slowed her horse to a walk and stood up in her stirrups, looking around. 'It is nothing to be alarmed of,' she said, but she did not sound convinced. It was strange – of course, we all knew it was nothing to be alarmed about. It was just a bird. A normal bird, if a big one. And yet we were alarmed. We were uneasy. Skittish. It did not help that we could not see the raven anywhere, either.

'We will go to that little hill,' Hulda said, after a moment, pointing ahead, 'and then turn back.' She did not say whether that was the usual route or not.

The hill was not far away – maybe fifteen minutes' walk. As we approached, Hulda talked to us over her shoulder.

'This hill is a fairy house,' she said. 'Somewhere where the Hidden People live.'

'Wait,' Doug said, pulling Gretl up. 'I don't think I want to go.'

Hulda turned her horse around. She smiled a wide, slow smile. 'Why?' she asked. 'What do you think they will do? They will not show themselves to you. They will not do anything to you.'

'I don't know,' Doug said.

'It is good that you believe in them,' Hulda said.

'I didn't say I believed in them!' Doug snapped, glaring.

Hulda held his gaze steadily, and then turned back around. 'We will go to the little hill,' she said, her voice curt.

'Doug,' I said quietly, once we were back in single file and moving forwards. 'Are you OK?'

'Don't you start,' he muttered back, his head turned so that it was, to me, in profile.

'I thought you were OK,' I said.

Doug did not respond.

We got to the hill and we rounded the hill and we disturbed the raven, which made that sound again, that sharp cawing that set something discordant resonating inside me, and it scrambled skywards from its resting place.

'Oh no,' Doug said.

Hulda said something soft and breathless.

The raven had been sitting on – plucking at – the corpse of a chestnut-brown horse. It was in a strange state of decomposition. The process must have been slowed by the cold. It was still decomposing though. Its face in particular was pitted and rotting, the damage no doubt helped along by the poking and prodding of the raven's beak. You could see the holes it had made around the eyes and nose and mouth. There was no smell. Parts of the corpse were slightly submerged in ice – puddles of water that had frozen around it.

Hulda looked up at the raven that was now circling high above, a black silhouette against the yellowing sky, and shouted something in Icelandic. The raven answered with another shriek. Hulda's eyes were wet but she was not crying, exactly. She dismounted from her horse – all of the living horses were wary, now, shifting from hoof to hoof – and knelt by the body, stroking its mane. She murmured words that neither Doug nor I could understand. We both dismounted too and stood holding our reins. I didn't know what to say.

The hill was on its own, a long way away from any other hills. It was small and almost perfectly conical. Beyond the hill – to the north – was an expanse of black rock. The hill itself was mostly black rock too, apart from a kind of ring of yellow grass around its base. It looked like the hill had simply erupted through the surface layer of earth, which it probably had.

The Hidden People.

That night we ate at the hotel in Reykjavik. The food was disappointing. We'd ordered different fish dishes but they were both so bland and wet that they were more or less interchangeable. The view, though – the view was incredible, because the restaurant was on the top floor of the building and had one glass wall that faced out over the harbour towards Mount Esja on the other side of the bay. We knew that already, and had marvelled at the view every morning over breakfast, but this was the first time we'd been up there at night. We had a good view from our bedroom window as well, as that was quite high up, but the bedroom window faced the other way, over the city. After pushing our plates to one side we both went to the door in the glass wall and stepped out onto the balcony. It was cold out there, and we were only dressed for the dry heat of the rooms and corridors of the hotel, but the chill was exhilarating. There was a breeze up and our hair – we both had long hair – streamed from our heads.

The hotel had a square base and was very tall. It was a new building, but due to its simple shape and its exterior of hard, black stone, it had the imposing presence and gravitas of a tower or castle from a fairytale. The structure descended beneath the ground where a *heittur pottur* (or 'hot pot') and sauna tapped into a natural hot spring.

From the balcony, the view was much more immediate than it was from the dinner table. There was no glass to cast reflections, there were no other diners taking up space in your field of vision, there were no warm, foody smells detracting from the effect of the glowing blue mountain that stood opposite us, across the water. The sounds of the city drifted upwards, but they were not overbearing; Reykjavik was a small city, and the vast darkness surrounding it on all sides seemed able to swallow all human noise effortlessly.

'I can't stop thinking about that horse,' Doug said. 'I know I should forget about it, but I can't. I'm sorry. The horse and the raven.'

'Don't apologise,' I said. I thought about saying more, about trying to reassure him, but I didn't know how, because the effects of the horse and the raven were the kind of things that really you just have to let fade away. I'd almost forgotten about them to be honest.

I was woken that night by a voice. It was a thin and high and rusty voice. It was saying words that I did not understand. As I regained consciousness fully I wondered if they'd been words at all, or just sounds. I thought I'd dreamed them, whatever they were, because there was nobody else there, apart from Doug, and he was asleep in his bed. The room was bitterly cold. I slowly realised that I could hear the wind roaring, and I opened my eyes to see the blackout blind from the window was curling and bouncing back into the room, twisted and buffeted by the gusts coming in. The window was open.

I sat up.

Apart from the blind and the pages of a book I'd left on the desk, everything in the room was still. There was nothing else, really, that would blow around. We'd been quite organised with our clothes, put them all in the furniture provided. After all, we were in Reykjavik for two weeks. The furniture was heavy, dark, wooden. Stocky and solid and simple.

I swung my legs to the side of the bed. When I put my feet down, the floor felt like ice. I padded quickly around the end of Doug's bed to the window, and leant out to grab the handle. We were actually a long way up. The street below was quiet, but I could see the main road further away, lit yellow, with the occasional car moving along it. Looking out over Reykjavik was like looking out over the modern, real-world version of a small town out of a Disney film or something. The electric lights did not look electric; they looked like candles or other flames. I pulled the window back in, and fastened it shut. Doug must have opened it earlier and then gone back to sleep.

On my way back to bed I glanced down at Doug and saw that there was something wrong with his face. He seemed to be wearing an unusual expression for somebody asleep. The room was dark now that the blind was back in place, so I bent down closer in order to see.

His eyes had been removed, his optic nerves left lolling from the sockets, and there were numerous deep, messy incisions around his nose and mouth. His tongue was swollen and bloody and there was a large puncture wound at his temple. I touched it, briefly, thinking 'Wake up, Doug,' thinking that such intimate contact maybe would do the job. But at the slightest brush of my fingertips against that broken skin I recoiled, and I realised simultaneously that of course he was dead. Otherwise he would be breathing, moving, screaming.

I sat down on the edge of my bed for a moment and then stood up again. I went over to the desk so that I could call reception, get them to call the police. But I couldn't find the phone. I didn't really want to put the lamp on, because I didn't want to see Doug's face any more clearly, but I did put the lamp on and just avoided looking in his direction.

I lifted up the phone receiver once I could see it, but there was no dial-tone. I thought maybe it was something to do with its being a hotel phone. I wasn't used to them, the way they worked. I dialled anyway but nothing happened. I felt like I was trying to use a toy phone or something. I double-checked the instructions in the information booklet, but I was doing it right. It just wasn't working.

I went to the door of the hotel room but it wouldn't open.

In a conscious effort not to look at Doug, I turned to look at my bed, and saw that my body was lying there in the same state as Doug's, blood wet on the white sheets. My eyes had been plucked out and my tongue bitten at, my lips punctured and nose hacked. I gazed at it – my body – and then at Doug, and then back at myself. My body, that is. It was dead.

I didn't fully understand the situation. I was thinking, Where is Doug? I mean, there was his body, and there was my body too, and I was there, so where was he? Was he in his own similarly occupied hotel room? He must have been in his own hotel room, timidly fingering the wounds in my head. I mean, his own version of this hotel room, his own afterlife. Really we should have been together. We should have been in a relationship, a romantic one. Looking at our dead bodies lying there like that, our separate beds seemed ridiculous, prudish, inhuman.

His own afterlife. I moved over to the window and raised the blind and stared at my dim reflection. I was a dark cut-out framed by the lit room behind me. Through the glass I heard the raven shriek. I thought it might have been out there, bloody-beaked and full of eyeballs. I tried to open the window so that I could look out, look up and see the sky unimpeded by glass, but I couldn't, it wouldn't open, it was like the door, the telephone. It had been open before but that was before I'd seen myself, before I'd realised, before I'd thought about it.

Huginn and Muninn. It was one or the other. Maybe we had seen both that day. Maybe one through the day and another at night. Maybe one had got Doug and another got me. I didn't know. I still don't know. And it has been how many years, decades, millennia maybe, since that night I woke up. Neither raven ever came back. I am quite sure that one or the other is watching me here, watching Doug too, wherever he is, or maybe not, maybe they have too many victims to watch over, too many brains just floating, doing nothing, nothing to do but remember, alone, and wonder, and think about it, what is it, some kind of entertainment for an old god? Or what? What is it? Maybe one of the ravens has Doug and the other has me in our totally exclusive existences now.

I thought a long time ago that I would go mad and looked forward to such a thing, thinking at least then there would be a change. But I have not gone mad. I have just remained here, in this room, looking out and down sometimes over the lit city that may as well be a painting or something. I would rather have died out there on the plains with the horses, with Gretl and Krabí, and the ice and the bitter wind and the lava fields and the Hidden People and the trolls – we never mentioned the trolls, we never asked about those. And the raven. Or the ravens. Out there, watching that raven ascending and descending through the golden light like that one thing you always think of that you always wish you hadn't thought of.

When the Red, Red Robin …
Regi Claire

After her release from prison, Sarah G changed her name to Toobad, bought herself a second-hand laptop and got broadband. Just for fun, she Googled 'terrorists'. And came up with literally millions of websites, news reports, blogs, profiles, images. Then she typed in 'revenge bomb', which produced nearly as many results – until she refined her search.

One morning a week later she hears a knock on her front door. It's a well-dressed young man, smooth-shaven, smooth-talking. He introduces himself as a sales rep for computer virus protection. When she says, thanks, she's already signed up with one, he puts his foot in the door and pushes his way in.

Sarah has learnt a thing or two in prison so she steps aside, pretending to be quite unfazed.

'Your computer was stolen from a government research facility – where is it?'

'Look at my children.' Sarah points to the framed photo on the wall. 'They're fine, upstanding citizens: a lawyer, a linguist, a banker. I always cared for them. Cooked, washed, cleaned the house. They'll come back.'

The young man rams his fist into the picture, shattering the glass. One of the shards slashes the children's faces. 'There's a virus on that computer. You need to be quarantined.'

'You'll regret this, believe me,' Sarah says.

The laptop is on the kitchen table, the screen saver showing a close-up of the robin she has downloaded.

'Tweet, tweet, little bird.' The young man grins as he pulls out the cables.

'I did warn you.' Sarah is no longer afraid. The air in the room has changed. It has thickened and started to pulse with a life of its own. The young man, too, has noticed the change, judging by his more and more frantic attempts to leave. It's too late, of course.

Sarah smiles at him poised over the laptop, unable to move a single muscle in his body, unable to take his eyes off her, or to scream even. Then she tells him about the dead robin she'd found in her garden fifteen years ago.

The bird had gagged on its entrails and shat itself to death. It had died in agony. She buried the remains under the hedge. Her husband said he'd tried out a new poison to kill off the mice in the shed, adding with a laugh, 'Poor wee bastard was too greedy.'

Next day she'd seen the robin's mate leave its nest of cheeping chicks and flit about in the pouring rain, from shed roof to washing line to forsythia and back, trilling so hard its tail dipped and rose in distress. Two days later the chicks stopped cheeping and the robin lay by her back door, a hole clawed in its breast. The hole was black, a festering blackness that seemed to leak into the flame-red feathers like something alive.

She buried the family of robins in a row.

'A divorce?' her husband exclaimed as he followed her into the kitchen that night.

She didn't answer, just gave the onions in the frying pan an extra-hard stir.

Was she menopausal or what?

She'd watched the onions getting burnt.

'The children have flown the nest so now you think it's your turn?'

Her fingers had clamped round the pan's long handle, lifted it off the gas – and swung it at him.

'And that was that.' Sarah falls silent.

Almost apologetically, she shakes her head at the immobile young man with his fixed stare. Then the air around him shudders and tears open, releasing him at last. There's a whirring sound, like wings beating furiously, and he screams in terror as he tries shielding his eyes from the series of flame-red flashes.

A Nestling
Jack Trevor Story

The boy had been in the tree half an hour before he discovered that he could not get down. Part of the time he had been fascinated by the birds' nest, and part of the time he had been enjoying the incredibly long view across the fens.

Both parts had been quite satisfactory, and well worth climbing a tree for, even though the birds' nest had, in a way, disappointed him. Instead of eggs, there had been baby birds, barely feathered, yawning for food and moving around and peering out over the side, recklessly, hungrily. And then he had got round to the view, twenty miles or more on every side; flat lands, elevated rivers, irrigation dykes, even tiny specks fishing at Vaseford Locks and tinier specks gathering reeds for arrows in the black reed-beds towards the bay trees which hid the village but not quite the church spire. All fascinating, amazing and enjoyable, till you suddenly and sickeningly discovered that you could not get away from it. That you were thirty feet high, isolated from the world and only nine years old.

The lesson he had learned immediately was that it is easier to climb than to descend. Especially if there is some important achievement just above your head. He had but lately suffered a tragedy and this had blinded him to everything except the small nest in the crutch of branches half-way up the tree. The tragedy concerned his perfect collection of blown birds' eggs which had lain carefully packed in cotton wool in all their blue, green and speckled loveliness. He had taken it down from the

81

loft two days ago to find that all he had was a large flat box full of blue, green and speckled dust and bits and pieces. There were certain clues which enabled him to deduce that mice had been there. Not one perfect shell remained of a whole season's collecting and swapping and even buying.

'That'll teach you to rob birds' nests,' his sister had said.

This had been unfair, for he never took more than one egg from any clutch and even then only when he had none of that kind.

'Just the same,' his sister had said (she was fourteen and very humane), 'you don't know where your swaps come from.'

Well of course a chap couldn't guarantee the integrity, or whatever it was, of other collectors, but he reasoned that whether he had swapped for an egg or not, it would still have been taken. Anyway, his year's collection had gone for mice diet and he had to start all over again. Almost immediately, hoeing garlic from a wheat field near the artificial manure factory, he had found twelve plovers' eggs in a nest on a grassy bank. He had taken one. Blackbird, mavis, sparrow, martin, two-finger Tom had followed pretty closely. And now, with the season getting late, he had seen this nest.

The tree, as he remembered now, sitting on the stout bough and staring down, had presented no difficulties. With his young face turned expectantly upwards, his hands groping high, his joints cracking heedlessly, his toe-caps scruffing unforgivably on the rough bark, he had been blissfully unaware of height. And then at last he had scrambled up within arms' reach of the nest, to find that he was too late to prick an egg through with a thorn at either end and blow it dry. Life had come before him. Four small, big-headed but exquisite birds were in occupation.

He had stood there five minutes or more, his lips parted, his nostrils dilated in an effort to subdue the noise of this heavy breathing. Of course he was fascinated. He had seen newly hatched birds before, scores of dozens of them, but he had not ceased to be amazed and fascinated. The boy was not aware yet of any thoughts about the meaning of life and where God was, but somewhere, unexpressed, hardly even a thought, was the deep conviction that newborn birds were a part of it all.

Twice he watched them fed by a briefly visiting parent seemingly conscious of the boy a few feet away. But still they remained open-beaked and shrill, cuffing each other, fluttering around and coming perilously near to falling from the nest. Several times the boy was terrified for them, his hand jerking involuntarily towards them, but each time it was all right. It was quite all right. The baby birds, although born not much more than a day ago, knew what they were doing and how far they could go. And that was amazing in itself.

Then the boy's legs ached, standing there on the bough, and he sat down. This meant losing sight of the baby birds and so he glanced around at the view. In no other part of the country could it be more impressive – spacious, anyway – than it was from this tree in the fens.

The tower at Soham you could see, the church at Isleham, Vaseford Locks and the anglers, a distant horse towing an unseen barge, straining forward against no more than early summer air, it seemed. The boy had lived in the Fen country most of his life and although he had never been bored with it – take the fishing alone – it had never been as engrossing as this. It was like sitting on a relief map, a green and black map. Here and there stood a lonely windmill, sails derelict and upflung as though in supplication, or slowly turning for cattle meal.

It was all – the birds and the view and the moment – fascinating. There was no other word for it. Until you suddenly glanced round for the sun and remembered the time.

Remembering the time and the distance he had to go across

the fields and along the driftways, the boy stood up for one last glance at the birds. Then, looking down, he knew he was stuck. Even without trying to climb down he knew he could not do it. Although up here the sun still poured down a tunnel of green leaves on his face and body, the bole of the tree was already lost in shadow. It was not dark exactly, down there, but it seemed at least three times the original distance. He tried just the same. For one thing he had to get to Scouts.

He hung by his hands for seconds that seemed like hours, stretching his legs, straining his feet, his toes, for the next branch below. But there was no feel of it. When he looked down, which is difficult in that position, his own body screened the part of the branch he needed for foothold. He contemplated dropping for it, knowing it was only a matter of inches. He relaxed his fingers, began to slip, remembered what had happened to Ron Chapman – and with a fierce effort scrambled back on to the bough.

He sat there, panting a little, a little faint, a little frightened. The view was no longer fascinating; it was vanishing into evening, distance, shadow, the map vast and obscure and without horizon. Vaseford Locks were now only a few specks of white paint. He did not bother to look up at the birds' nest, although he could hear that everything there was unchanged. They at least were already safe home.

He made three more resolute attempts, each less effective than the one preceding. Finally, his strength going, he slipped, badly; clutched a green branch which bent and whipped through his fingers; grabbed at a dead twig that snapped and went falling to earth – down, down, down, ages before it hit the hard knotted roots. Then with a desperate, clawing, dog-paddle at the trunk and a snatching of everything green and brown he was back on the bough again, exhausted, finished, stuck.

It was then he made his special call; a warbling yell in

the throat. Usually it was loud and strong enough to bring protests from all over the village and PC Badcock up to see the headmaster. But now it was feeble, useless, unechoed, wasting itself in a lot of distance with nobody to hear.

But somebody did hear. Suddenly, in a silent moment of reaction and despair the call came back across the fens, the same cracked notes, warbling. The boy let it fade away then replied louder – hopefully, desperately.

Again the call came, louder. Then another call mingled with it from a different direction and soon from the village and the river and the reed-bed boys were calling to one another, quite meaninglessly and, as the boy in the tree sadly realised, as they did whenever somebody liked to start. For them it was a game. For him it was a cry of distress, like the drums of Africa, the hilltop bonfires of threatened Elizabethan England, the smoke signals of the Indians. It was a game for them because they were walking by the river, or fishing, or gathering reeds, or even swinging on their orchard gate, none of them stuck thirty feet high in a tree in the deep middle of a darkening fen.

Glooming alone amid the leaves he was startled by something that hit him on the head, a terrified squeaking, a flutter of tiny talons over his face, the brush of feathers. Then it had gone down past him, still squeaking, rattling through the leaves below. The shrill sounds stopped. There was an awful quiet on the world as though something important had died.

He thought at first it was a bat, but realised immediately afterwards that it was one of the small birds which had dropped out of its nest. What could not possibly happen had happened. One of those tiny, perfect creatures had fallen to the ground. Through anger, or ignorance, or overconfidence, or miscalculation or something.

The boy looked down but could not see the small bird on the dark earth, although he knew it was there, lying motionless, kicking perhaps, perhaps looking up at the nest, wanting to be fetched back. The baby bird, the nestling, was in a much worse predicament than he was. Something had to be done and he did not hesitate. He forgot that he was stuck.

The boy swung down by his hands, dropped perfectly to the branch below, slithered down on his stomach, felt the branch below that with his feet, stood on it, dropped again on his stomach, followed the crooked line of the bough out to where it drooped towards the ground, edged himself along, quite rapidly and confidently, still fearful only for the bird, wondering if it was in pain or whether something was threatening it, or how you could tell if a bird's bones were broken. In less than three minutes after leaving his unleavable perch he dropped lightly to the ground and went in search of the bird.

'What's happened?' his mother said, when he came in. Something obviously had happened. He was late home on Scout night to begin with. He was white, strained, dark-eyed – though the dirt and general depreciation were no more than usual. But there was the look of a job well done about him as well. A good deed look.

'I found a nest,' he said.

Without looking up from her book his sister (the humane one) said in her guardian tone, 'You cruel thing.'

'They were hatchies,' he said. He would not allow his sister to detect that he had been at all delighted.

'Good job,' his sister said.

His mother cleared a space for his tea, the boy got out his Scout uniform and his father tried the hat on as he always did. Over a hurried tea the boy told his mother about the bird falling from the nest. He forgot to mention his own predicament.

'Was the bird dead?' his sister asked.

'I don't think so.' (He knew it was not even hurt, but only a little disconcerted.)

'"Don't think so". Where is it?' His sister had laid aside her book.

The boy finished chewing a mouthful of food and swallowed hot tea.

'I put it back in the nest,' he said, briefly.

Barren Clough
Neil Campbell

Don't you love the way that sunlight in spring makes everything stunning, when the grass is arrayed with sprays of light, birds' flight catches the colour, the stillness of budding trees is changed slightly by the evening breeze and the fresh air is filled with trills?

It was the coldest winter for thirty or forty years; a winter where snow covered the high hills almost constantly for three months from November and the council's JCB didn't get to grit the road until the day before the defrost, the day the village began to murmur with the mention of heads.

It was when the farmer from Portobello went out into his fields after the thaw that he saw them. The road up out of the village had been thickened with snow and then that snow had iced over, and the same thing down in the village meant sprained wrists and ankles, and an old boy called Magic aggravating a hernia.

Jack lost his wife some years before, and sometimes you would see him in the tractor with his grandson on his knee as they drove up and over the hills. The farmyard held a high flagpole with a flag of St George at the top, and in its flapping or oblong shadow there was a pond, collected at the bottom of Barren Clough. It was a pit stop for geese flying between reservoirs, and the heron from nearby Black Brook.

Jack's black and white cows farted all winter so that when

the wind blew in certain directions you'd think the tin roof of the cow shed might blow off with the force of accumulated methane. In summer when he let them out they wandered black and white across the hills, chewing their way across the skyline, eating the low slung branches off the blossoms in Barren Clough. Sometimes the same noises that came from the shed rang out across the moonlit hills as a strangulated plea that seemed to send a shudder through the leaves.

It was an evening by the pond as Jack tinkered with his tractor that he saw the moonlight shining on something unusual by the bottom of the Clough. Half in the flagpole's shadow, it floated like a sponge, sinking only slightly as the water's weight collected and slowly sucked it down.

Because of the pond and the sight of the others after the snow's thaw, Jack got out his shotgun and donned his deerstalker cap and started roaming across the fields. On the Whaley side of the hills the wind struck him as he squinted across to the trees above Disley. He looked down at the houses on Western Lane and thought of how most of his old friends had died quietly of old age, wondered at the new occupants he didn't know, the youngsters that pulled their faces in their cars when they had to wait as he drove down the lane with hay bales the same way he'd done for forty years.

As he looked down at the houses on Western Lane, Jack thought of his own youth, when he'd moved from Whaley to Bugsworth. He'd got to know a couple of old boys in the Navigation and they played dominoes in the evening. George and Jim scoffed at the notion of Jack calling himself a local when he came from Whaley. Jack asked how you qualified and George told him to come back in twenty-five years, and when he did George was dying. Jack went in to the Navvy and asked for his usual Guinness and the landlady came back with a double whisky from George.

Jack spent all his days on the farm, working harder and harder to get less and less for what he produced. So the shotgun came out and he carried on searching every morning. One night he dreamt his washing line was filled with yellow spiders, bats flew back and forth in the sky and all his windows were covered by mosquitoes.

What Jack couldn't know at first was how it had been done. As a farmer he knew that the threat had been eliminated by many years of killing. He couldn't envisage that coming back, but after weeks and weeks of wandering, after talking to anyone in the village old enough to know what he was talking about, it came to him that maybe, just maybe, they were back. So he started to listen as well as look and it was that that gave him confirmation as he lay in bed listening back to the tenor of his dreams.

In his youth Jack had seen them and wondered why they'd had to do it. And when he went out looking for them again and couldn't find them, all those years later, he started to have nightmares about his youth, his boyish clean-shaven face reappearing among collages, collages like those in the paintings of Hieronymus Bosch.

He knew not to frighten them off by making them aware of his presence, and he guessed he'd have to act fast before they moved away. So he began to observe them from his vantage point in the conservatory, his binoculars trained on the skies above the cow shed and Barren Clough at the horizon line. Night after night he sat there looking at the changing colours of the sky, a sky sometimes white, sometimes blue, often a pervading grey, sometimes a sedentary fire, sometimes yellow, sometimes pink; all the time shining through the trees. And for a time he couldn't see the patterns.

Eventually Jack saw them from the conservatory and grabbed his gun and deerstalker cap and set off out the back of the farm and straight up Barren Clough to the trees on the hillside. He felt the climb in his legs like he never used to, but annoyance and adrenalin hastened him higher until he got to a hiding place behind the trunk of an oak he'd seen rise over forty years.

The shotgun was ready and Jack lifted its weight higher but he had to be sure before starting to blast. And then one of them landed briefly in the branches of the oak and Jack shot upward and brought down great branches on top of himself.

After bringing down the branches it seemed to Jack he'd missed his chance and the red skies went quiet for a while. But inexplicably, tauntingly, they came back in numbers, the red winter sky filled with spiralling blackness and the silences of the hills gone to their gliding, accumulated call.

Jack blasted at the sky, shell after shell, the shotgun ramming his shoulder with every cannonade. He stood there in the growing red, the strength draining from his arms, and then the blackness turned thicker before turning in a wind gust to white. The snow came down heavier and heavier, and though a part of his mind kept telling him to turn around, a stronger, louder part told him that this was something that needed doing now, and so he kept blasting into the snowfall, blasting until the snow stopped and the sky cleared and all was covered by stars.

The flight of black eagles covers the Peak District sky in black glory. You don't see them because the years of persecution are ingrained. And in those bygone days there were reasons above and beyond deeper concerns like the flight of poetry. But now, if you are lucky, maybe a child on an old man's knee on a tractor, you might see them, their wingspan covering counties, their flight from hilltop to hilltop faster than any bullet train you might imagine, faster even than a bullet train of the skies and much quieter, infinitely more elegant than any invention.

And if you get close enough you can hear the vastness of that wingspan as a heavy brush on the sky, and you will know you have seen it and heard it because you will feel it deep down inside yourself, know that the blackness will never go to grey, know what is beyond all government control, and you yourself will fly beyond bullets into the limitless vistas of the sky.

Shrike
David Rose

Redstart on my local patch, darting across Longwood Ponds. A stopover on its trip back to Africa. Late, though. Today's the 28th of October. Should have been well on its way by now. Mustn't allow myself to read too much into it.

Heard today that we have been granted start-up funding for the pilot project on advances in morphic resonance. Now if we can demonstrate a possible link to changes in migration patterns, thence to climate change, we might secure full Project Funding from the European Ornithological Survey.

The link is possible. The concept of morphic resonance – force-fields of memory, like the force-fields round a magnet, directing group behaviour – does have application to migration. Flocks follow established routes laid down many generations ago. Sometimes the routes change, departure times change. Why? How is the new pattern learned? This is culturally, not genetically, transmitted behaviour.

What we hope to postulate, and devise tests for, is the way a few, or even a single bird, can act as pathfinder, establish a new route or timetable, altering the force-field, the group memory. Others follow, strengthening the resonance, reinforcing the field for the species mass.

Flash of red and yellow as I enter the common. I've disturbed a green woodpecker ground-feeding. Long-tailed tits flittering in the hazels. Single blue tit. Scarce round here now.

It was blue tits that started it all. The classic example of individual behaviour affecting group behaviour – the starting point for the concept of morphic resonance. Blue tits suddenly, in the 1920s, learned to peck through milk-bottle tops for the cream. The phenomenon was widely observed in a short time. It died out during the War, when milk bottles also disappeared, both reappearing afterward. Between 1945 and 1947, individual instances were found to occur, then spread rapidly throughout the area, but often well beyond individual breeding ranges. How did they all learn so quickly, almost simultaneously? Not, obviously, by simple imitation, because of the distances between outbreaks.

My own personal interest currently is in establishing the possibility of cross-species alteration in morphic resonance. So far it's been applied only within species – blue tits as an example. What if such alterations in group memory could jump species?

I've been canvassing and collating individual observations for some time. It needs anecdotal evidence to reach a critical mass, then proper observational field studies instituted. If we could just secure project funding, how much difference it could make.

Wettest November for some years. A group of what I took to be dabbling mallards in a run-off pond turned out to be teal when they raised their heads. I worked closer, could see then the yellow undertail. Cheered my day.

Rumours of a brown shrike on Staines Moor. My God, that's fantastically rare. Only two recorded in the British Isles before: one in the Shetlands, one in Cornwall. Now – assuming it's substantiated – one right on my doorstep.

Resisted the temptation. There have been – as expected – hundreds of twitchers inundating the site. Nothing will be seen of any scientific value. It may, on some opinions, turn out to be a woodchat shrike – rare enough, well out of its European range and season, but not the equivalent of a brown, en route from Siberia to India. Ah well. Besides, one vagrant doesn't make a resonance.

Six teal and a pair of gadwall on Shortwood Pond. Plus a male shoveler. Worth braving the cold for.

It was, it's been confirmed, a brown shrike. *Is*, possibly, since there have been recent sightings, latest on New Year's Day. It may well be here now for the duration. But the twitchers have departed. Just a few dedicated birders out there weekends. Worth my while now.

Onto the moor from Hithermoor Road, through the wicket gate, over the boardwalk bridge, then due south to the hawthorn hedge, according to my informant. At least the ground's firm now it's frozen. Sea of mud with the twitchers churning about.

No sign of it here. I've quartered the whole area. Should have brought a spare flask of coffee.

I'm sure it's not here now. I'll risk a closer look in the hawthorn before I go. Maybe a telltale impalement.

Insects, small birds, mammals, impaled on a thorn for later consumption – classic sign of a shrike's presence. Hence its nickname: the butcher bird. But there's nothing here.

Roar of aircraft from Heathrow merging with that of traffic on the M25 as I cut back along the reservoir perimeter. To be added to by the high-speed rail link to the airport if their plans go through. Poor little shrike. All the way from Siberia to end up here. No wonder it's moved on.

*

Sheep still out on the reservoir embankment, despite the cold. Well insulated, I suppose. The fence certainly won't keep out the wind – only trespassers. It's six feet high and topped with – my God. Here on the barbed wire. A wren firmly impaled. Another, along a bit. So it is still here, just found a better larder. Note the coordinates, come back tomorrow. Light's giving out as well as body heat. Swift tramp along the bypass, cut across Shortwood Common and home.

It's not just a tick on a list, you see. Offers a possible observation project. To end up here, on a route from Siberia to India or China, the vagrancy would have to be caused by strong easterlies. But the prevailing winds in November were westerly. A fluke misdirection, or a pathfinder? Time will tell. If, over the next, say, ten years we detect others following the same route, we could establish an altered morphic resonance, a new migratory group memory. Which could, speculatively, relate to climate change. Or not.

Frankly, I don't care, as long as we get the project funding. What would excite me would be for other species to be affected by the force-field; olive-backed or pechora's pipits, say, or dusky warblers. But at least I have a positive observational proposal to strengthen our claim.

God, it's cold, despite my excitement. Shortwood Pond frozen solid. Coots picking through the pasture. A grey heron staring forlornly at the ice. If the cold keeps up like this, the heron population will drop drastically, as in years past. The recent mild winters may be at an end for a while. Could be precarious.

Crisp morning but at least the sky's brighter. No point traipsing round to the Hithermoor entrance. I'll cut across Shortwood and along the bypass, retrace my steps along the fence.

Reeds fire-frosted in the sun.

Caught a glimpse of a barred flank. Shadow of the reeds or – no. It is. A water rail. Scrambling over that frozen trunk. Wonderful. Never have broken cover if the pond weren't frozen over. Ill wind... Heron in the distance. Seems to have found something this time. Angler made a hole in the ice? Need a sledgehammer to do that. Besides, no sign of any one around. In fact, I've seen no-one apart from a girl with a pram, one of those with the fat all-terrain wheels, trundling along the footpath earlier.

I've startled it, it's trying to take off. Struggling, though. Something in its bill. A fish? Big one. Carp perhaps. I've not known herons take fish away. If it's too big to swallow whole, they'll eat it piecemeal on the bank. It's airborne at last. Something flapping. It's the fish. Tail, maybe. Get the bins up.

It's – no, appears to be some sort of wrapping. Paper? Maybe it pinched it from the chip shop. It's heading up, toward the pylon.

No sign of the shrike. Carcasses still there. It's either eking out its food or it's gone. At least I've confirmed its presence. Head home.

Water rail's vanished too, deep into the reeds.

The sun, dropping, dazzling off the pylon, along the cables strung with starlings. I can count thirty ... forty ... fifty-seven on that one stretch from ... something up on the pylon. Not a bird. Skewered there.

Around the legs of the pylon, twenty feet up, there are strings of oversized barbed wire, to deter any suicidal climbers. It's impaled on one of the barbs.

Even with the scope I can't make it out. I'm against the light, distance is too great. Can't get any closer, the pylon is beyond the common, across the allotments.

*

Shrike

There's something caught in the scrub round the pylon's base. White. Whiteish. It's not paper, too limp. Cloth. Looks for all the world like a small square of yellow-stained towelling. Flecked with a pin-glint of light.

The Candling
Deborah Kermode

Chosui took his morning draught before dawn, when the birds were still sleeping. The liquor scalded through his bowels, making him strong, purifying him. He would be fully purged within the hour. As he drained the last drop, the sun was staining the edges of darkness grey and he could hear the peacocks stirring. His heart quickened at the sound: another day of wonder was about to begin.

His routine changed only slightly to accommodate the seasons: the birds ate dried food during the winter and Chosui's potion was also of dried roots and leaves, pounded in a mortar then soaked in hot water; in the summer he dug the roots fresh from the garden and picked the leaves from the blossoming plants. Now, it was spring and the buds were full of promise, showing a glimpse of the tightly furled flower within.

He arose from the long wet grass, barely aware that his trousers were clinging damply to his thighs. Chosui cupped the buds carefully in his hand and bent to sniff them, even though he knew it was too early in the year for them to have an odour. He inwardly reprimanded himself for his impatience; although it was not a named delusion it showed an incontinence of spirit that he must attend to later.

The first cry sounded loud and bright on the morning air and, smiling with pleasure, he turned to greet his teachers. It was the largest male that had cried: he strutted slowly about the garden, his colours muted in the early light.

The others emerged from the shelter and followed him, the males fluffing their feathers against the cool air, displaying a hint of the glory to come, reminding him of the hidden flowers soon to burst from their buds. The females came last, brown and dowdy, looking for all the world like big ducks waddling in the wake of gods. A familiar darkness clouded his happiness.

Chosui stood quietly with his head bowed and waited for the big male to approach him. The peacock lowered his crested head until his long neck briefly touched Chosui's in greeting, then he untwined himself and strutted into the forest of flowers, leaving Chosui drenched in bliss.

He shook himself out of his self-indulgent reverie: the birds must be fed. Already they were pecking at the tight buds, but these were not enough; though the plant was nectar to them, it could not give them the sustenance they needed.

Chosui prepared the peacocks' morning feed while they clustered around the trough, then left them to their meal. As he stood back, he felt light-headed: it was some time since he had eaten. He disliked food; it made him feel bloated and impure, but it was a necessity. He would wash himself, eat, then meditate before reading the sacred texts.

His meagre breakfast of rice and beans was interrupted by a loud banging on the front door which made him catch his breath with shock. He waited silently; perhaps they would go away. But the knocking came again, insistent, so he steeled himself for the encounter and opened the door.

A woman stood there: a dowdy woman, like a peahen. He looked at her. She was not young. Heavy-haunched, wearing wellingtons and a green jacket. Red cheeks; thick wiry black hair threaded with grey. She was smiling. He had never seen her before.

'Hello, I'm Ruth,' she said and stuck out her hand to shake. He ignored it. She thrust both her hands into her capacious pockets, her smile wavering. 'Oh. Well, I'm sorry to drop in unannounced but I haven't got a phone number for you and …'

'What do you want?'

'Feathers, actually. Peacock feathers. You know my daughter, Kelly? She runs that little jewellery shop in the village, Bits N' Bobs. She's just had another baby and I'm minding the shop for the next few months.'

A vague image formed in Chosui's mind: a vacuous pale-skinned girl who made earrings and necklaces from the feathers. His dealings with tradespeople were a necessary evil: they all had to eat.

'Wait here.'

He brought the feathers to her; a fan of iridescent eyes.

'Aren't they beautiful?' she said, stroking them with a stubby finger. 'How do you get them from the peacocks: do you pluck them? I can imagine they'd put up quite a fight.'

'No, of course not,' said Chosui, stiffly. 'They moult. When the summer's over.'

She counted out the notes carefully into his hand; he held his breath and looked away: the sharp stink of money bothered him.

'Please could I see the peacocks?' she asked. 'Sometimes when I walk past I hear them crying; they sound like babies. It makes me sad.'

'They're not … not sad. They're all right.' Unused to talking, he stumbled to a halt. He willed her to leave. There was a smell coming off her; it wasn't just the odour of bank notes, there was something else …

He turned and strode blindly through the house, followed closely by the woman. Her proximity made his skin crawl. He quickened his pace to escape her, flung open the French windows and ran to the bottom of the garden.

'How wonderful; this is more like a field really; isn't it big?'

panted the woman. She was stumbling through the weeds and nettles but catching up quickly. 'I suppose you need all this space for the peacocks. Where are they? Is that their house?'

She pointed at the large, rickety construction of wood and tin at the south end of the garden.

Chosui ignored her, plunged his face into the foliage and breathed deeply until he was calm. When he emerged she was still there, watching him.

'What beautiful plants,' she said. 'I've never seen them before.' She bent over the dark, glossy leaves and gently separated the purple sepals to expose the clusters of blue flowers within.

'You shouldn't touch them,' he said harshly.

'I'm sorry.' She stood back. 'I didn't hurt it.'

'It's dangerous. Not for me and the peafowl. For you. You should keep away from them.'

'How strange, my fingers are tingling.' Ruth examined them, then rubbed her hands on her jeans. 'What is it?'

'Wolfsbane. Monkshood. *Aconitum ferox*. It's deadly poisonous; it kills in minutes.' Chosui smiled, a taut grimace of excitement, enjoying her shocked expression. 'Don't worry; you'll be all right. You have to drink it or eat it. Just stay away.'

She laughed. 'Don't worry, I will.'

The woman had recovered her poise quickly: she was brave. Chosui felt compelled to continue, to impress her: the words tumbled from his mouth, more words than he had uttered in months.

'The birds eat it; it makes them strong and pure. No other creature can survive it. "In jungles of poisonous plants strut the peacocks. These brave ones are never attracted to pleasures, but thrive in the jungle of suffering and pain." That's a quote from the master, Dharmaraksita. And the bodhisattvas are like peacocks: because they are pure, they can take the five poisonous delusions and transform them into enlightenment,

102

which opens as beautifully as a peacock's tail.'

He stopped suddenly, panting with the effort of speech. The woman regarded him with bemusement. 'So you're a bodhisattva, are you?'

Before he could answer, a mournful cry rang out and they both turned to see the large male strut slowly out of the forest of wolfsbane by the shelter. As a peahen emerged from the dark doorway, the cock lifted his train of feathers and spread them into a glorious halo of colour.

'Beautiful,' breathed Ruth. 'Is he...'

'Quiet.' Chosui took her arm, shivering at the human contact, and pulled her down onto her knees with him so that they were both hidden in the long wet grass.

The peacock turned his back to the hen and shook his tail feathers at her with a sound of dry leaves rustling in the wind. The female, apparently uninterested, pecked at the ground, looking for snails or worms. The cock called again to her and Chosui felt the woman beside him shudder at the strange cry.

The hen gave up her pretence and went to him and the peacock mounted her, his wings beating the air. When it was over the hen resumed her search for grubs and the cock, his feathers no longer erect, wandered over to the feeding trough.

'That was incredible,' whispered the woman. 'Will she have babies now?'

'Chicks,' he corrected her. 'Who knows? Sometimes the eggs are fertilised, sometimes they're not.'

'And do you sell the chicks?'

'I sell some of the peacocks; no one wants the females.' He tried to quell the contempt in his voice and failed.

'The males do,' she said, smiling. 'Look at all the trouble they go to, with their beautiful displays and their screaming. They'll do anything to get the girls' attention.'

She was making them sound importunate, desperate. Chosui

103

bristled. 'It's all hormones,' he said tersely. 'They're attracted by the female's hormones. Doesn't matter what she looks like.'

He suddenly became aware that they were still kneeling on the damp earth. 'You can get up now,' he said.

As the woman rose, she pressed deliberately on his shoulder for support. 'Yes,' she said. 'Hormones. They've got a lot to answer for, haven't they?'

He caught something in her expression, a hint of coquetry, and swiftly looked away.

They walked in silence to the house. As he opened the front door to let her out, she picked up the bundle of feathers, raised them to her face and smiled at him over the swaying fan of eyes.

'Mustn't forget these,' she said.

'Come tomorrow, if you like, early,' Chosui heard himself say. 'At dawn. I'll be candling the eggs.'

After she had gone he ran to the garden and sat among the plants, his head in his hands. Why had he said that? He recalled his voice echoing in the narrow hall like the voice of a ventriloquist, inviting the woman to the most private of his duties.

He tugged at the long matted ropes of his hair in self-disgust, his distress growing as he recalled his thinking earlier that morning: that he despised the peahens. The delusion of jealousy. He craved the love of the beautiful ones who were in thrall to them; who in their desire to mate would turn from him as though he ceased to exist the moment a female signalled her acceptance. And then he had repeated his disdain in an effort to impress the woman: the delusion of pride.

That night, he prepared the concoction and left it to brew for ten minutes longer than usual. Only the pure can eat the wolfsbane: the impure must suffer. And he suffered, but his body and his spirit were strong. When he was purged and the shaking had stopped, he felt empty and light. Tomorrow, he would fast.

Chosui slept badly. His dreams were rich and exotically coloured and full of images of a woman: the same woman; no longer plain, but sultry and alluring. He awoke long before dawn, walked naked to the birch tree that grew by the rear wall of the garden to cut himself a rod and flogged himself until the unclean thoughts were driven from his mind.

He barely had time to dress before she arrived. He noted with relief that she looked the same as yesterday: a middle-aged woman with coarse hair, weather-reddened cheeks and an open smile.

Saying nothing, he walked through the French windows and across the rain-filled garden to the shelter. Inside, it was just light enough to see the high perches on which some of the birds roosted. As he entered, Chosui picked up a battery-powered lamp and an old piece of cardboard.

'Over here,' he whispered, and she crouched beside him. The peahen nested on a bed of fir branches and dried grass with two scrawny chicks beside her.

Chosui slid his hand under the bird and eased her off her eggs. There were three of them. She fluttered her wings a little but sleepily settled a few inches away and watched. Chosui switched on the lamp and a blue halogen light glared from the metal cage, so bright that the woman winced and covered her eyes.

He took the piece of cardboard and laid it over the light, so that the beam shone through a small hole in its centre, and held an egg over it.

'This one was laid ten days ago, but you see, it's clear,' he said quietly. 'Should be blood vessels at seven days if it's fertilised.'

He carefully set it aside, out of the peahen's sight.

'What will you do with it?' asked the woman.

'Feed it to the birds. The shells are good for their digestion.'

The woman said nothing, though he felt her disgust. He

could smell her again; that maddening smell filtering through even the odours of wet feathers and birth.

Breathing through his mouth only, Chosui held another egg to the light so that she could see the blood vessels through the thin shell, then returned it to the nest and picked up the remaining egg.

'This one could be overdue,' he said hoarsely. 'I'd say she laid it a month ago; should have hatched by now.' He held it to the narrow beam of light. 'Can you see?' he asked. 'That dark thing in there, that's the beak.'

He held it to her ear and she heard a faint cheeping.

'It wants out,' he said. He turned the egg over; the shell was broken where the chick had pecked it. Chosui carefully inserted his fingernail in the crack and picked a piece of shell off. Blood bloomed onto the smooth surface and the woman recoiled.

'It's all right,' he said. 'Just not quite ready to hatch. It means there's still blood flowing through the umbilical cord, bringing it food from the yolk sac. I'll give it till tonight then come and see how it's doing.'

He placed it back in the nest, then unable to bear her proximity any longer he jumped suddenly to his feet, picked up the unfertilised egg and strode to the door of the shed, the lamp beam jagging wildly around the walls, startling the roosting birds. For a few moments the woman could see nothing but a bright image of the pinhole beam, then she stumbled to the doorway and saw him running across the grass, pausing to hurl the egg into the trough where it smashed into the side and bled yellow yolk.

When she caught up with him, he was sitting cross-legged in the jungle of wolfsbane facing the wall, his bony back to her.

'Are you all right?' she panted. 'Was it something I did? I'm so sorry ...'

'Please, you must go now.'

She saw that he was shaking. 'OK, if that's ... well, thank you anyway. I hope the chick is all right. I'll let myself out.'

He sat for many hours, the aching of his back and thighs a small discomfort that gave him some relief. The woman had asked him if he was a bodhisattva, and he had believed that he was. For like the peacock eating plants that will kill any other creature, he had the power to absorb the five poisonous delusions that fill the mortal body – the delusions of lust, fearful and angry revulsion, ignorance, pride and jealousy – and suffer no harm. Drinking the lethal potion without damage was further evidence of his purity.

He knew he was a bodhisattva no longer. The woman had caused him to fail catastrophically, but through penance he would make himself strong again: only then he would resume drinking the sacred wolfsbane. The thought of the pain he was about to inflict on himself consoled him, and he could almost put out of his mind the scent that had filled his nostrils as the woman crouched beside him in the candling light: the earthy reek of sex.

Ruth thought of him often over the weeks that followed, that strange, gaunt man, burning with a fever whose origin she could not understand. What was his name again? Chop suey? Her daughter told her he had changed his name from Keith, and they'd had a laugh about it. Poor man.

She thought also of the candling; his gentle hands; the bloody membrane beneath the shell. She would never look at an egg in the same way again. And the beautiful spread of the peacock's train as he mounted the hen while they knelt silently together in the long grass. She had felt the man vibrating next to her like a bass string.

The urge to see him grew stronger. He was so pale, malnourished; perhaps she should take food. One evening, she closed the shop early and went to the local supermarket. She bought bread and cheese, rice and canned beans, fruit and vegetables.

He said nothing when he answered the door to her, but turned abruptly and as before she followed him into the garden, dumping her shopping bags in the hall.

'I brought you some food,' she offered. 'Just a few things; I know you don't get out much...'

He turned to face her and she stepped back in shock. His eyes glittered, sunk deep in their sockets; the skin stuck to the skull, no flesh remained.

'I have fought my delusions. I have done penance. I have meditated on the Lord Dharmaraksita's sacred teachings. If you came again, I was going to turn you away. But I cannot, I cannot.'

Chosui tore off his stained white cotton trousers and shirt and threw them to the ground. Naked, he stamped his feet in rhythm and chanted:

'Batter him, batter him, rip out the heart
Of our grasping for ego, our love for ourselves
Trample him, trample him, dance on the head
Of this treacherous concept of selfish concern
Tear out the heart of this self-centred butcher
Who slaughters our chance to gain final release!'

Panting, he turned his back to Ruth, spread his arms wide as though crucified, bowed his head and displayed to her.

Ruth saw a skinny white man pirouetting like a cadaverous ballerina in a parody of *Swan Lake*, his welted ribs and bottom and the backs of his thighs covered with a tattoo of a peacock's tail feathers and train. He tried to scream the cry of the peacock, but his voice was hoarse and it came out as a croak.

'Cluck,' she said. 'Cluck, cluck.' When she started laughing she couldn't stop. 'Cluck,' she wheezed. 'Oh God, I'm sorry, that's too funny.'

By the time she had recovered, he had disappeared into the shelter. Two peacocks raised their heads from the trough and looked at her disdainfully.

'Stupid bloody birds,' she said, tears of laughter still running down her cheeks. 'Stupid bloody woman.'

She walked into the large, dark space. He was kneeling by the nest of the peahen she had seen before, holding a small bird in his hands. She still couldn't remember what he called himself. Keith, that was his real name: it would have to do.

'Keith,' she said, 'I'm sorry. Is that the chick that was about to hatch last time? How is it?'

He turned and threw the darkly feathered carcass onto the straw. 'It was a female,' he said. His voice was back to normal. 'You see?' He picked up another chick. 'This one's a female too, you can tell by the feathers.'

He wrung its neck and discarded it, then picked up another. Ruth put her hands over her mouth.

'Male. Reddish colour; not dark brown like the hens.'

He carefully replaced it, squawking, then picked up the mother peahen and pulled its head off. That took longer. Ruth was weeping.

'Don't worry; the chick will be all right. He's old enough to fend for himself now. That was the last female.'

Chosui threw the bodies into the corner by the door, where they landed with a soft thump on an untidy pile of feathered corpses.

He rose and left the shelter. As Chosui ran towards the house, the large peacock flew down from the trees and took a few tentative steps towards him, but Chosui turned his head away and continued. Ruth jogged in his wake, the tears blurring her vision. By the time she had followed him through the open French windows into the spartan room beyond, he was sitting cross-legged on the floor, a glass of brown liquid in his hand.

She closed the doors behind her because the air was still cool and he was naked, then crouched awkwardly beside him on the bare floorboards.

'Keith, I'm so sorry; I didn't mean to upset you, it just seemed funny at the time…' Her voice petered out. 'It wasn't funny, I was behaving like a stupid child.'

Chosui said nothing; he seemed unaware of her presence. He downed the potion in one, throwing back his head to expose the Adam's apple bobbing between the corded muscles of his throat. His face drained of blood; his jaw clenched and locked. As Ruth put her hand on the cold skin of his back, he vomited bile.

'Keith? Keith! Oh my God, what have you done?'

Led by the big male, the peacocks strutted across the garden and converged on the house, beating their wings against the French windows, the grease from their feathers on the glass like an imprint of angels' wings. Time and again they hurled themselves at the windows, bleeding onto the panes, crying their unearthly cry.

And Ruth could do nothing but run from one side of the room to the other and back again as Chosui convulsed and moaned and the peacocks' heavy bodies smashed into the glass; then they at last fell silent, a mass of broken birds, their intertwined blue necks no longer shining but dull with death, and Chosui was silent, too.

A Revelation of Cormorants
Mark Valentine

'Cormorant, from the Latin for "sea-raven". The Tudors saw the bird as a symbol for gluttony: Shakespeare refers to hungry Time as a cormorant. It may have gained this reputation because of its proficiency at catching fish. Milton, however, invested the bird with a dark glamour: he likened Lucifer sitting in the Tree of Life to a cormorant, no doubt because of the bird's habit of standing with its black wings spread out to dry. The satanic image stuck. The occultist and poet Ludovic Horne wrote of his "Cormorant days/dark and sleek". The atheist essayist Llewelyn Powys refers to the birds as "satanic saints" in Parian niches on the chalk cliffs of Dorset, but he celebrated them too as manifesting the ecstasy of the moment, as they plunge into the sea after the silver-scaled fish of their dreams. Conan Doyle alludes to an untold Sherlock Holmes case of "The Lighthouse Keeper and the Trained Cormorant". Isherwood cites them in a nonsense poem. Folklore about them is much barer than the literary record.'

'Crow. A 15th-century Northern ballad tells of a Crow King who rules by magic. The title may involve a punning reference to the "croaking" of the birds. Scott records a Northumberland superstition which counted crows' caws for purposes of divination. As carrion birds they were associated with gallows and gibbets. Ted Hughes…'

William Utter put down his pen upon his labours at *A Flock of Myths: the Legends, Lore and Literature of the Birds of Britain*, and rubbed his eyes, transferring some of the black ink from his fingers to his eyelids and giving them a bruised, shadowed look. This had the effect of accentuating the length and angularity of his face, which a disobliging acquaintance had once compared to a coffin-lid, with a brass-plaque brow. Utter was in fact quite proud of his brow, which he felt was of the sort once described as 'lofty'. His hair had shrunk from it some years ago, leaving certainly a bare plate upon which Utter would sometimes write with frowns.

He had taken white-walled Watchman's Cottage, on the sea at a little haven in Galloway, for a quarter of the year, to write, or rather (he supposed he should say) compile this book, a commissioned work, which was really a gathering of greater men's titbits, as if he were a tame bird being fed by hand. Contented: perhaps; replete, but unfree. He had been asked to do it, he knew, only because he was a competent cataloguer of facts who could be relied upon to deliver to deadlines. He longed for the time when he would have reached whatever bird it was that began with 'Z'. Zanzibar finch? But that was a long way off, as he worked now through the 'Cs'.

He sighed heavily and the exhalation blew the white slips of paper containing his carefully garnered quotations into the air, where they fluttered for a moment before returning to the surface, in disarray. He muttered to himself and got up impatiently. They could stay like that. Even after just the few days of his stay, settling in, putting everything in proper order, getting in provisions, he felt the need already for some time away from the study lamp.

The only person he had seen to talk to since his arrival was Mr Stair, the caretaker of the cottage, who had let him in and explained its (fairly basic) facilities. Utter had at first wondered if he might undertake a little original research with his new acquaintance. Having established, via a series of cautious pleasantries, that Mr Stair was a local man and had lived in the little fishing harbour most of his life, Utter had mentioned in passing the book he was intending to work on. Then he asked, as he hoped conversationally, if Mr Stair knew of any local sayings about birds. This attempted foray into folklore fieldwork had not proved a marked success.

Mr Stair had lived up to the sound of his name, giving Utter a sombre glare. Then he had run his long fingers through his jackdaw hair – black streaked with silver – and slowly found his way to what proved to be quite a long speech, for him, in that it contained more than one sentence.

'There would be some, I suppose,' he had conceded. 'But myself I give them no heed. You would be better, I'd suggest, just watching what they do. That's the way, I find, to learn about their habits.'

He said this as if he imagined that the visitor really wanted to find out about the local bird-life rather than learning what it was people said about birds, but Utter decided not to pursue the distinction. Politely he had let the conversation run in the direction the caretaker had taken it. He had asked where on the shore might be best for watching the widest range of birds. Mr Stair had regarded him as if this was not a question he was minded to answer. But at length he had said: 'If it's the seabirds you are after, I would go over by the White Strand. But watch for the tides, mind. They come in fast there.'

Now Utter turned over this piece of advice in his mind, like a gull examining a piece of litter for its edibility. As he gazed out of the window to the long grey skies and the hissing ripple of the murky waves, he admitted to himself that he already felt jaded; and now his quotations were all upset. A walk among the rocks on the shore would do him good. He might, indeed, observe some of the birds, as Mr Stair had suggested, though quite what he would be looking for he was not so sure. He supposed there would be crows, and cormorants, and there might be some glimmer of a point of interest about them that he could work into the entries he was writing. He looked at the illustrations of these two birds, and a few others, in a pocket guide he had bought, and got their shapes roughly fixed in his mind.

Then, picking up a raincoat, the notebook containing his work so far from 'Albatross' to 'Crow', and a black umbrella, he left the cottage. As he pulled the door to, his strips of other men's sayings rose up once again for a brief flight above the desk.

Often in Galloway the land only dwindles down to the shore, slowly descending in peterings-out of rocks and last gasps of grassy tussocks. But, following the caretaker's directions, the pensive editor found that the path to White Strand rose from the cove where he was staying to higher ground, and he was walking among heather and dying bracken upon a sheep track above the sea. There was a keenness in the air, the way was lonely, and the calling of the seabirds (which ones he did not exactly know) was sharp and plaintive. The great grey clouds all at once struck him as like closed eyelids, and he frowned at the thought that he was now inventing his own quotations, which would not do at all. But perhaps, he reassured himself, he had merely remembered the image from some more notable source.

After a half an hour's quiet walking upon this ridge, Utter judged that he must have reached the region Mr Stair had described. And indeed down below the sands did seem to have a finer, creamier look to them than their tawnier counterparts of earlier in his wandering. Not white exactly, despite their name: more a wan yellow, they stretched, it seemed to him, like a palimpsest, a piece of wrinkled, blurred papyrus. And those grey rocks: they were surely the residue of ancient writings, all but unreadable now, the characters of some lost language. If one gazed long enough, Utter thought to himself, perhaps the script might be deciphered and the pale pages of the sands would yield up their secrets. And then the sturdier part of himself intruded and made his fingers clutch his raincoat more closely about him so that its flaps did not rise in the wind like fawn wings and carry him soaring off the cliff-top. Puckered up inside his mackintosh, and perched carefully upon a mossy rock, he let the fresh wind buffet him about a bit while he looked to see what birds there might be.

He could only just see over the green lip of the cliff but it was enough for him to descry after a while the flights of birds busy about the shore. Gulls, jackdaws, curlews, he thought he could make out and distinguish. And then – yes, surely: that serrated dark shape, that long neck and the angular form of the wings: they must be the cormorants whose quotability he had just this morning been exploring. They would emerge from the shadow of the sheer tower of rock that he was sitting upon, soar down to the rocks and then launch themselves into the sea to graze for fish. These glides upon the unseen currents of the bright air, followed by the descent to the shore, soon had a fascination for him, as if he were watching an elaborate ritual or piece of theatre, and he found (despite himself) that he was drawn into an eager absorption in the birds' activities.

After a while he began to feel the chill of his exposed perch upon the cold rock and also the pull of seeing the birds at closer quarters. He saw that there was a worn, winding path from the headland to the beach, a narrow channel between the heather and the tall grasses. Carefully, stolidly, he began to follow this down. The wind died about him as he did so, and a greater silence fell for a while, cut only by the cawing and croaking of the birds. The way was not easy: he had to place his boots firmly and sometimes cling on to whatever lay to hand in the undergrowth. Once or twice this proved to be a crop of spiny gorse and his fingers received a sharp tingle followed by a seeping of blood. He cursed and sucked at his maimed hand, but he was not dissuaded and continued to lumber down.

He reached the shoreline at last and from the final ledge of the path gave a little ungainly leap upon the sand, leaving a scuffed imprint. It came to him then as he made his way across the little inlet that, seen from above, if there had been another Utter watching this one, he would look as if he was writing upon the parchment of the shore. There was a quotation, he knew, one of those sonorous Victorian ones no doubt, perpetrated by men with a level stare, yes, and a lofty brow, and a preponderance of whiskers, about footprints in the sands of time. He knew it because it had always seemed to him an absurdly mixed metaphor. The sands of time, surely, are those that run through an hour-glass, showing our moments as they run away. But you can't put footprints in those sands: they are forever running on and, moreover, are generally encased in a glass funnel. But perhaps he was being too literal as well as too literary. The thought was pursued by another, about the moving finger that writ and having writ moved on; and from the high vantage he had just quitted, he supposed he must seem like just such a scribbling digit.

He took a deep breath of the quickening salt breezes and looked all about him. The birds, disturbed by his presence, set up a more clamorous calling, which echoed away at last as he stood still, clutching his umbrella, and they became more used to his presence. He craned back his neck and looked up to the defile he had just negotiated. The cliffs rose as a great looming shadow, but they were cut by vertical gashes into nearly separated columns, so that the effect was like looking at the spines of a vast case of dark basalt books. There was even gilt tooling upon these volumes, made by clusterings of ochreous moss, and perhaps their titles might be read by discerning the

116

imprints and indentations left by the narrow hollows and niches in the rock. And then Utter saw how right the Powys fellow had been: for in many of these hollows he could make out the forms of cormorants, with their black loop of neck and long beak and their upright, inquisitive stance. Even as he observed them in delight, one dropped from its niche and landed on the rocks, looking inquisitively about before suddenly, with a supple twist, taking to the shadowy sea.

He walked further into the bay and settled himself once more upon a rock, this one grey and salt-crusted and festooned at its base with black bladderwrack. White Strand was certainly a favourite habitation of seabirds, and their calling, and the crash of the waves upon the shore, set up a constant background noise like a wireless broadcast from some great station in the clouds. The cormorants were here in great assembly too: not only sheltering in the hollows of the steep cliff-side, but strutting on the shore and standing thoughtfully upon rocks further from him. They were roosting, perhaps, or resting, pausing before one of their fish-seeking dives; or holding out their wings to dry in that Luciferian posture old Milton had evoked; or pecking at their undersides; or simply regarding with their keen dark eyes the world as they found it: a world, he supposed, consisting chiefly of winds, waves, sea-currents, enemies and prey. A world simplified, but also stark and dangerous, where, as Powys had supposed, the bird might take an instinctive pleasure in its own being, in the craft of its fish-catching rituals, in the thrust of the air upon its pinions and the burst of the sea upon its sleek face.

Utter felt a sea fret waft about him, drew his raincoat more closely over his torso, and clung to the bamboo handle of his umbrella. But he did not abandon his study of the cormorants. He felt he could watch for hours their descents, their sea-dippings and their wing-dryings, their apparent glinting-eyed meditations upon what to do next. There always seemed something new to notice. You might think, if put to describing them, that their plumage was black, and there was nothing more to be said. But he soon found this was not wholly true. Beneath the sheen of their scaly cloak of black there was another hue, a subtle tint of malachite when the light was full on them, a hard green mineral gleam only seen at certain angles.

Then what of their wings? We speak, he thought, of birds' wings as if they were all alike, but he could now see that those of the cormorant had indeed something archangelic, and heraldic, about them. The way they were raised by the bird made them seem like shields of silver held in readiness by a knight's squire for a great tournament.

All the time he watched them he stayed still upon his rock regardless of the lappings of saltwater that found their way around him in little thrusting rivulets. And after a while it was as if the birds became almost used to him, and came to regard him as just an odd outcrop of rock. They began to land and to rest quite close by him and he was able to see their fine malachite-black cloaks and their mythic wings at the closest possible quarters. He became entranced too by their gaze. One great old cormorant stood on the next rock to him, in its tilt-headed attitude, with its long hook of neck, and glared at him from its black eye with its rim of silver. He could not free himself from regarding the dark grace and the saturnine stare of the bird; he saw now exactly why those writers wanted to make it a myth or a metaphor, for it seemed to belong to some other, plutonic dimension, some strange black gulf of a different time. He looked long upon the preening, prying bird while a wild roar grew around him, as if indeed he were on the brink of entering some other plane of existence.

And when he stirred at last from this reverie, he found that the little foaming streams around his rock had been fortified by a greater advance of the waves, and, gazing more widely, that in fact the sea had burst in upon the shore in great grey drives. He had better get back. He saw that he would have to hop from rock to rock if he were not to get his feet wet. Balancing himself with his umbrella like some seashore Blondin, he began to wobble from one rock to another; and then found that there were no more left, and he was not yet on what could be called the shore; indeed, that there was not very much at all that might now be called shore, for the sea was upon it all. He looked for where his cliff path was, but he could not make it out; and he realised that even if he did, he could not get to it, because the sea between where he was and where the path might be was now surging in strong currents. Annoyed with himself, he teetered back to where he had been and began to wade through the still traversable tide, feeling its cold claws clutch at his feet, tugging at him. He pushed on as hard as he could toward the base of the rock face but found that the pull of the tide became greater almost at each heavy tread. At last, thoroughly wet and worn out, he made ground on a flat rim of rocks immediately in the lee of the cliff.

He turned and saw the waves pound towards him. He looked down and saw the salt encrustations and the marine weeds even upon the rocks where he stood. These, too, then would be engulfed, and he did not know with what force; he must go further up. Perhaps there might be another path, a way across the face of the rock; it was steep, certainly, but he could make out hand-holds and boot-hollows. Possibly people had been up that way before. He took hold firmly of a chunk of rock and hoisted himself up, then looked about for another and made a diagonal line across the bleak surface. The sea crashed below him and made a greedy sucking noise at the base of the cliff. He scraped his hands and knees as he scrambled further up.

And then his burst of resolution gave way. No obvious places to grip presented themselves to his view. It still seemed a very long way up the cliff and the dim track he had hoped for was no longer apparent. Yet the sea was still roaring against the rocks and thrusting its pale tentacles of spray up towards him: it might only take one really big wave to dash him away. He inched very gingerly onwards until he felt he could go no further. He thrust himself in a sudden imploring hug against the cliff, as if its very nearness made him more secure. And then he tried to think.

But absurdly, all he called to mind was a questionnaire he had been sent the year before in preparation for giving a radio interview about one of his books. Amongst the many trivial and vulgar questions was one which had asked when he had come nearest to death. He had been tempted to answer on the form: 'While doing this: by boredom', but supposed that the answer would not be original. In fact, the question might be better than it seemed; for it had perplexed him. In his forty-four years he did not know that he had ever been close to that highest risk of all. Well, perhaps now he was; now, if he survived, he could certainly quote this experience. He even began, to distract himself and delay taking any decision about inching further up the severe rock face, to compose how he would now word his answer: 'Questing for cormorants, I...'

But that supposed, of course, that he would live to tell the tale. A sudden fevered surge of fear leapt up in him and his whitened fingers clung even more tenaciously to the little rims of the rock face. A cloud cleared the sun and he saw outlined in a film of light every crevice, every crack, each striation and scratch upon the adamantine surface. It was like looking at a strange map. But the effect, far from giving him a sure route, was that of casting him into despondency. There simply were not sufficient wide enough and secure enough hand-holds for him to claw at, still less sockets or ledges where he might rest his feet. And even if he did succeed in negotiating the hazardous way, he could not deny that at the very top of the climb there appeared to be a great overhang, thrusting out from the vertical column he was on, so that he would have to work his way at an acute angle over and around it. A very seasoned climber, with all the right impedimenta, might manage it; he knew that he could not.

Very, very slowly he manoeuvred his feet upon the bare outcrop and cautiously turned his body around, keeping his gaze at first straight ahead. Don't look down, he told himself, don't look now. He pushed his palms against the merest hint of pillars on either side of him, and his raincoat unfurled its fawn wings. There was nothing further he could do. There was no question of descending again, for he could not trust himself to do it: and there was no hope of ascending all that terrible way he had seen illumined around him. He would have to wait until somebody came. Perhaps the caretaker might at length wonder that he had not seen him all day, and, remembering their conversation, set out to search for him. He clung to that dim hope as to the rock, with a forlorn desperation.

At intervals he gave a hoarse cry in case there should be anyone passing above, and he was answered by calls quite like his own, coarse and shrill, from the seabirds he had disturbed.

The day darkened; he could see he would soon be benighted here. In the gloom it would be harder to keep his balance, harder to stay awake. It already seemed many hours that he had been here and he was very tired. Inevitably after a while he started to imagine, though he knew he must not, what it would be like when – if – he could hold on no longer and he dropped into the churning waters. Could he even then contrive a graceful dive, or would he simply flop? Would he strike his head on a rock, and end things insensible? Or struggle and gasp against the force of the waters until his breath gave out?

In the last of the light he thought he saw a dark flicker of movement come to rest in the next niche of rock to his. There was a sense as of a supple sliver of shape, and a rank, fishy stench. A single bead of black light seemed to stare at him. He remained perfectly still. They were all wrong, really, he reflected, those great men. The cormorant was not after all an embodied vice, not a devil, a dandy or a pagan saint: it was, like his days, like all our days, a living dark question mark, a plunge from the edge of existence into the silvery glinting silence of the future. Yes, that was it. Furtively, with extreme care, he removed his palms from their place of steadying, and then righted himself, reached into the pocket of his raincoat, and took out his notebook and pen. After the entry on the cormorant, he wrote, slowly, gently, 'Myself, I have come to the conclusion ...'

The Brids
Bill Broady

Many people considered Pamela beautiful – regulation blonde and willowy, with a shy but confident air – but she never did much for me. Of course I fancied her – in a regulation way – but I wasn't prepared to jump through hoops for her and she was obviously the kind of girl for whom the hoops would be at least half the fun. Nevertheless, throughout my peripatetic college years, we somehow always ended up living together. Whenever I moved she would – as if by some ineluctable natural law – attach herself to one of my new housemates, then stay on after they had gone. It was all rather curious because she obviously did not fancy me in the least – not even in the regulation way.

Pam had lots of friends, mainly from her English and Drama course, but she also, for no apparent reason, moved in political circles. Our kitchen was always full of actresses advocating anarcho-syndicalism while the politicos extolled the Stanislavski technique. She was a brilliant cook, feeding the multitudes night after night on a budget of next to nothing. Although she loved to party, she abjured drink and dope: her shiny hatchback ferried our dishevelled crew at blinding speeds along the unlit roads of Oxfordshire. One night, when she had stopped to allow her passengers to vomit in a field, she turned her huge bright eyes on me.

'You *understand,* don't you?'

Her voice had an unusually deep and serious note. This

was evidently a significant moment but I had no idea what she might mean.

'Yes', I said. 'I understand.'

After graduation I didn't hear from her for a while but when she finally turned up at my double basement in Bayswater we both knew that she would be staying. I was struggling with the rent and her tyro theatre company had just received an enormous grant to re-enact the English Civil War in a condemned tower block in Peckham. The climax, Pam said, would be King Charles being decapitated in the descending lift, after which the dynamite charges would be set off. In the meantime she was dancing in the chorus of *Sweet Charity* at the Savoy.

As always, she had five or six boyfriends in attendance: she liked to be pursued. She kept an elaborate chart with ticks and crosses in the appropriate boxes; it was as if she was casting her leading man. She would send them out on quests – to obtain a glockenspiel or some properly oval Turkish cigarettes, to slay dragons and ogres or to lay the Holy Grail before her surprisingly large and knobbly feet.

Alan, an actor, appeared to be the favourite. 'He's going to be on telly,' she said, in tones that somehow combined awe and disdain, 'playing Abraxas Dingle in *Emmerdale*'. He was absolutely perfect for her, except for his phobia. 'Why is there always something wrong with everybody?' she complained.

'What exactly *is* this phobia?' I asked.

She handed me a small laminated card which read

I AM AFRAID

OF

BRIDS

'Ornithophobia!' she laughed, when I still looked blank. 'Birds! He can't bear to say the word. He can't even write it down.'

'My God,' I said, 'if we all started changing the words for things we don't like, where would it ever end?'

'Mind you,' she conceded, 'I'm nearly as bad about redips.'

It was true. 'Killitkillitkillit!' she would scream if she even suspected that there might be a spider in the room. I didn't really kill them, though I told her I did, just gave them a good talking-to and released them in the garden.

'He told me that he only became an actor because he thought that inside the theatre he would be safe from birds.'

'What about *The Seagull*?' I asked.

One Saturday morning I found a note pinned to the fridge: V. IMPORTANT. MEET ME MIDDAY. NAT. GALL. STEPS.

When I got to the gallery I nearly walked straight past Pam, masked as she was by a pair of Edie Sedgwick-style shades – round, white plastic-rimmed – with her hair piled up under a satin bipperty-bopperty hat.

'You're just in time.' She grasped my arm and pointed out across Trafalgar Square. 'There's Alan now.'

A very tall, very thin man was crossing Northumberland Avenue. He looked around – Pam ducked behind a pillar – then carefully placed a newspaper on a bench and sat down.

'I'm meeting him,' Pam whispered. 'Or, rather, I'm *not* meeting him.'

It was as if the birds had been waiting for Alan. From north and west and east they came, fast and low. The beating of those shimmery wings combined into a great sigh of infinite compassion. Alan did not react as they were landing around him but his immobility was now of a different order.

I had never paid much attention to the pigeon. What varieties there were! What subtle gradations of green to blue to purple, from black to white through grey! They were moving forward with a regal, ruthless motion, like catwalk models crossed with stormtroopers. Some appeared to already have blood spattered on their breasts. The legs were horribly shrivelled but the talons looked razor sharp. I didn't blame Alan for being afraid: they reminded me of my grandparents.

He leapt to his feet and began to run. The pigeons chased him clockwise all round the square and then back again, widdershins. They no longer seemed to be flying, it was more as if they were being thrown at him by invisible hands. One of them clung to the instep of his right foot; kick as high as he might he still couldn't shake it free.

When they finally broke off to regroup there was something heroic about the way Alan walked back to his bench, sat down on his paper and recrossed his legs. When they returned he shut his eyes and clapped his hands over his ears but then a white, yellow-streaked dove alighted on his head to peck into the dark curly hair and he was up and their dance began again.

Tourists were applauding and photographing them. Under the impression that Alan and the birds had choreographed this whole routine, they were looking for a hat into which to drop their money. A couple of black-headed gulls chased the pigeons away, but only so that they could torment him themselves. I had to admit that it did look funny; up on his pillar even Nelson appeared to be smirking. At last Alan stopped running and just stood in the dead centre of the square, beating at his own head, as if the birds were now mainly inside it.

'Perhaps you should go over there now,' I suggested.

'No.' She began pulling me up the steps. 'Let's leave him to it.'

We ended up in front of Titian's *Death of Actaeon*. I didn't like it so much since they'd cleaned it and you could see what was actually going on. It was just a pack of dogs tearing apart a stag-headed man. I became aware that Pam was looking at me, not the painting.

'You *do* understand, don't you?'

I was not in the mood for revelations.

'Absolutely,' I replied.

That evening Alan rang; he apologised to her for getting the time wrong. I was feeling guilty so I decided to give the poor devil some help. I told Pam that in two days' time the great migrating streams of geese – barnacles, brents and greylags – would be making their annual convergence on Hampstead Heath, to land on the sward between Kenwood House and The Pond.

'The skies will be black with them,' I told her, 'honking and flapping away. It'll be dangerous, of course: they'll be fractious and hungry after their long flight. Every twitcher in London will be there.'

'It sounds ideal,' she said. 'What's a twitcher?'

She dressed herself up for Kenwood in a blue and white retro twinset I had never seen before. Her newly cut hair was now lacquered into a silver helmet. She twirled round, flapping her arms. 'So, do I look like Tippi Hedren in *The Birds*?'

'More like Patsy Hendren.' I looked her up and down. 'Crossed with Tippoo's mechanical tiger.'

Her smile vanished and her eyes filled with tears.

'No, no,' I said hurriedly. 'You're perfect. Drop-dead gorgeous. Absolutely the bride of the brids.'

That was the thing about Pam: she couldn't bear being teased.

'Your geese never turned up,' she said that evening.

'The wind changed,' I replied. 'And they landed on the pitch at Lords. It was on television. Hundreds were killed. The Second Test Match has been abandoned.'

'Anyway, it all worked out fine.' She started trying to unstick her hair. 'There was this robin that kept following us, making a sort of weird choking noise. Alan said it was ancient Aramaic backwards; I was getting quite scared myself. I left him in Highgate: he went into a phone box and refused to come out.'

I assumed that Alan was out of the reckoning until a fortnight later when he turned up on the doorstep, carrying a litre bottle of rosé. He really was a remarkably handsome man: a pale glow seemed to come off his perfect skin. Unlike most tall people, when confronted by someone shorter than himself he did not dip at the knees but instead threw back his shoulders and stretched out his neck as if heading an invisible football. At this moment I stopped feeling sorry for him.

'Don't go!' Pam mouthed at me, so Alan and I were left to make increasingly awkward conversation while she, white-gowned like a surgeon, worked her magic in the kitchen. He didn't seem to share my taste in music. 'What *is* that disgusting racket?' he asked. I held up the album cover on which Charlie Parker's head had been appended to the body of an enormous sparrow. '*Brid Lives*!' I said.

It was a relief when dinner was served. Individual poussins stuffed with chestnuts, diced carrots, cream cheese and seven other things beginning with 'c'. Alan merely prodded at it with his knife.

'They're poultry,' I reassured him. 'They can't fly.'

'They've got the eyes, though,' he mumbled. 'That's the thing.'

'Now you're getting ridiculous,' said Pam. 'I didn't cook their eyes.'

'I love pigs,' Alan said defiantly. 'And cows. And I like eating them as well.'

Things did not improve. Pam was trying to persuade him to play Charles I in Peckham while he insisted that *Emmerdale* would be taking up all of his time. I was surprised to hear this;

I'd thought that they just threw that shit together. 'No!' he finally yelled. 'He's a king and he's a midget! I just can't play it!'

I decided to go to bed but Alan got up too. 'I'm driving up to Yorkshire tomorrow, early.' He tried to kiss Pam goodnight but only succeeded in pecking her shoulder. I could tell by the way she crashed around her bedroom afterwards that she was not happy with how the evening had gone.

She was beginning to worry me. Of all the flats and houses we had shared this was the first time that we'd had a common dividing wall. I could hear everything: the drawers opening and closing, her shoes hitting the floor, the click as her wristwatch was laid on the bedside table. She always murmured some indistinct prayer before pulling the light cord. Her breathing was regular and deep with only the occasional growly snore. I wasn't embarrassed or aroused; if anything I found it rather sad. What *was* strange, however, was that on the three occasions that a man stayed overnight for the final test – which they all failed presumably, because none came back again – there had been no sound whatsoever. Even her clock had apparently stopped ticking. I tried to convince myself that I had fallen asleep and merely dreamed that silence.

When I got home late on Friday I was greeted by Pam in what could only be described as a baby-doll nightdress. 'Alan's coming!' she said triumphantly. I wondered what she might have been cooking: there was a funny smell like when you're in the zoo, approaching the big cats' enclosures. And there was an even stranger sound: a high-pitched formless twittering – I'd never thought that Ligetti or Messiaen would be Pam's cup of tea. She threw open the door to her bedroom; it had seemed to become larger after she had moved in. Now it was full of birds, all singing away, happy as Larry. Their wonderfully ornate cages gave the impression of a scaled-down Kew Gardens. I guessed that the greenish ones might be canaries and the bigger ones mynahs or macaws. I knew the toucan; it looked like a cartoon of itself. Its beak was so yellow that I just had to laugh. One spiky-feathered little chap seemed almost beside himself with fury.

'What's that blue thing like a demented budgie?'

'I think it's a budgie,' said Pam.

A tremendous heat was coming off the birds. It was like being in a jungle: I was afraid that I might be about to sweat.

'Wherever did you get them?'

'From Luther down at *Feather and Fur.* Fifty quid for overnight hire. He'll pick them up tomorrow morning.'

'Didn't he find it rather a strange request?'

'No. He never batted an eye, just asked me what I'd like them to do. So I said I'd like them to kick up an almighty fuss for an hour or so and then go silent as the grave. "Fine," he said. "That's what folk usually want."'

Then Alan arrived and she wasted no time on preliminaries. Hooking her thumb under the fancy buckle of his belt, she drew him inside the bedroom and firmly closed the door. I expected him to come straight back out, screaming, but nothing happened.

I put on the headphones and turned the music up. For hours I tried to read but couldn't concentrate. When I finally went through, the silence from her room was absolute: she must have draped the birdcages. As I lay on my bed I couldn't even hear my own breathing or my heartbeat or the low humming of my circulating blood. I could clearly discern waves of ever-deepening darkness pulsating across the ceiling. I got up and sat at the kitchen table, squinting through the railings. During the day our street was virtually deserted but at night it was surprising how many pairs of dark-trousered legs passed above. Some of them paused for five minutes at a time, as if they were watching or listening for something. Surely they couldn't all be burglars?

At seven, Alan appeared. His face was grey and he seemed to have somehow diminished inside his clothes. It looked as if every bone in his body had been broken and then badly reset. He positively snarled at the sounds emanating from my poor pink plastic Dansette. *Klactoveesedstene* was obviously not his idea of an aubade. Without a word he drained my coffee cup and then ran up the stairs. The engine of his car took some time to start and I heard him hit something as he pulled out: Pam's Volvo, presumably, as he had parked close behind it.

An hour later Pam herself emerged. The birds were still silent.

'That was fun.' She yawned and stretched luxuriously. 'But I don't think I'll be seeing Alan again.' She sighed. 'Anyway, at least I've cured him of his fear of brids.'

'Yes,' I said, 'but now he'll be terrified of women instead.'

She scraped the cold coffee grounds into her cup: Miles Davis hurtled into 'Bird Gets the Worm'.

'But I thought you said you understood, my dear... That's how it's *supposed* to be.'

Rarely Visits Gardens
Juliet West

It is very cold, and the snow is still falling. I'm standing at the french doors in my dressing-gown. Birds huddle in the maple tree, feather-fat and freezing. I think they must be hungry. A bowl of dry cornflakes lies half-eaten on the kitchen table. I grind the flakes into tiny pieces, unlock the french doors and walk onto the white lawn in my bare feet. Snow flattens under my toes and sends discs of pain up through my heels, into my ankles, the cold so extreme it is like being branded with ice.

I scatter the cereal crumbs across the lawn. My head feels spacious on this January morning; big with silence. No cars on the road. No children walking to school.

I like this day.

The starlings arrive first. They strut about like evil bastards, attacking the flakes with their dagger beaks. A blackbird flies down, then a pair of chaffinches. They don't seem to notice me, sitting on the bench under the pergola. I'm keeping as still as I can. Trying not to shiver.

On the shed roof another bird perches, watching the feast. It's speckled like a thrush, but it has pale yellow stripes above and below its eyes and chestnut-red under its wings. There's something rakish about this bird – it has the look of a highwayman. Its head jerks up, and a black eye stares straight at me. For a long time we look at each other, and my vision separates into blocks of colour. White snow, black eyes, red flanks. A thick slice of snow slides from a branch of the maple tree onto the shed, scaring the bird away. It flies over the neighbours' gardens, disappearing behind the church hall at the end of the road.

Something flickers inside me: a spark of energy.

I find a picture of the bird on the internet. It's a redwing. The website is very informative. *Redwings roam across the countryside, feeding in fields and hedgerows*, it says. The text is broken up by a picture of a redwing on a leafless branch, eyeing a cluster of ripe red fruit. *The redwing rarely visits gardens, except in the coldest weather when snow covers fields.*

Rarely visits gardens.

For a change, I decide to get dressed. I even take a shower. The shampoo suds are grey with dirt and grease and they slick down the plughole with strands of my dark blonde hair. I bend down to pull at the strands and they come free from the plughole with a clump of black hair tangled up underneath. This hair belongs to Kesh. Instead of crying, I smile and tease out the Kesh strands, laying them side by side on the edge of the sink. When they are dry I put them in my reliquary with the other items: his toothbrush, a chewed fingernail, the book he was reading.

Deciding what to wear takes until lunchtime. I start off in Kesh's clothes, but I don't want my smell to infect them. This has happened to two of his shirts already. Finally, I squeeze into a black jumper dress, cashmere, with burgundy ribbed tights and black high heels. I even apply make-up, and when I look at myself in the mirror I smile at the stranger gazing back with kohl eyes and glossy hair.

Downstairs, I find a bag of raisins. I plump them in warm water from the kettle then step out into the garden, dropping a trail of raisins as I walk. The bench under the pergola is pillowed in snow. When I sink down onto it, the snow squeaks.

It doesn't take long for the starlings to crash in, then the blackbirds and a song thrush. A flash of red lands on the ivy, but it's only a robin. I have time, though. I can be patient. Darkness falls, and I am still waiting. He's a highwayman bird. Maybe he'll come out at night.

There's a movement in the maple tree. I think I can see the stripes of the redwing, but in the gloom it's hard to be sure.

When the sound comes, a quiet *hello*, I jump up from the bench too fast. My feet slide from under me, a sickening lurch. I gasp as the man breaks my fall, one arm around my back, the other gripping my wrist.

He looks very pale. Perhaps it's the reflection of snow on his skin.

'So sorry,' he says. 'I didn't mean to frighten you.'

'It's … terribly cold,' I say.

'Yes.' He releases his hold, takes a step back. Is he going so soon? Then he looks me up and down, fixes on my eyes. 'You're all dressed up, with nowhere –'

'– Cocoa?' I ask, and step carefully towards the french doors.

He follows close behind, stamping his feet and sprinkling snow crystals over the wooden floor.

I don't care what he thinks of the house. It's filthy, of course. Dust veils the living room; it dulls the coffee table, the mantelpiece, the hardened pools of melted candle wax. The peaches in the fruit bowl have been there since July. On the day Kesh died, they sagged with a sudden grey mould. Over the months I've watched their transformation. Just black-brown lumps now, smelling of earth.

The man takes off his hat and I'm surprised to see he doesn't have any hair. It's shaved close against his scalp. He has wide amber eyes and his lashes are long, like a child's. His mouth is beautiful, and when he smiles I have the strange sensation that

I am seeing the whole of him – boy, adolescent, lover, old man. He is tall like Kesh, six feet one. I cannot breathe.

'I'll warm some milk,' I say, gesturing for him to sit on the sofa. In the kitchen, I lean against the worktop, mind racing. There's no milk. All I can offer him is hot water, or the brandy Kesh's friend brought round after the accident. Paul has stopped coming now, like everyone else. I told him it was for the best.

I reach for the brandy in the top cupboard and suddenly I'm hot in my tight woollen dress, my body fizzing and prickling as the icy numbness wears off. Blood is rushing to my cheeks, and I grab a pile of unopened Christmas cards I'd left on the windowsill, splay them into a fan and feel the cool breeze on my face. Calmer now, I take two glasses and place them on to a tray with the bottle.

He has chosen Kesh's side of the sofa, next to the bookcase and the orchid which I've managed not to kill.

'I'm afraid there's no cocoa,' I say. 'Is brandy okay?'

He scrutinises the bottle.

'Brandy would be perfect,' he says, unzipping his black fleece jacket.

We sit next to each other on the sofa, a few empty inches between us. He stretches out an arm and squeezes an orchid flower. I imagine the scar it will leave, a brown mark against the white fleshy petal. Then he gestures towards the photograph of me and Kesh. We're on top of Stoodley Pike, laughing into the wind.

'Your husband?' he asks.

'Yes,' I tell him, and he nods.

We're onto our second glass of brandy when he leans over and brushes my cheek with the back of his hand. The touch is like a jab, a hypodermic shot through my skin; such exquisite pain I could cry with pleasure.

135

I lean towards him, put my hands up to his face. But he pulls back.

'Later,' he says, running his hands down the cashmere, assessing the curve of my breasts, my belly. 'I'll come back.'

Next morning it has stopped snowing but there's no sign of a thaw. I scatter raisins again, hoping to see the redwing, but the starlings peck up all the food and then there's nothing left to offer.

I decide to do a little housework. I clean out the fruit bowl and empty the ashtray. There were six cigarette butts in there, sticky with my mum's pink lipstick. The last time she came was some time in late October when she caught the bus down from Keighley. Sat there chain-smoking. 'I knew no good would come of it,' she sighed. 'You marrying a ...' She took a deep drag to stop herself saying Paki. '... an outsider,' she said.

At two I boil the kettle for my soup.

'Tomato and lentil?' I say to the birds, who can't hear me. I imagine the red powder tipped onto the snow, sinking in like blood specks.

I add the boiled water and take a few sips. As the liquid hits my stomach I feel nauseous with guilt. What am I thinking, cooking for myself while the birds outside are starving and shivering to death?

The village is almost deserted, but the hardware store is still open. At the back of the shop there are two shelves stacked with bird food. Mealworms, suet cake, fat balls, raisins. It's hard to choose, so I take everything. The shop assistant packs them into two plastic bags and tells me I'm generous. 'Nice to think of the wildlife,' she says. Her hands seem very large.

The pavements are icy, but my shopping bags are like anchors or counterweights and I glide home without falling.

In the garden, the shed door is wedged shut with snow. I kick away the icy lumps and slide back the bolts. The door creaks open and Kesh's blue jacket is hanging over the handle of the lawnmower. I almost fall onto it, gathering it up to my face, then thrusting my hands into the pockets. There are some dried grass clippings which cling to the wool of my gloves, and a crumpled brown envelope with a shopping list on the back. *Olives, feta, basil, bread,* in Kesh's small loopy handwriting. My mouth floods with saliva and I can almost taste it, the food we ate that summer Sunday. It was our last weekend together, and we sat outside drinking white wine, closing our eyes to the sun and dozing on the picnic blanket until Kesh said, *The air is starting to chill,* and we went straight up to bed, refilling our wine glasses on the way.

I place the grass clippings inside the envelope, fold the shopping list and tuck it carefully into my pocket. Something new for the reliquary.

It's tempting to go inside now, to curl into bed, but a bird is singing at the bottom of the garden. A single note; clipped, erratic, hungry. I rip open the packets of food, fling raisins and mealworms around the lawn and loop a fat ball onto a low branch of the maple.

I wait inside this time, on a wooden stool which I've pulled up to the french doors. I've only been there a few minutes when the redwing arrives. It's back on the shed roof, watching me, ignoring the food and the other birds which dart about on the ground below. I feel dizzy again, but not sick. Excitement is aching in my gut and when the doorbell rings I stand up so fast the starlings take off with an outraged chatter.

He smiles when I open the front door, and walks into the hall without speaking. He kicks snow clumps off his boots and unlaces them slowly. The brandy and the glasses are still on the tray in the living room. I splash brandy into the glasses as he sits down on the sofa. His fingers slide across mine when he takes the drink.

I ask him if he is hungry, but he shakes his head. 'Tell me about your husband,' he says, looking again at the photograph next to the orchid.

His family were from Kerala, I tell him. Kesh was a prince – no really – way back, he was descended from a long line of princes. He worked as an architect and we were almost rich. This upset my family more than anything. *They come over here, they take our jobs…* But we were so happy, nothing could touch us. Life was wonderful until that day in July.

'July?' the man asks.

A little girl was crossing the road, on her way to school. She was nine years old. He hit her and then he hit a grain truck. Death was instant, the coroner said. Nobody felt a thing.

'You must have loved your husband very much,' he says.

I nod, but I am not choked by grief. Only desire, which rises in my throat so powerfully that my body sways towards him and my hand moves onto his thigh.

He puts his heavy hand over mine. Now he will kiss me, I think. But he lifts my hand from his and drops it onto the sofa like a hunk of dead meat.

'You loved him so much that now you are throwing yourself at a stranger who has come into your house without even telling you his name. You loved him so much you would betray him in an instant – even while his unborn child is kicking inside your womb?'

He picks a petal from the orchid, rolls it between his thumb and forefinger. I put my hands over my ears and clamp shut my eyes. My moan turns into a scream. A sound I don't recognise. He has noticed, so it must be true. But – a baby? It is grotesque. It is Kesh I want, not a baby. What good is a baby with a dead father? A baby with me for a mother?

I must talk to the man, make him understand, but as I open my eyes he stands, shoves his feet into his boots and steps out through the French doors. His footsteps crunch across the lawn in the afternoon dusk.

'Please...' I shout through the open door. But now the garden is empty. The snow on the lawn is smooth as milk.

The silence is tight now, small and oppressive. I need to feel the ice on my skin once more, the expanse of cold, the surging energy of it.

I take off my socks and step barefoot into the creeping darkness of the back garden. In the snow-white night my belly looks huge, round as the moon, and when I press my hands against the taut bump the baby kicks hard, deep inside like a hammer pounding into velvet.

Under the maple tree there is a depression in the snow. I move closer. The redwing is lying on its side, yellow stripes luminous around its unblinking eye.

My baby kicks again and I know it is time to go inside. Tomorrow I will buy food. Apples and eggs. Milk, bread.

But first I must bury my poor dead visitor. I pick up a handful of snow and scatter the flakes over the small body on the lawn. They make the tiniest sound, *tat tat tat*, on his stiff brown feathers.

All Our Dead Heavens
Conrad Williams

I was convinced I saw a star die as the 747 made its final approach. You missed it because you were asleep and I didn't tell you when you stirred because I knew you'd ridicule me. How often have you told me I live with my head in the clouds? Perhaps I'd learnt by then not to provide the ammunition with which you often shot me down; a lesson it had taken me long enough to take on board.

Maybe I should have recognised that collapsed light as a sign, a symbol of what had happened between us. Hard not to with hindsight but at the time I was still hopeful, untouched by your cynicism. A cruel part of me still whispers that you accompanied me not because of the prospect of reconciliation but for the free holiday it was for you. Fitting, wasn't it, that the dead should have paid for all this? It was no holiday for me, more an attempt to revive something between us that had once been so alive. The trip took a big bite out of my share of Dad's estate but your smile, your hand in mine as we stepped on to the tarmac at Plaisance Airport rallied my optimism, justified the expense. We drove the rented car to the Shandrani – a quiet little hotel on the south-east coast of Mauritius – with the windows open, your cheek resting on my shoulder. The smell of burnt sugar cane made you hungry and me tired. Remember we stopped for a few minutes to look at the Southern Cross? It reached for the Earth's curve beyond which England lay beneath skies these stars would never visit. The sky was at once darker and more alive than any other I'd seen. There was a low flash of pale white, like the inside of an eggshell: a bird of some sort. Nightfishing, maybe. Flying purely for the fun of it.

It was too dark to go for a walk so we ate a light meal at the hotel before I hunted for our room. You stayed in the bar: there was a jazz band playing – piano and lazy brass – so I missed you coming to bed. Some time before dawn I felt your mouth moving upon me and we made slow, sleepy love though I'm not sure how far from sleep I strayed, for the next thing I knew, a honeyed patch of light was where you should have been and I had to convince myself I'd not dreamt the whole thing.

A set of shadowed prints in the coral sand led down to the sea. I waited beneath a parasol near the portion of beach which met the leading edge of filao trees, hoping you would appear soon so we could breakfast together.

I was ten when I first came here with my parents. The Shandrani was known as Le Chaland then. We would sit on the hot sand and eat toasted cheese sandwiches or so much fresh pineapple it made your teeth itch. That dead tree on the outcrop of rock separating this beach from Blue Bay still clawed towards the Indian Ocean. I felt it must mean something that in the time before knowing you and meeting you and loving you and now, the tree stood through it all. I'd walked this beach with an Australian boy who gave me a dead starfish for helping him hunt for snakes that we never found. *Here, turn that rock over. Edge of the beach ... try under that deadwood.* Over there was the verandah where my father cut his hand on a broken bottle (I'd hunted for the scar as he lay in his coffin; it had been the thing that persuaded me it was really him). Further along – I could just see it from here – were the scorched lawns upon which I'd played chess with an old man from Düsseldorf who called me The Maestro. At the time he was just a German with gallstones. Eric, his name was. Now my memories of him were

141

polluted with suspicions of what he might have done in the war. *Did you kill anyone? Did you watch somebody die? Did you lift a finger to sanction a death, or prevent one?*

You surfaced then, holding a conch, naked save for bikini briefs. The sea water clung like beads to your oiled body. I pretended to be Sean Connery singing 'Underneath the Mango Tree' in *Dr No* and your laughter was a green light. I kissed you, your warm, salty mouth softening under mine, your breasts and belly gluing to my shirt. I was a kid again, suddenly engulfed with need, but you broke away and frowned at the yearning you saw in my eyes. Breakfast was a quiet affair.

Your mood lifted when we travelled inland to Curepipe, but you didn't believe me when I explained the town was so named because French settlers used to stop there for a rest to clear out and refill their pipes. The shower surprised us till I remembered the old joke Mauritians relate about there being only two seasons in Curepipe: the rainy season and the season of rains. The lack of signposts made it hard to work out where we were going but eventually we found the Plaines Wilhelms Road. Indian and Chinese shops vied for attention with European boutiques. You took a photograph of the Royal College before we moved into a noticeably modern area of the town full of souvenir arcades. We had lunch at a French restaurant called La Potinière before visiting the Botanical Gardens on Sir Winston Churchill Street where great swarms of Novembrier lilies loosed seeds into the air.

And all this time there was so much I wanted to tell you, so many promises, assurances and insurances I needed to discuss, but I knew that to broach these subjects was to jeopardise the détente at which we'd arrived. The knowledge that our week here would pass quickly only made me more desperate, more confused. You must have sensed my frustration but chose not to help assuage it. Didn't you realise how much we had to straighten out? Mauritius was the site for our peace summit.

Or was it simply that you knew we were beyond rescue and that debate could only widen the rift? Did you consider that an acceptable condition: that we were close enough to be lovers but out of reach for love?

My need for an either/or pushed you too far that night; I saw a fury in you that frightened and reassured me. The rest of the week we spent apart. Did you think of me at all on your visits to Port Louis, Quatre Bornes, Mahebourg?

I wonder if it was loneliness that brought you back to me on that final day. At first, your amiable mood set me hoping again but I soon noticed a difference in the way you looked at me, the manner of your voice. Everything about you contained a distance. The dawning that I'd never kiss you again or feel your body accept mine filled me with a loss so acute that I felt my face grow chill as its blood drained away. How could you chat to me like that when six days earlier your mouth had milked mine of passion, your skin had been a blanket for my body? I was a cosy bit of banter over the back fence, not one half of a warmth, an understanding, a compulsion. *We'll still be friends*, you said. *We'll write*. The words were clearly formed by your lips but all I could hear was *goodbye ... goodbye...*

Towards dusk we skirted the town, confused and enchanted by neon playing on the breakers. You ignored the sea at first, electing to stroll up the beach towards a spot where heat haze softened the edges of the beach huts and turned trees to ghosts. Somewhere beyond all that, deadened by thick, tropical air, music was bringing people on to the streets. We were alone here, despite the detritus of dozens gone before us this afternoon. The sand, ruined by footsteps, looked like a solid cream sea. Cool ocean breezes sucked the smells of coffee and cinnamon down from the front. I could see sails burning on the horizon.

In your wake, I watched you stop and kneel to examine a shell and grasp some of the sand – still warm from the midday

143

heat – and let it dribble from your fingers. From here I could see your hair tumbling to one side, the ripples in your loose skirt, brown moments of skin. Your mouth would taste spicy now, your eyes swimming with a sunset you'd prefer to witness alone. The sky behind us was moon-shy, bruising with night. There was to be a party later on; I could see people organising the barbecue. Laughter can be disorienting, disturbing, when distance distorts it.

I waited for you on the black line of kelp where the sea had reached that day. It exploded beneath my feet like pine knots in fire. The sea blazed and whispered, trapped between two shoulders of rock which also shackled the beach and threw motes of light on to it. Parties were going on up there too. I watched you edge towards that lava sea, loving you for the way you arched, trawled your hair with sudden fingers. You turned to me then, beckoned me over.

The seagull was dying, its wing crushed. But that wasn't what you wanted to show me. 'Look, there's its mate.' I followed your gaze and saw a whitish scrap wheeling above us. Its cry sounded plaintive enough to bear out your words.

You grabbed my hand and led me away to the soft dry sand at the top of the beach. I tried to put my arm around you.

'No, watch.'

We watched as the bird wailed and swooped over its prone mate before landing by its destroyed wing. I thought for a horrible moment that it was going to start pecking at its eyes but it settled into the sand beside it. I looked at you, about to suggest a final drink in the bar but you were smiling, eyes wet.

'My God, that's beautiful. He's waiting with her … he's waiting till she dies.'

We waited too, until it was too dark to see, then walked back to the hotel, trying to ignore the shrieks that swept into the night.

Tsipporah
Adèle Geras

Here is something I've noticed: as soon as candles are lit, as soon as night falls, my grandmother, my parents and all my uncles and aunts start telling stories, and the stories are often frightening, meant to send small shivers up and down every bit of you. When the grown-ups talk, I listen. I never tell them *my* frightening story, even though it is true. They wouldn't believe me.

A few weeks after my eighth birthday, my grandmother took me to visit her friend Naomi. Why, I wanted to know, had I not seen this friend before?

'I never take very young children to see her. She might frighten them. The way she looks, I mean,' said my grandmother.

I imagined a witch, a giantess, or some monster I couldn't quite describe. I said, 'What's the matter with her?'

'Nothing's the matter with her. She's very old, that's all.'

I laughed. 'But you're very old and I'm not scared of you.'

My grandmother said, 'Compared with Naomi, I'm a rosebud, I promise you. Wait and see.'

She was quite right. Naomi was ancient. Her head was like a walnut, or a prune, perhaps, with eyes and a mouth set into it. She wore a headscarf and I was glad of that. I was sure she was bald underneath it. She sat in a chair pulled up to the table, drinking black coffee and smoking horrible-smelling cigarettes. She spoke in a voice like machinery that needed oiling. After I was introduced to her, I was supposed to sit quietly while the ladies chatted. I couldn't think of anything worse, so I said to my grandmother, 'May I go out into the courtyard for a while? I'll just look at things. I promise not to leave the house.'

My grandmother agreed, and I stepped out of Naomi's dark dining room into the sunshine. The rooms Naomi lived in could have been called a flat, I suppose, but it wasn't a flat in a modern block. It was in a part of Jerusalem where the houses were built around a central courtyard, and four or five families shared the building. In this courtyard there were pots filled with geraniums outside one door, and some watermelon seeds drying on a brass tray outside another. A small, sand-coloured cat with limp, white paws was sleeping in a patch of shade. Naomi's rooms were on the upper storey of the house. It was about three o'clock in the afternoon. All the shutters were closed. Perhaps everyone who lived here was old and taking an afternoon nap. The sun pressed down on the butter-yellow flagstones of the courtyard, and the walls glittered in the heat. Suddenly I heard a noise in the middle of all the silence: a cooing, a whirring of small wings. I turned round to look, and there, almost within reach of my hand, was a white dove sitting on the balcony railing.

'How lovely!' I said to it. 'You're a lovely bird then! Where have you come from?'

The bird cocked its head, and looked exactly as though it were about to answer, then changed its mind and in a blur of white feathers, it flew off the railing and was gone. I leaned over to look for it in the courtyard, and thought I saw it, just there, on a step. I ran down the stairs after it, but it was nowhere to be seen.

A girl of about my age was standing beside a pot of geraniums.

Where had she come from? She wore a white dress which fell almost to her ankles. I thought, She must be very religious. I knew that very devout Jews wore old-fashioned clothes.

'Have you seen a white dove?' I asked her. 'It was up there a moment ago.'

The girl smiled. She said, 'Sometimes I dream that I'm a dove. Do you believe in dreams? I do. My name is Tsipporah, which means "bird", so of course I feel exactly like a bird sometimes. What do you feel like?'

I didn't know what to say. I was thinking, This girl is mad. My name is Rachel, which means 'ewe lamb', but I never feel woolly or frisky. My cousin is called Arieh, which means 'lion', and he's not a bit tawny or fierce. I said, 'I just feel like myself.'

'Then you're lucky,' said Tsipporah. 'Sometimes I think I will turn into a bird at any moment. In fact, look, it's happening … feathers … white feathers on my arms …'

I did look. She held out her arms and cocked her head, and I blinked in the sunlight which all at once was shining straight into my eyes and dazzling me … but in the light I could see … I think I saw, though it's hard to remember exactly, a flapping, a vibration of wings, and the krr-krr of soft dove-sounds filling every space in my head. I closed my eyes and opened them again slowly. Tsipporah had disappeared. I could see a white bird over on the other side of the courtyard, and I ran towards it calling, 'Tsipporah, if it's you, come back … come back and tell me!'

The dove launched itself into the air, and flew up and up and over the roof and away, and I followed it with my eyes until the speck that it was had vanished into the wide pale sky. I felt weak, dizzy with heat. I climbed slowly back to Naomi's rooms, thinking, Tsipporah must have hidden from me. She must be a child who lives in the building and likes playing tricks.

On the way home, my grandmother started telling me one of her stories. Sometimes I don't listen properly when she starts on a tale of how this person is related to that one, but she was talking about Naomi when she was young, and that was so hard to imagine that I was fascinated.

'Of course,' my grandmother said, 'she was never quite the same after Tsipporah died.'

'Who,' I asked, suddenly cold in the sunlight, 'is Tsipporah?'

'Naomi's twin sister. She died of diphtheria when they were eight. A terrible tragedy. But Tsipporah was strange.'

'How, strange?'

'Naomi told me stories … you would hardly believe them if I told you. I know I never did.'

'Tell me,' I said. 'I'll believe them.'

'Naomi always said her sister could turn herself into a bird just by wishing it.'

'A white dove,' I said. 'She turned herself into a white dove and flew away.'

My grandmother looked at me sharply.

'I've told you this story before, haven't I?'

'Yes,' I said, even though, of course, she never had. I didn't tell her I had seen Tsipporah. I didn't want to frighten her, so I said nothing about it.

Now, every time I see a white dove, I wonder if it's her, Tsipporah, or perhaps some other girl who stretched her wings out one day, looking for the sky.

Dead Bird
Socrates Adams-Florou

It's a quiet day. There is a washed-up bird on the shore; it is dead. A child is pointing at the bird and laughing and saying to Mummy about how the bird is trying to swim. Mummy is pulling the child away from the bird. It is covered in mud. The mud is from the sea and it is old and wet.

Two men are playing a game with the dead bird. They pick it up and are throwing it for miles across the beach. They call the game Bird Ball.

The first man picks up the bird and throws it as far as he can and then the other man chases after it. As he chases the dead bird he is shouting, It's flying, it's flying. He is excited. The other man claps heartily as his friend chases the flying bird. They play for hours and hours until the tide comes in and the sun goes down.

They leave the dead bird on a piece of concrete next to the sea. They want to come back tomorrow and play Bird Ball again. The dead bird has bits missing from it. It has four feathers left. Its guts are hanging out. Its eyeballs are broken.

A cat mistakes the dead bird for a kitten; the cat is blind. The cat picks up the dead bird in its mouth and carries it into a den where it lives with its kittens. The dead bird rots.

A man finds the skeleton of the dead bird in the cat's den months later. The cats have died because of diseases from the dead bird;

they were so busy snuggling up to it and loving it that they didn't realise it was a rotting, dead bird. The dead bird skeleton is attached to the dead mother cat's nipple. It looks like it is suckling at the cat's nipple.

The man is a stand-up comedian. He looks at the skeleton attached to the dead cat and starts laughing. He laughs and laughs and laughs! It's hilarious. Ha ha ha ha ha ha ha ha. He takes a photo of the cat and skeleton, in between huge, hard laughs. He thinks that the skeleton is sucking the cat's tits. They are both dead. A dead bird is sucking a dead cat's tits, he thinks. He gets out a notebook and writes down this line. He will use it as part of his act.

The wind, over many months, blows the tiny skeleton out from the den. It is on the pavement. It is raining. The skeleton is getting wet and blown all over the place. An artist sees the skeleton and is stunned by its fragile beauty. He takes photos of it in the rain. There are tiny bits of hard rotted flesh still attached to it. The artist is happy. He grabs the skeleton and pulls it apart into individual bones. He takes a small white plastic bag from his larger black shoulder bag and puts the wet bones into it.

He looks into his bag and smiles.

The bones from the dead bird are used as decorations around the artist's house. He likes bones. He has put all of the bones in different places, stuck to the wall and on top of different pieces of furniture and on the table and he just scatters some on the floor. Whenever he sees some of the bones he thinks, I am an interesting guy.

He is an interesting guy with great taste in bones.

He throws a dinner party and his guests all crowd around the delicate bones and they say things to him like, I love these bones, and, You are such an interesting guy. They say, I love these bones, and, You are such an interesting guy, so many times that the artist starts to get an over-inflated opinion of himself. He puts on a pair of sunglasses.

He has sex with a woman at the party.

After two weeks the artist gets bored of the bones and throws them out. He redecorates. He paints the walls of his house with a wash of orange paint with some of his own blood in it.

A bird is searching through the rubbish bins of the artist and finds the bones poking out from the black plastic. The bird doesn't know what the bones are and ignores them. It flies off leaving the bones lying on the pavement. Three years later the bones are just a tiny little powder.

The powder is sucked into the nose of a man and makes him sneeze. He sneezes one more time and his wife says 'Bless you' to him. He says to his wife, Shut up. He looks angry. He looks very angry and dangerous. The rest of the bone dust flies around on the wind of the world. It makes it to every continent.

More birds die. They are all washed up on to the shore. The next day the town wakes up to a hundred thousand dead birds on the shore. Everyone can play Bird Ball.

The Beautiful Room
RB Russell

Maria said to him, 'I'd be tempted to rent the house for just this one room.'

'It is lovely, yes.'

'The way that the light comes in from that window, through the curtains on to the plain walls…'

'What is that material?'

'Muslin,' she replied. 'It's not very practical. It would be too bright in here in the mornings but who cares? Look at that view down over the town. I wouldn't mind being woken up early just to stare at that.'

'I suppose it *is* magnificent.'

'You can trace the pattern of the old streets in the shapes made by the rooftops. I could sit here at this windowsill for hours on end, just looking out, contemplating this view, losing myself in it… And if I had to return to the real world, I wouldn't mind because I'd be coming back to this beautiful room.'

He frowned, and looked around him, suspicious: 'This house may be a couple of hundred years old, but they've done exactly what they do in brand-new show-homes; it appears big and airy because there's only this bed in the middle. There're no cupboards, no chest of drawers… Once you've hung a few pictures, maybe put up some shelves or added a bookcase…'

'But we couldn't do that. It would ruin the room. The other bedroom would have to become a dressing room.'

'And what about guests?'

'They'd have to sleep downstairs.'

'We have to be practical, Maria. When we get a new place sorted out I'd be expected to do quite a lot of entertaining. We'd need at least one decent-sized guest bedroom.'

'But the walls are so good in here, so bare and white. The light coming in through those crooked window panes, through the curtains moving in the breeze … It's so cool in here although it's baking outside.'

'But what about the winter? Then it'll be bloody cold.'

'Why can't you be positive for once?'

'What do you mean?'

'Well, we've looked at a dozen apartments and houses in the last few days and they've all had their good and bad points. And there've been things about each that we've disagreed on, but for once we've both decided that this is a beautiful room.'

'But we've got to be realistic. It would be cold up here in the winter.'

'There's a fireplace.'

'That small grate wouldn't give out enough heat! And even if we stoked it up in the winter it would mean carrying fuel up two flights of stairs. And every morning it would have to be cleaned out and the ashes taken back down. I can see you starting to complain about that pretty quick.'

'It'd be a small price to pay…'

'So you say right now. But when the January winds are blowing and the few hours of daylight only give us a view of driving rain over wet rooftops…'

'So which one of the properties that we've looked at so far do you actually like?'

'The ones in the city. They were all far more practical.'

'But I don't want to live in the city.'

'There'd be so much more for you to do there, while I'm out at work.'

'Look, John, I don't know this country and I don't know its language. I'm willing to follow you here, and learn. It's a lot less daunting in a small town like this, and it's so picturesque. It's no further from the vineyards than if we were in the middle of the city. In fact, I think you'd get to work quicker from here.'

'But you agreed to come abroad to support *me* in *my* job. I need to get us somewhere to live and I won't have much time to go looking once I've started work on Monday. I've indulged you. I've shown you these ramshackle old places out in the middle of nowhere and you still won't understand how impractical they are. Let's just go back to the city, rent that apartment with the three bedrooms that I liked with the view towards the airport.'

'You've *indulged* me?'

'Yes. I've shown you the pretty little properties in the countryside that you wanted to see.'

'Just to keep me quiet?'

'I'm the one earning the money and paying for our new life, so I think I should have the casting vote.'

'But I've given up my job to follow you here, to support you.'

'Yes, so support me now... We'll go back to the city and sign the contract on the flat that I liked.'

She sat down on the bed. At that moment there came an odd noise from behind her.

'What was that?' he asked. 'It sounded like a bird, in the wall.'

'These'll be solid stone walls. They won't have a cavity.'

She got up from the bed and walked over, putting her hand on to the wall gently, carefully. As she did so there came a scuffling, almost a fluttering, that did remind her of a trapped bird.

'We've got to get it out of there,' she said.

'And how do we do that?'

'I don't know.'

She backed away from the wall, glad that for a few moments

they were not talking about where to live. She had known John like this before. She knew that he was worried about his new position with the company and she could see the old behaviour returning. She had hoped that moving to a new country would be a fresh start, but was now considering that she might have made a mistake.

'I'll bang on the wall,' he said. 'If I make a noise just behind where the bird is, it'll drive it back along to wherever it came in.'

'But we don't know *where* it got in,' she replied cautiously.

He walked to the window, opened it wide and hung out. However, he could see only a couple of metres of the stone wall before it turned the corner, out of sight. He came back inside the room.

'It'll probably have come in through the eaves,' he suggested. 'We'd best just leave it.'

'No, not if the poor thing is trapped.'

'It's just a bird.'

'But it might die in there.'

'So what? It's not as though we're taking this house. If it dies and rots it's somebody else's problem.'

'That's not good enough. We must get it out.'

She saw the old anger for a moment, but he controlled himself: 'If we bang on the wall under it, maybe that'll frighten it back up and out.'

With the flat of his hand he slapped the wall low down, under the spot where he thought they had heard the noise. There was a frantic scrabbling around and the sound of debris falling. He repeated the action twice more.

'Stop!' she shouted. 'You're frightening it.'

'That's the idea, isn't it?'

When he did it again there was yet more frenetic activity from within the wall, but it appeared to have divided into two distinct sources either side of him.

She put her hands over her ears: 'I don't like it. I hate to think of it being so scared.'

'*Them* being scared,' he said. 'There's more than one.'

'I'm scared.'

'But they're just birds. They're not mice or rats.'

'I'm not scared *of* them, I'm scared *for* them. I wouldn't care about rats. Maybe there was a nest in there and the babies have fallen out and down into the wall?'

The sound continued, although intermittently.

'No, they're making far too much noise for babies. Now I come to think of it … of course … this wall is lined. They're in between the lining and the stone wall.'

He slapped it again in confirmation and the sounds resumed, louder than ever and startling him so much that he took a hasty step back.

'I think it's best to leave them,' he decided. 'We'll let them find their own way out. We're just making things worse.'

'I'm sure they seemed higher in the wall that time.'

'I don't know…'

He walked forward decisively and slapped the wall hard. Maria felt that the whole room had shifted slightly out of alignment at that moment. The noise suddenly intensified and appeared to be coming from all of the walls all around them.

'Stop it!' she shouted over the din. 'You're upsetting them.'

'Me?' he shouted, and this time the sound did not seem to want to die down. 'Whose idea was it to try and help?'

Now the scuffling, scratching, beating racket seemed not only to be in all the walls, but under the floor and in the ceiling. It was even more insistent, faster, almost enraged. It was as though all the furious activity was actually in the room with them, although there was nothing to be seen.

'We'll leave,' he decided, surprising her by taking her hand and trying to pull her to the door.

She resisted and so he repeated his words, shouting. When she shook her head he threw his hands up and went to the door. It was closed and when he tried to turn the handle it would not move.

'Just go,' she insisted, afraid more of his rising anger than of the birds.

'I can't,' he shouted back over his shoulder, furious with her. 'The bloody thing's stuck.'

'Why won't it open? Is it locked?'

'It's wedged in the frame.'

And all the time the sound seemed to become yet louder. He left the door and strode back to the open window. He looked out over the bright, idyllic view and decided that although there was no way down for them (they were four storeys up), he could at least call for help. He had only to wait for somebody to pass in the street down below. It was marginally quieter with his head out of the window but his anger would not subside. He couldn't see anyone immediately but he shouted for help anyway.

A few moments later Maria tapped him on the shoulder and made him jump.

'What?' he demanded.

'You try the door again; you're stronger. I'll shout for help.'

He was reluctant to turn back to the room but did so. The noise within the walls seemed to be worse still, the ceaseless scuffling and scrabbling of wings and claws. As he walked to the door his mood shifted finally into its old, familiar deep groove. When he turned the handle and pulled at it roughly he found that the door still would not move, so he pulled at it again with all his strength. He had hurt the muscles in his arm and so kicked at the door, which stayed firm.

He looked around and could see Maria hanging out of the window and could hear her shouting, although her actual words were lost to him. He shouted as well, sudden profanities, but they did not make him feel any better. He couldn't believe that anyone else in the building hadn't heard the noise as well.

Maria left the window and came over to him warily. 'There's nobody out there to help,' she shouted, her eyes darting from wall to wall, putting her hands over her ears. 'We've got to do something.'

He looked around and then walked over to where he thought the noise was possibly the most extreme. He kicked the wall with his shoe and decided that the lath-and-plaster really would be quite old and fragile. He turned, and with determination he kicked back at the wall with his heel and felt it give way.

She watched as he kicked again, and twice more, creating a gaping hole. When he bent down and started tugging at the plaster whole sections came away with rotten strips of wood and billows of dust. And then that part of the wall suddenly seemed to explode.

Birds fell and flew out, taking to the air all around them. Large, ungainly, filthy things flapping and churning the dust from rotten wood and plaster in the confined space of the room. Frightened creatures with desperate wings surrounded him. He tried to grab hold of Maria, but she had moved away from his grasp. It was suddenly hot and hard to see or breathe with all the buffeting birds, the feathers and particles of plaster. He instinctively fell to the floor to escape the pandemonium.

He put his hands over his face, head down, trying to filter the air that he strove to breathe calmly and deeply. With his eyes closed against the detritus he relied on hearing and was relieved that almost immediately the sound was reducing. There was still an uproar in one part of the room and he opened his eyes nervously and looked up. He stood carefully, watching as the last few birds were throwing themselves towards the window. In just a few more seconds there was only one left trying to escape. It was almost white, covered in the dust from the debris.

It crashed against the frame, recovered in a confusion of wings and falling feathers and then somehow made it out.

It wasn't quite quiet in the room; at least three birds were thrashing about on the floor, exhausted and broken, unable to follow the others to freedom. Around him, the fragments of birds and decades of fine litter thinned out and settled over the room.

He wheeled around in a full circle, wondering what was missing, confused. He remembered the need to escape that had so recently preoccupied him and he tried the door again. It was still stuck fast so he directed all of his force into a kick. A panel split but did not immediately give way. It took several more kicks before he had made a gap wide enough to get through. He was about to leave when he remembered the open window.

He did not know why but he felt compelled to go and look at the view one more time. He peered out, uncertain, and it was unchanged. The street immediately below was empty, and the roofs of the town spread out before him haphazardly. Up in the sky there was a flock of birds that were just distant shapes becoming smaller and smaller. All that he could do was watch, alone in the silent room, as they became so distant that they disappeared into the deep blue sky.

Gulls
Nicholas Royle

I never dreamt, when we retired to this old house by the sea, what trouble there'd be with the gulls. I'm talking about the big ones, the new urban thuggish variety that have been buying into the heart of seaside towns and establishing themselves willy-nilly, come hell or high water, in recent years, that mug you for your sandwich or ice-cream, peck and tear apart rubbish bags, wheel over you too close, screeching incessantly. These are the type that have learnt to stand their ground, with violent yellow eyes that don't blink or bear looking into. Like a new breed of rat, only gulls, super-gulls. In the space of a mere couple of decades they seem to have been morphing into some new species altogether. That's what my wife thinks. As if a genetic trigger were being released, part of a plan, like a government experiment. Or, she thinks, if it's not the government, it's climate change, unprecedented evolutionary acceleration thanks to a tipping effect. All this feeding on human garbage, heavy metals and other nutritional goodies, it's thrown the bird-world off kilter, resulting in a new phenomenon along the south coast, a geneticist horror story unveiling its frightening face before our very eyes but with most of us too dim or drugged up on everyday crisis management even to notice.

In any case, it's not the seafront muggings or ripping into litterbins or daily screeching. It's to do with the night turning into dawn. Someone told me it started with the old school they knocked down, the gulls no longer able to build their nests on its extensive rooves. Rooves, roofs. Which is it? Neither sounds right to me. But who cares any longer about proper language or pronunciation?

At first we were hardly aware. But then the breeding season came. The house is narrow but tall. What possessed us to buy a place with so many flights of stairs I'm not sure. Space for the grandchildren, my wife said. We don't have grandchildren, I said. And then, she said: if you're going to be by the sea you want somewhere characterful and solid. My wife always wanted to live by the sea and now she has her wishes. We sleep at the top, in an attic room that looks out over all the other roofs for miles around. Or rooves. Roofing. The roofscape. There's the odd tiny triangle of sea in between, but the principal vista is rooftops, flat and sloping, in every direction and, for weeks now, they've been covered, I kid you not, with nesting gulls. It's been crazy, an open-air mental-hospital-cum-hotel-cum-departure-lounge for squawking, mewing, frantic birdlife. Even before the day begins we get to hear them scuffling and sliding on the roof above us, landing and taking off, pattering and skittering about dislodging tiles, besmirching the windows with their filth, making their cacophonous din.

It's never one sound, but a swirling ubiquity. It keeps shifting, whining, whinnying like ponies, cheeping like chickens, cicadas, a cockerel or two, a goose, a swamp of frogs, mallards, mewing, trilling, screeching a siren, human infants crying. There's something diabolical about it, an auditory *ignis fatuus*, a sound-shifter. It's a barrage of sound, an erupting of bar-rage, vicious sheep *baa*-rage, at once distant and near. It's a gluing, a galling, a sawing of plastic with a quiver of backsound, a *koo-ip* that flips into scoffing. It's an aggressive self-cajoling, a plaintive parody, ridiculing the plaintiff. It's a cawing triumph of maniacal croaking, a black magic wedding, an apocalyptic glutting. I connect it with the image of a descent quickening, as of something dropped or thrown down the stairs: unspeakable gullet.

It's been weird weather too, hardly a splash of rain. And every beginning of the day it's identical, the cacophony of the gulls and this feeling of the end of the world. I can't say it any clearer than that.

Woken up, a tympanic attack, an assault of sound: what is it? where am I? who's making this racket? I'm taken in every time. Have I been drugged, transported through the night and woken in the depths of Amazonian jungle? Or in a fairytale with peacocks? Or surrounded by penguins and sea-lions in an Antarctic nightmare in which everything is melting from my face? Or is that a human baby in agony, horribly close by? The sounds are appalling, incomprehensible, pipers gulping oxygen twisting asphyxiating struggling curdling cries at every window because in the heat you have to leave them all open, and I've been gulled again.

Waking up used to be a kind of freedom. Even setting an alarm on your bedside clock you're waking up on your own terms. But this is waking up on theirs. Every daybreak, or still earlier. More regular than clockwork, quicker than time. No alarm can beat their larum. *Larus* larum *laridae*. I'm caught out, duped every time.

It's not even morning, it's this dark milky nothing and: what is it? where am I? who's making this racket? Ethel and I have stopped talking about it. We know what the other one's thinking. We're on the same page.

Happy as Larry they make a mockery of Latin and every other language I ever came in contact with. Larum *larus*, *larus* larum, *laridae* never die, Larry larynx never say die. *Larus argentatus*: silver gull quicker than quicksilver. It doesn't matter how little or well I sleep, how hard I try to anticipate them, they are out there in advance, tripping the light, screeching ahead. The other day I was reading: 'Herring gulls are very noisy and famed for their raucous laughing sound...' Laughing? Who's laughing? And famed? Is this a new TV series I've been missing? What's the name of it, *Celebrity Rooftops*? Ballard writes somewhere of the 'sea-wearying gulls': a charming turn of phrase. Don't worry, be weary. But be wary of this weariness, it will have you for breakfast.

It's truly an omnivorous word. Gull (verb): cram, gorge: hence (possibly), delude; (noun) cheat, impostor, but also the one cheated or duped. Gull: throat, gullet. Gull (verb): to swallow, guzzle, devour voraciously. To wear down or wear away.

I wake up in an underworld of shrieking monkeys, a ferocity of broken piped music, elderly folk groaning on their deathbeds in some twisted NHS Hieronymus Bosch dystopia.

I'm worn down completely. In the past few days I've scarcely slept. If I shut my eyes it's to the horror-tilting yellow of gulls.

Gull sounds have clocked, clucked, clotted everything. I hear voices below me in the street, but they disintegrate into gulls echoing in the gully: donkeys braying, flooded engines turning over, coyotes and hyenas. There's the incessant *kyow-kyow-kyow*, as ornithologists call it, trying to sound scientific. But goodbye to all that, I say: it's looping loony tutti-frutti tutting, tooting, tooting bec beckoning, screeching as if the rooftops suddenly were awash with fish, herring, herring aid, hearing gulls, and of a sudden pterodactyls, crooning, craking, creaking, squawking, strafing, the demented snatch of a band of Native Americans crying off across a vanished prairie two hundred years ago, it's warpathological screaming scrying genetic transformation, swallowing hole, a phantom downloading generated in the gullet. It's drunken arid chanting charging changing, oneiric pestering bickering busking bantering, murderously battering wearying sound into a new source, new sauces, pickled hearing aids, a human cry, collapsing walls of sound.

It's dry as dust, too hot to go outside. I've confined myself to the house, in mew as people used to say, wandering from one floor to another trying to settle in a chair somewhere for a few minutes, unable to read or think. Then I look out of the window again at neighbouring rooftops. Young ones, silent or mewling, all brown and downy, I see: armadillos on stilts, gigantic artificial insects, moths obviously manufactured in China.

The fledglings stand about, bored out of their miniature brains, waiting forever to fly. They stoop their shoulders when they mew, in a mimicry of the old and vulnerable.

A few weeks ago Ethel called them 'the new lot' and wondered what'll they be like a year from now, with a further genetic shift, I mean: what are the *next* new lot going to be like?

Too much life, she went on to remark, gazing out.

But we've stopped speaking to one another now.

I just passed her downstairs. She was sitting still at the table with the sunlight streaming in. You need help, I thought to myself. I looked around for something. As if she were a hawk, I've put a sheet over her head. I'm letting her sit like that for a while.

Snow
Marc Werner

We left the car in a layby. It was only drizzling, but spring was some weeks off and the weather was unpredictable. By the time we were halfway up the first valley, the drizzle had turned to light snow, which fell in tiny flakes, like grated parmesan. When the path turned a corner, I stopped, and as we set off again I found that we had switched positions and Nixon was now in front.

I watched his broad back.

We had talked a little in the car. He had asked me why I had got in touch after so long and I had said that I couldn't really explain. His name had popped up and I had acted on impulse. We had been good friends at one stage, I had said, as if he needed reminding.

'Yeah,' he said, 'and then we weren't.'

I looked at him at that point, but his eyes remained fixed on the road.

When we reached the ridge at the top of the valley, larger flakes were falling, and as I looked along the uphill path we would now follow, I could see that the snow was sticking just a little way ahead.

'For every three hundred feet of ascent,' Nixon said, 'the temperature drops by one degree centigrade.'

He walked on and I followed. My boots, more used to tramping city streets, provided just about sufficient grip even once we reached the snow layer. Nevertheless, I found I was having to keep my head down to watch where I placed my feet, so it was a shock when I finally looked up and saw the ground fall away in front of me, sloping down to an enclosed body of water.

'Scales Tarn,' said Nixon.

'Do you … come here often?' I joked, pausing to get my breath back.

'Ever since I moved up here,' he said, 'I go walking in the fells every weekend, often during the week. I've climbed this a dozen times. There are more routes up it than most.'

I didn't know what I'd expected when I'd contacted him. He'd said he'd meet me at the railway station and I was to bring walking gear.

On the far side of the dark, choppy water, the mountain rose steeply to a craggy ridge.

'It reminds me … of that painting by Magritte,' I said. *'The Domain of Arnheim* … It was in that book Mr Bell kept in the art room … Remember?'

Nixon didn't reply. He just stood facing away from me, staring at the mountain.

'You're married,' I said.

For a few moments he said nothing, remaining still, but then he turned and looked at me. His eyes were as dark as the water of the tarn.

'I was,' he said, his eyes meeting mine for the first time since we had left the car.

He said nothing more, but held my gaze.

'Right,' I said, finally looking away. Then: 'That was the first Magritte painting I ever saw.' I looked at Nixon again and he looked away. 'A steep mountainside with lots of snow and exposed rock – like that.' I nodded towards the mountain. 'And part of the ridge, in the painting, is shaped like the head of an eagle – *is* the head of an eagle.'

Nixon's head turned back towards mine and the intensity of his stare made *me* look away and as I did so I saw a large black bird soaring over the ridge. My first thought was that it was an eagle. It looked big enough, with a huge wingspan and 'fingered' tips.

'Raven,' Nixon said.

We both watched it soar and drift into a patch of low cloud and reemerge, then turn on to its back and tumble, losing altitude rapidly. Within seconds it was level with us, to the left of the tarn, and we could hear it calling, a low, guttural croak followed by a lighter repeated sound, like laughter, and then it was gliding down the course of the beck that drained the tarn. From there it disappeared. I realised I'd been holding my breath. I breathed out, shivered.

'Normally I'd go up Sharp Edge.' Nixon pointed to a razor-like arête that climbed steeply away from the right of the tarn. 'Not today. Wouldn't get more than halfway up.'

I suddenly wanted to go that way, but could see it would be treacherous. Snow and ice, and Sharp Edge was well named, plus when I looked back the way we'd come there was little to see, as wispy grey cloud was drifting up the valley. Conditions were unlikely to improve the higher we went.

I followed Nixon as he skirted the foot of Sharp Edge and we took a gentler route for the next half-mile.

'Turn left here,' Nixon said when we reached the head of the valley. 'Gets a bit steeper. There'll be some scree, a bit of scrambling. The wind will increase.'

I looked at the rosy patches on his prominent cheekbones, his pinched cheeks, and tried to remember when we had stopped being friends. If I could remember when, I might remember why.

We followed a rocky path that zigzagged its way up the shoulder of the mountain. To begin with, the width of the path allowed us to walk side by side.

'*The Domain of Arnheim*,' Nixon shouted over the increasingly blustery wind, 'is named after a story by Poe.'

'Really?'

'About the search for paradise on earth.'

'Doesn't sound much like the Poe I've read,' I shouted back, leaning into the wind.

Nixon stopped and leaned his weight on one leg, bent at the knee. I was glad of the rest. The gradient had stealthily become steeper and we were having to work a lot harder.

'Some people say it's about death,' he said, looking up the slope.

It was impossible to see more than twenty yards, mist or cloud obscuring the summit. The snow on the ground was six inches thick and more was falling.

'Better press on,' he added.

The slope became steeper, the snow deeper, the wind stronger, but I just kept planting one foot in front of the other, occasionally looking up for reassurance beyond Nixon's footprints. Out of nowhere came a memory of staying at his house in the suburbs. We had planned to go night fishing at a pool in a park close to where he lived. His mother insisted we get some sleep before we went. I could picture his bedroom, the warm glow of an orange lampshade, brown and yellow covers on the bed. One bed or two? I couldn't remember.

I did remember clambering over the park gate in the early hours, one of us handing over a fishing basket to the other, a rod bag being slotted through the railings.

I remembered walking behind Nixon through the trees, consciously stepping in his footprints. Somehow the distance between us had increased and I glimpsed him as he emerged from between two trees and then disappeared behind another one. This had reminded me, at the time, of another Magritte painting from Mr Bell's book, *The Blank Cheque*, in which a horse and rider had been rendered partly visible and partly invisible while passing through a group of trees – but the normal rules of visibility and invisibility had not been applied. At one point the horse disappeared behind the space in the background between two trees. It was not possible. It didn't matter how long you spent looking at the picture, it didn't – couldn't – make sense.

I had eventually caught up with Nixon and then shortly afterwards the pool was revealed, nestling in a shallow depression like a miniature foreshadowing of Scales Tarn.

Once we had tackled up, we saw a magpie – just one – and this was back when magpies were a lot less common than they would become and if you saw one you would go, *One for sorrow* ...

It hopped on the opposite bank while we fished, cocking its head and appearing to stare directly at us with its oily black eye, and we wondered if it would bring bad luck, but Nixon hooked a decent-sized tench before dawn, so we figured it hadn't.

When we reached the cairn I thought we were at the summit, but Nixon explained about the distinctive saddleback shape of the mountain. It effectively had two peaks and this was the lower of them. The next bit, he said, was mainly level, but the conditions were deteriorating. If it got to be a whiteout, we would have to retreat.

I supposed I could imagine what a whiteout was, but I asked him all the same.

'It's when you're in the cloud and the ground is covered in snow and almost all the light it receives is reflected. You lose visibility and the ability to judge distance and direction.'

He set off and I followed. Even when we had been friends, Nixon had had a tendency to be brusque and unpredictable. He could suddenly turn. I tried to remember getting back from the fishing expedition and couldn't. I couldn't picture us dismantling the rods or arriving back either at Nixon's house or at my own. I was unable to pinpoint when I next saw him.

I wondered, then, if it was after that that we had stopped being friends, as if one of us had stepped behind a tree – or even in front of one – and become invisible.

I watched my boots move forward one by one through the snow as if they were not attached to me. They had slowed down, in spite of the reduction in gradient. In fact, there was no gradient. This was a plateau. The cloud had closed in all around. Nixon was presumably in front of me. I just couldn't see him. All I had to do was quicken my step. But I wondered about the extent of the plateau and how gently or otherwise the ground fell away when you reached the edge. I wondered how you knew when you'd arrived at the summit. There would be a trig point or another cairn, I imagined. I could still see the line where the cloud met the ground: it was right in front of me. Wasn't it?

No. There was no line and if I thought there had been, I'd been kidding myself. For how long? Seconds, a minute, five minutes? I was surrounded by benign white light. Both the air around me and the snow beneath my feet sparkled with a glittering uniformity that was either a genuine phenomenon or a complex hallucination. At any moment, the cloud would clear and the sunlight that I could sense infusing everything would strike me directly.

I stopped and looked around. Every direction exactly the same. In fact it made no sense to think about direction. There was no direction, right or wrong. In city streets I had always known where I was on the map, even if the street was one I had never walked down.

I started walking again, then stopped. In my head was a picture of the route I'd taken since leaving the cairn, the line

I'd walked, but I knew it didn't correspond to the actual route followed. I didn't know how I knew. I just knew. I knew I was lost as surely as normally I knew I was not.

I heard something off to the left. Voices. It was definitely voices talking, rather than one voice calling. It figured that there would be other people on the plateau. It was a popular mountain among fell walkers. I was near the summit. People congregated at trig points.

'Hello?' I shouted, taking a few steps in the direction of the voices, which had fallen silent and then started up again, but in another direction, straight ahead, and this time it sounded less like two people having a conversation. It sounded more like laughter. A strange, guttural laughter, softened somewhat by the cloud and the snow.

Flight of Fancy
GA Pickin

I strained my eyes, searching amongst the river's boulders for a sign of movement, willing him to be there. I'd seen him every single day for the last three weeks, once I got to know his territory. After a few chance sightings I began timing his habits so that I wouldn't miss him.

But two days ago I couldn't find the heron anywhere, nor yesterday, nor today. I realised I was clenching my fists, digging my stubby fingernails into my lined, unlovely hands, repeating 'He must be here, he must be here' over and over under my breath like a prayer. It seemed that whichever deity watched over me, and over herons, had defected to the other side.

I searched the sky, looking upstream, the direction he inevitably chose for his morning flight. You can't mistake him for any of the other birds that inhabit the riverside. He's so free and solitary, never darting or swooping but travelling in a long, gentle glide full of quiet dignity. The pale, almost bluish colour of his underparts as he flies over always reminds me of my own eyes when I was young.

'Neither grey nor blue,' my ma used to say, 'but full of promise.'

Like my heron. I've got to the point now where it's a matter of survival. Somehow, no matter what mood I was in when I came out for my walk, everything is put right if he's there. I know it's silly, and childish, and impossible, but when I catch sight of him, even if it's only for a moment, I can feel something lifting inside me.

I can't believe I even tried to explain it to Jim. He was cleaning his rifle when I told him, polishing the already gleaming stock with his special gun rag. He keeps them locked up, 'out of harm's way', he says, although he means out of *my* way, as if I could ever want the use of them.

'Like a lucky mascot, this heron?' he asked me.

Although it's not really what I meant, I agreed. He probably never needs to escape from himself, the way I do, so he wouldn't understand how important the heron is to me.

'Where did you say you saw him?' Jim now gave me his full attention, using that keen look he gets when he thinks he's striking a shrewd deal with some tourist in the shop.

'Along the pebble beach, and upstream by the little island,' I told him. I saw him narrow his eyes and nod slightly. 'Why?'

'Because this may be our lucky break, Ailsa. Mr McBride from the George Hotel is turning his function room into a posh restaurant. He wants to call it "The Heron", and serve exotic fish dishes at jumped-up prices. He's asked me if I can do him a stuffed heron.'

'You can't,' I clutched at his arm, pleading with him. 'Not my heron, not my lucky heron.'

'You'll be able to see him whenever you want, once they've put him in a glass case. I've never done anything with a long neck. It will be quite a challenge.'

I opened my mouth to protest, the tears of anger and frustration coursing down my face. But Jim gave me one of his warning looks.

'Ailsa, no nonsense. The price is right.'

I knew then what a terrible mistake I'd made, and, after my unwitting betrayal, it was up to him to survive Jim's gun for as long as his heron's wits would serve him.

Although I tried to keep an eye on what Jim brought in with him after each hunting trip, it was impossible to catch him every time. I was too busy serving customers, fetching dried peas off the top shelf or rummaging through the drawers behind the counter for fishing line or shotgun shells.

Jim and I had taken over the shop when a hunting accident put paid to his job on the ferry. I admit that his idea to turn half the space over to fishing equipment and hunting accessories had been a smart move, for the 'leisure' side of the business turned out to be the most lucrative.

But then Jim got this bright idea of stuffing 'trophies'. He got a grant and learned off a man in Dumfries, travelling down on Tuesdays and Thursdays, bringing back road kills, dead pets, anything he could use to practise on. I've got to hand it to him, he's quite good at it now, and lots of the locals and a fair number of tourists make use of his skills, adorning their dens with the stuffed skins of creatures they have murdered. Or 'bagged', as they put it.

He's done a range of game birds – grouse, pheasant, pigeon, even a ptarmigan. As for me, I won't even have cut flowers in the house. I see nothing decorative or nostalgic in filling a room with dead things.

The whole idea of my heron, filled with wire and kapok, or whatever it is Jim uses, made me feel physically sick. The shiny glass eyes gazing sightlessly from within a glass box would make him look stupid, witless. And after the novelty wore off, the patrons of the George would cease to notice him. Perhaps Mr McBride would think up a new theme for his restaurant, or move on to some other pub, consigning the heron to a storeroom somewhere, where mould and insects would take their toll. The poor bird won't even have served the fleeting purpose of providing someone with a full belly.

All those people who will see his dead form won't know him as I know him. His slow-motion flight and awkward body camouflage a master fisherman. When they see that distinctive crest on his head, glued into place, they won't be able to appreciate the speed and grace his neck had as he caught his prey.

'Model your movements on the swan,' my ma had advised me, inspecting my own long, gangly limbs. But I'm sure she would have included the heron in her advice, had she ever seen one. Not raucous nor flamboyant, just quietly competent, that's the heron.

But today, I couldn't find him anywhere. Not up the creek, or by the island, or round the bend by the old mill. Even though I know it might be coincidence, I also know that Jim's been busy in his workroom these last three days. I haven't had the nerve to go in and see what he's up to, although he's been humming and singing all round the shop when he can spare the time to help with the serving. Instead, I've haunted the riverbank, hoping to get a glimpse and put my heart at rest.

I headed back up the lane, past the holiday cottages and the village green, down the little path by the church into Drove Road, where the shop is. And there they were. Mr McBride and Jim, standing in the doorway, shaking hands, big smiles on both their faces showing lots of even gleaming white teeth, their arms pumping and pumping as they congratulated each other on a deal well made. I stopped for a moment in the shadow of the church, and felt my insides go cold and hollow the way they do when you're anticipating the worst, and lose that last warm kernel of hope inside.

Then, something took over inside of me. I gathered my spindly legs beneath me, ran in long loping steps, and pushed past the two men, breaking through the clasped hands and the nodding heads. I dashed through the shop and back into Jim's workroom, flinging the door wide with a bang and slamming on the light switch. The room was a mass of wire and feathers, and gave off an odour of glue, chemicals, and offal. But my heron wasn't there. The two men were still staring into the shop, wondering what had hit them, when I flew out again, straight to the van at the kerb, with the big green and gold logo of the George painted on the side. The rear doors were unlocked, and I wrenched them open, my arms flung wide with the effort as if to embrace the contents of the van. There on the cold metal floor was a box, a crate really, just the right size for a heron's coffin. I must have screamed, because Jim was shaken into action then. I could feel him trying to restrain me as I ripped off the lid of the crate, my fingers catching and tearing on the rough wood and cheap staples.

And there he was, sighted at last. He was resting calmly on his side in a bed of Excelsior, gutted and stuffed. Not my heron, but the skin of my heron, crude and dead, with those dopey glass eyes staring out at me. His shape was unnaturally thin, and the once-graceful neck was slightly lumpy, as if he'd caught a fish down his throat in mid-swallow. I shook off Jim's fingers and grabbed up the mutilated corpse, heading back the way I had come, towards the river.

Jim and Mr McBride followed me, but even with my awkward burden I outdistanced them. The heron was light, and I let my gawky legs use their length, so long kept in check, stretching out to cover the distance in even, fluid strides. I was strong too. My daily rambles have built up the muscles while Jim's have become weak, standing in the shop or at his workbench all day. God only knows what exercise Mr McBride may get, but it doesn't include his lungs, for he soon stopped, doubled up and panting, before he even reached the edge of the wood.

With the inner compass that guides a hunted animal, my legs took me through the hedge at a thin spot, and I scrambled up the bank. I ignored the brambles, letting them rake and catch along my clothing and skin, but being careful to keep my heron high above the lethal thorns. Then I found his tree.

This is the tree where he and his mate had their nest last season. I climbed up, using my sweater to tie the heron to my back as best I could. Higher and higher, then out over the river, to the same fork where the nest lies, empty now, waiting for the next season's eggs.

So here I sit with my heron, his glass eyes gazing into mine, waiting to see what we shall do next. Jim is calling from below, shouting for me to come down, begging and threatening and screeching. He has raised the crows, and they circle above, mimicking his anger in their sarcastic way. I can see Mr McBride too, making his way down the path, his shiny shoes going matt with mud and leaves. I inch along a bit further, and let my legs dangle into space. The river's loud rushing noise drowns the human sounds, and my heron and I look out, first downstream, to the beach, then up, away towards the source of the river.

This is the way he has seen it countless times, this view high above the mud and turmoil. Perhaps he has been up into the mountains and even caught fish from the head waters.

Like an out-of-focus picture come clear, I see it. Instead of being alone, trapped in glass boxes that cramp our limbs, we could launch ourselves off this branch, my heron and I. We could spread our wings and soar away, high above the river, the village, and Jim. We would be so distant that it would take the best field glasses in the shop to make out any details of our features.

I take one last look below, and throw out my arms, my heron beside me. We circle once, then turn upstream, our legs dangling behind us, and slowly, tantalisingly, we disappear from view.

The Wounded Bird
Michael Kelly

The man is old, infirm.

The man is lonely.

He hasn't always been old, or infirm, but he's always been lonely.

The man is sitting in his favourite chair, drinking tea, when he hears a small thump. He eases himself up, and totters over to the window, peers outside. He sees something small and red in the grass. A ball, perhaps. He goes out to investigate and finds that it is a bird on the ground. The bird is alive. The bird cannot fly. The bird hops and stutters and falls. Hops, stutters, falls again.

Maybe it's an old bird, the man thinks. Blind.

Maybe it's lonely.

The man lifts the bird, holds it. He has never before held a living thing in his hands. He brings the bird inside.

The man puts the bird in a cardboard box lined with tissue. He gazes admiringly at the bird in the box. It is a beautiful bird: red like his heart. He puts a lid on the box and punches breathing holes in it. Then he sits in his chair, thinking, sipping tepid tea.

The bird is quiet.

The man is quiet.

Then, from the box, comes a low metallic sound, a *chit chit*.

And the man smiles, happy that he isn't so old that he can't hear. Happy that he is no longer lonely.

But the man doesn't know anything about birds, so he gathers his coat and his cane and he takes the subway to the library. He gets a library card. He borrows books about birds. He even buys a book-bag so he can tote the books home. He sits on the subway and looks at the other passengers. The man feels good.

At home the man goes straight to the box and lifts the lid. He looks at the bird. The bird, unblinking, looks at the man. It is a beautiful bird, the man thinks. Red, like his blood.

The man reads the books. He learns that the bird is a Northern Cardinal. It is a male. It is a song bird. *Chit chit* it sings, and *purdy purdy purdy*. He loves the sound of its song.

That night, the man sleeps on the sofa next to the cardboard box. He keeps a table lamp on, so the bird will have some light. In the fitful night he thinks he hears rustling and a soft, insistent thumping sound.

When he wakes, the man goes straight to the box and lifts the lid. The bird flies out, past the surprised man. It hits the window, falls. The man gasps, reaches for the bird, but it rouses itself and flies away before he can reach it. The bird circles overhead, round and round, a red ring, before landing on the edge of the cardboard box. Quickly, the man snaps the lid back on the box, trapping the bird.

The bird is quiet.

The man is panting.

Then the man has an idea. There is a pet store two blocks away. He walks to the pet store. He doesn't even bring his cane. He buys bird food – seed, grains, insects. He buys a cage.

The man sets up the bird cage. He could not carry a large cage, but it has a perch and a feeder. He lifts the lid on the box just a little. He puts his hand in, feels around blindly, then snatches the bird. He puts the bird in the cage.

The man fills the bird feeder, stares at the bird, smiles. Again he thinks about what a beautiful bird it is. Red. Like his love.

The bird stutters along the bottom of the cage. *Chit chit. Chit chit.* The bird is talkative in its cage: *chit chit purdy chit chit purdy.* The man even thinks he can hear another songbird outside his window, as if in answer.

For many days the bird is talkative and busy. It launches from the perch and hits the cage, chattering, wings fluttering. The cage shakes. The man feels hurt. He tries to soothe the bird. He coos to it, placating. After a time, the bird is quiet. It rests on its perch, silent and unblinking. The man smiles.

In the following weeks the man talks to the bird, tells it he loves it. He reads to the bird. He plays music for the bird – Debussy. But the bird remains silent and songless. The man feels his heart breaking.

Then one day the man goes to sleep and something opens up inside of him, something red, and he doesn't wake.

The house becomes silent. Dark. It stays silent and dark for some while, then there is a *chit-chitting* in the dark. *Chit chit. Chit chit.* And the bird continues its chatter for some days. *Chit-chit.* But the house is silent except for the bird's insistent cry.

Then, after some time, the bird is quiet.

Corbeaux Bay

Geeta Roopnarine

It is their summer holidays. He has gone for a run along the beach, early in the morning, every day except today. Last night he slept uneasily, disturbed by the peculiar sound of a night bird.

Sunday, and the beach is already swarming with people gaily mapping their domains with rectangular pieces of scraggy matting. The fishermen have returned from their trawling and Christine is at work in the lean-to. She slits, disembowels, and segments strange sea creatures that she has picked up from the nets; they may not be marketable but they do make nourishing soups. She looks like a Pied Piper but with a flock of black scrawny corbeaux, turkey vultures, some as tall as their youngest son. She throws the inner parts of the head, the gills, and the shining entrails to them without looking and they eagerly scoop up the offal, their curved beaks slicing, spilling the juices of the soft material. They are fast eaters, intent on their portions and defensive of their territory, fiercely pecking.

He is uneasy that she feeds the birds while the children watch from the balcony but she laughs and says it is because he is from the city and does not understand the ways of nature, that when she was a girl her mother did the same and she sees no reason to change.

As he hurries along the pathway to the garden, one of the corbeaux, intent on feasting, on staining the cement red, is unaware of his approach. He aims a kick at it. The bird staggers

181

a few feet away with a weird sidestepping gait and gazes at him. The flock also pause for a moment, their heads cocked to one side, and look up. Christine continues to pull, to stretch, to empty.

When he is almost at the gate, she notices him in his sneakers and tells him to take his mobile phone.

'What?' he says. 'And have you calling every five minutes to tell me which child is using dirty words, or which one is making his kaka?' He goes back inside and puts away his phone and his watch.

Then he bares his arm at her. 'I am on holiday.'

He goes for his run but soon returns. The sun is high in the sky and the people on the beach upset him, playing handball and shrieking as if the beach belongs to them. Tomorrow, he promises himself, he will leave early in the morning, and explore beyond the coconut trees on to the shoreline bordered by the jungle.

The birds have gone and he is pleased that he doesn't have to look at their bare wrinkled necks, their curved beaks, their staring eyes.

Next day he leaves at 6am, before the sun is up. He takes a small bottle of water, strapped to his waist. He picks up his mobile phone, remembers his conversation with his wife the day before, and puts it back down.

The beach is white, pristine. There is not a soul in either direction. The sea is grey, untouched yet by the morning sun. It looks fresh, newly formed.

He pulls off his socks, balls them up, places them in his sneakers and runs in the fine sand, his feet caressed by the soft swell of the water. He leaves no trail, and in front, the beach stretches out clean, unmarked.

He goes further and further until he leaves the swelter of houses, humped together like ticks. After an hour he reaches the end of the long beach and the sand gives way to a rocky outcrop. Here, the coconut palms surrender to the tangled growth of the tropics. He dries his feet, puts on his socks and sneakers, and climbs the rocky incline. Another, shorter beach stretches out in front of him. In the distance, beyond a protrusion of blood-red rocks, a second bay shimmers.

The small village has vanished behind the curve of the sea. He drinks the rest of his water and decides to go as far as the red rocks, maybe take a small sample for the boys. In the sky, a bird circles lazily.

He jogs slowly, taking care. The sand is littered with debris: broken plastic, bottle tops, a single rubber flip-flop. He looks at the orientation of the shore, at an angle to the long beach, and it appears that the sea rages through here at intervals. As he goes on, it becomes rocky. He wonders whether he should turn back. The sun is already high and Christine would be looking towards the beach. Then he reasons it is a pity to come so far and not see what is on the other side.

The liver-coloured rocks are jagged with thin spikes and he is amazed at the different shades of red, rust and brown that swirl through the small peaks. He is dizzy from the long run, not having had breakfast, and the hot sun, but he is determined to climb to the top, to master this wilderness.

The top does not disappoint. It is wild and rugged. In the forest, the trees seem alive, listening. Here, too, he sees that the ocean comes in with a vengeance. Large logs are piled up at the edge of the narrow strip of beach as if it protecting it from the forest or something unknown.

The tip of the rocky outcrop is covered with huge globs of white with black feathers sticking out here and there. He looks up. More birds are circling but they are too far away for him to identify. Probably those damn corbeaux looking for another gullible housewife to feed them.

183

He peers down. On a ledge cut into the rock, he sees nests with broken shells but one has two eggs. They are large, speckled with grey. An image of Christine's face, frowning, passes across his mind as she sees him with the egg, when her monopoly on nature is broken, and the boys touch the egg with their small, sensitive fingers.

As he balances himself and stretches precariously to get at the egg, his attention is caught by some markings on the beach below like symbols in a strange language.

He falls and as he moves through the air, slowly, he sees a multitude of black figures huddling under a projecting ledge. He hits one of the tall spikes in the rocks below and feels something ram into his stomach. Then, the spike breaking, he falls again.

He is lying on the beach. He takes a deep breath. There is no pain yet. He sees himself take a hold of the spike with both hands and pull hard. He flings it away and at first there are no fluids, no blood, no acids.

He rolls onto his stomach, closes his eyes and gives in to the pain, his face pressed against the sand. When he opens his eyes, the markings, the symbols, are no more than hundreds of v-shaped footprints of birds.

A stain spreads across his T-shirt and he pulls it off, tears it and makes a bandage of sorts. He reaches towards his pocket and then his hand falls away; he pictures the mobile on the table where he left it.

A movement above catches his eye. On the hidden ledge, something is causing the birds to stir. They raise their heads and seem to sniff at the air. Then they are quiet, watchful, their heads cocked to one side as if listening to some signal.

They take to the air, fly high. He exhales slowly. He turns his head towards the forest. It looks dark, impenetrable. The only way is back over the cliffs. He tries to move forward, but the pain leaves him weak.

He hears a movement and moves his head slowly. A corbeau is on the beach, side-walking like a bashful virgin, its beak contained, quiet.

Another movement, and more feet making v-shaped symbols on the sand.

His mouth is dry; the hot rays seem to pour down his throat.

He wishes he could talk to his sons, listen to their little squabbles falling around his ears like soft rain.

Then, a stirring of wings blots out the sun.

Husks
Stephen Bacon

When he made the inevitable decision to return to the cottage, he realised that he'd have to make the journey itself without the booze.

The memories almost suffocated Haddon as he drove south, staring through the windscreen with eyes that felt too big for their sockets.

The incident at the service station was a mistake; he'd taken the photograph from his wallet for the first time in years, believing he could handle the act of seeing them. For a few moments he'd felt an overwhelming surge of love as he'd stared at the picture of his wife and daughter. Then all at once the sense of regret bit like a snake, and it became imperative that he reach the cottage as soon as possible.

The motorway felt perilous; cars roared past with scant care, oblivious to his fragile state. Haddon gripped the wheel with focused intent.

The aviaries are busy with exotic birds, shrill cries, fanned tails and jerky movements. Eager to spot the exhibits, they crowd the cage, entranced by the strange kookaburras.

It's feeding time and the birds are restless. The gloved keeper is inside the aviary, distributing limp, fluffy bundles – dead chicks.

The natural brutality of the kookaburras is mesmerising; how they grip the chicks in their razored bills, pounding the tiny bodies against rocks or branches. Then they tip their heads and swallow the carcasses inch by inch until every part of the chick is consumed.

Cerys is disturbed by the sight and Jill quickly moves to comfort her. They hurry away, aghast, the insane mocking laughter of the kookaburras ringing in their ears.

The legacy of this will be several weeks of sleepless nights.

It was evening before he left the A338 and began his final approach to Christchurch. The Dorset scenery was vaguely familiar even after all these years, redolent of late summer. The images evoked memories of happier times, languid holidays at the cottage before the darkness swept in.

He almost missed the turn-off from the B-road; it was only the presence of the pub opposite that alerted him to the proximity of the lane, virtually obscured by overgrown grass and shrubs that had sprouted in the intervening years. He drove slowly along the bumpy track, switching on his lights to banish the shadows created by the canopy of trees. The cottage waited at the end of the track, made ghost-like and malevolent by the car's beams.

Once he'd switched off the ignition, the ticking of the cooling engine crowded his senses. The windows of the cottage stared back, challenging his gaze. It looked exactly as it had in his dreams.

Weeds had cracked the paving stones, as if nature was trying to claim the building. Ivy clung to the roof, smothering the chimney.

Haddon gripped the brass key and turned it with some effort, sensing the resistance of the lock. He pushed it open with a squeal of hinges and stepped inside.

Mildew and stale air conspired to mask the scents familiar from Haddon's previous visits. He clicked the switch and light flooded the entrance, prompting a vague recollection of agreeing to pay the bills by direct debit. He might have been thankful of this, but the truth was he couldn't have cared less. He'd brought a battery-powered lantern, nevertheless.

Dust motes trembled in the air as he moved inside. Everything looked *almost* the same. The table and chairs had been moved against the opposite wall, presumably to allow the paramedics easier access. He entered the kitchen. A spike of regret: the chipped coffee mugs had been hung on the mug-tree instead of stored in the cupboard like Jill would have preferred, probably by some well-meaning police officer who'd felt the need to wash up in the aftermath. The worktop looked bleached of colour. Cerys's old toys had been thrown together into a cardboard box.

He paused at the foot of the stairs, staring up into the waiting darkness. A click of the switch revealed magnolia walls, faded watercolours, yellowed skirting. He thought about that final visit, how they'd arrived as a living, breathing family, and left as lifeless husks. Even he – who'd been stretchered out hooked up to drips and a portable ventilator – had spent the last five years in his own alcohol-induced stasis.

He climbed the stairs. Both of the bedroom doors were closed but he could see into the bathroom, noticing the remains of several insects on the white lino. Dust had coated everything. The air felt grimy and stagnant. Too fragile to face his daughter's room, Haddon drifted into the main bedroom and collapsed onto the bed.

The sheets were chilled and starched, smelling of damp. And in the room in which, five years before, his wife had died, Haddon fell into a deep sleep.

Cerys is drinking her hot chocolate. He knows the sweetness of it will mask the bitterness. Jill waits downstairs. He can hear her weeping from up here in Cerys's room. He watches his daughter for several moments, still astonished by the volume of love he feels. She finishes the drink and he wipes the final remnants from her upper lip. He dims the nightlight and tucks her into bed. She's puzzled by the fact that he hasn't made her brush her teeth.

'It doesn't matter, love,' he whispers to her. 'Nothing matters now.'

She lies down and he strokes her forehead, watching her eyes flutter closed, noticing her breath deepening. His hands trace the dome of her skull, where wisps of hair still cling resolutely to the sallow skin.

Soon it's time to leave her. Jill will be coming up to say her final goodbyes, before they'll embark on their own journey. He can hear the chink as she stirs the mugs downstairs.

At the door he turns suddenly, hearing a light flapping sound from the direction of the window. There is nothing there. Maybe it's an owl, nesting in the eaves. He clicks off the light and his daughter becomes a frail shape in the bedclothes.

Haddon awoke, instinctively throwing a glance towards the window.

The thin curtains were still drawn, sunlight seeping around the ill-fitting fabric. Of course there was nothing there. In fact, his dream that night had been of a bird perched on *Cerys's* window-sill, not his own. But in dreams there is no logic.

He was still dressed. His limbs ached to a degree he'd never experienced before. Opening the curtains, he allowed the light to enter the room. The view into the trees accentuated his isolation. His eyes traced the line of a path through the woods. They'd imagined one day strolling along it with their future grandchildren, picnic basket in hand. They'd bought the cottage several years before Jill fell pregnant. He swallowed and turned away from the window.

In the bathroom cupboard there was a toothbrush with stiff bristles. He ran cold water over it before squeezing a centimetre of dried toothpaste onto it and brushing his teeth. It felt alien and obscene in his mouth.

Once he'd washed, he went downstairs and made a cup of black tea with bags that were orange and brittle. It tasted even worse than it looked.

Someone had propped the fridge door open and switched it off at the plug. A newspaper, curling at the edges, lay on the worktop, imparting news from five years before. He opened the cupboard that housed the boiler and flicked the switch. Vague knockings and a hiss from the pipes brought to mind veins coursing with blood; it was as if the house had been woken from its slumber.

The morning progressed at glacial speed. Haddon investigated the woodland surrounding the cottage, surprised by how far the vegetation had encroached. Remnants of yellow police tape remained tied to the spindles of the veranda; the words DO NOT CROSS almost obliterated by the elements. He found two curious objects on the wooden steps. They were small desiccated bundles of some unknown material. He held them close and examined their consistency. The husks resembled owl pellets – cracked, brown, oblong casts that crumbled as he touched them. Strangely there were no tiny bones contained within, merely brittle lumps of dried tissue. The remnants disintegrated between his fingers and were dispersed on the breeze.

He supposed he should have been double-checking that all his affairs were in place, but the simple fact was he couldn't be bothered. It was pointless. He had no other family except for a cousin he hadn't seen in twenty-odd years; Jill's family had shown him nothing but fury and contempt since her death. At the inquest they'd seemed angrier about Haddon surviving than they had about Cerys and Jill's deaths, as if it was further proof of his inadequacies; he hadn't even succeeded in taking his own life.

The overnight bag in the boot of his car crackled as he carried it into the cottage. He opened it on the bed, removing the packets of tablets that he'd been stockpiling over the past few months. This time there would be no – *backing out* – mistakes; he'd swallow enough to ensure there was no coming back.

The wall clock reminded him that it was lunchtime, even if his body was oblivious to the fact. He wasn't hungry, but felt his bedtime cocktail might sit better on a stomach already lined. He'd learned that in the suicide group-therapy sessions he'd been forced to attend. He was now a fount of knowledge where it came to taking your own life; he knew the best knot to tie in a hanging, how correctly to slit one's wrists in the bath, what kind of hose would be the most effective when attached to an exhaust. To use any method other than an overdose, however, would be cheating.

Haddon walked to the pub on the main road. The lane was frantic with bird calls and movement in the trees. At one point he thought he heard something laughing, but he reasoned it was probably just a chaffinch.

The pub was relatively empty. An elderly couple sat in the window pecking at their shepherd's pie, and a man who was obviously a sales rep was wolfing down a ploughman's lunch. Haddon ordered a small lasagne and chips and a pint of lager, and chose a table in the darkest recess of the room. While he waited, he tried to ignore the plastic climbing frame that was visible through the window.

When the meal arrived he ate slowly.

As he was leaving, he caught sight of a reflection in the chrome trim that edged the bar; something with an impossibly bloated head appeared frozen on four spindly limbs behind him, the pale, domed skull balancing on a frame of bones.

He gasped and turned. A dog-shaped plastic collection box for the RSPCA stared back, the eyes of the golden retriever rendered deliberately mournful. Its sentiment matched his own.

Soon, my love. Soon.

The walk back to the cottage was languid and considered. He'd purchased a bottle of whiskey from the bar, fighting the urge to moan about the price. He tucked the bottle under his arm as he walked. To shake the image of Cerys in her final days – the loss of hair, dark hollow eyes, the misshapen bulge of her head – he took the photograph from his wallet and braved a glance. The picture had been taken at some theme park, as Jill pressed close to Cerys, laughing at something out of shot. A month later the tumour had been diagnosed.

At first he and Jill had resolved to remain strong. They'd certainly never let Cerys become aware of her own impending death, despite the doctors' advice. After months of avoiding the issue, Haddon had finally realised that they both shared the same belief; life beyond Cerys was inconceivable. They'd refused to contemplate such an existence. So they'd hatched the suicide pact one drunken night, lost in their own sorrow at news that the cancer had spread.

Haddon's hands have now stopped shaking. He is lying in the bed, his arms wrapped round Jill. She is not moving; her breathing is shallow. He reminds himself that this is the only option. Cerys is already at peace. There is no going back now. He forces open one of his eyes and glances at his wife. Her skin is losing its colour. Her lips look darker, though her face appears unreal, synthetic. In the woods outside, a fox cries sharply. It sounds like a child.

For several minutes he lies still, eyes closed, willing his body to drift into the abyss. His mind is dimming, his brain becoming detached from its surroundings. He can imagine looking down on himself from above, sounds fading as he settles into the realms of sleep.

But what is that? A sharp cackle of laughter from his daughter's room. He is moving there instantly, propelled by fear. From above he watches as Cerys lies motionless on the bed. The laughter rings out again and Haddon's attention is drawn to a small hunched shape on the window-ledge. A flutter of wings and he realises that it is the kookaburra they saw at the zoo. Its jerky movement looks mechanical. The bird hops onto the bed and edges upwards with a shake of its feathers. It pauses as it reaches Cerys's pillow and cocks its head.

Haddon watches aghast as the bird leans in near to her skull and pecks sharply at a point above the ear. It repeats this action several times. Haddon screams silently in frustration as he is forced to watch. Soon he can see blood creeping across the pillow, the wound black and glistening. The bird continues working away at his daughter's head until it has opened a gaping cavity. The alabaster bone is stark against the scarlet. Then, in one precise fluid movement, the kookaburra reaches its pointed beak into the hole and plucks out a soft mass of black tissue. It tugs on the jellied flesh, stretching it in an effort to remove the quivering lump. Finally it is free of the skull. The bird flutters onto the post of the headboard, trailing spots of blood across the duvet. It shifts the lump of flesh until it is gripped tightly, then cracks the mass against the wood several times. Finally satisfied, it tips its head and the lump disappears down the bird's throat.

Suddenly he is back in his own room, images of his daughter's head still raw in his mind. He opens his eyes in alarm and flips off the side of the bed, landing heavily on the floor. He crawls across the carpet towards the door. He reaches for his coat, which is hanging on the back of the chair, feeling for the mobile phone in his pocket. The effort is exhausting and he drops back onto the floor, the phone almost jolting free of his fingers. He tries to look at the handset but his eyes are unfocused and watering. The number-pad feels too small, but he jabs frantically at the 9 three times. There is a burning sensation in his chest and he turns to his left and vomits onto the floor.

From the handset he hears the shrill static of a voice answering. He wipes the vomit from his mouth, clamps the phone to his ear and says, 'Ambulance, please. I need an ambulance.'

Upon his return, the cottage had an air of expectancy about it. The late summer sun cast long shadows across the ground. The air was warm and still. Haddon wandered the house, searching for something profound to do with the time remaining. He came away feeling unsatisfied, instead having to content himself with drinking the whiskey and looking at the photograph of Jill and Cerys.

The booze was as welcome as a long-lost friend. He relaxed into its embrace, sensing the edges of reality being smoothed, feeling the grip of oblivion tighten. The shadows slid across the bedroom wall as evening advanced. Soon the sounds of birdsong filled the air, pushing away all other noise. The shrill melodies and rhythmic calls were like a lullaby. Presently he realised he would have to swallow the tablets.

The meagre light was enough for him to see by as he pressed the pills free of the foil wrappers, collecting them together in the folds of the sheets. Soon there was a small pile of red capsules. He topped up the whiskey and began pushing them into his mouth, washing the pills down with a forceful swig. Haddon could feel them lodging in his gullet. The whiskey was helping. He felt a mild tingling sensation in his stomach. His body was becoming bloated and sluggish.

He rolled onto his side and rested his head on the pillow. Earlier, he'd thought about leaving a note but decided it was needless.

The sky was losing its final vestiges of light. The birds had fallen silent. His legs seemed to be vibrating. Eyes closed, he allowed his mind to settle, slowing his breathing to an absolute minimum.

And then he heard the sound of the front door opening; footsteps in the hallway, the creak of the stairs as someone ascended.

Haddon closed his eyes and tried to become invisible in the

tangle of sheets. The bedroom door opened and then he heard a voice:

'Daddy, where have you been?'

He opened his eyes and stared at Cerys in the doorway. She was wearing her favourite jeans – the ones with the pink piping – and her *Dora the Explorer* T-shirt. Her hair was tied into two neat bunches at either side of her head. She was smiling and her face radiated delight.

Haddon tried to sit up. He stared back.

She was still there. 'Mummy and me have been waiting for you.'

He swallowed and shook his head slowly. 'Where is Mummy?'

'She's outside.' She blinked. 'We've missed you, Daddy.'

He stood gingerly and limped over to the little girl. She took his hand. The window was still open. He looked out, seeing a dark figure waiting in the long grass. The figure seemed to hesitate and then waved. He returned the gesture.

'Daddy, are you all right?'

He turned to see Cerys's beautiful face. 'I'm fine, sweetheart. I just had a bad dream, that's all.'

She hugged his legs. 'Well – everything's okay, isn't it?'

'It is.' He put his hand on her shoulder. 'C'mon, let's go and see Mummy.'

At the top of the stairs he paused and threw a final glance back into the bedroom, doing his best to ignore the crumpled shape that lay tangled in the bedclothes.

His daughter capered ahead, skipping down the stairs. By the time Haddon reached the bottom, Jill had appeared at the door. They embraced and he breathed in the familiar scent of her hair, and the Haddons drifted out into the darkness.

Painful Hard Ectoplasm
Laura Ellen Joyce

Hart enjoyed the creak of his new grey boots on the stair. They were an early present to himself. He was looking forward to seeing some of the girls at the early evening Christmas service, Lori, Sarah, and plain little Nancy Peach.

'Just looking in on the chickens, Mom,' Hart yelled down the stairs. He didn't go at once to the coop on the apartment rooftop but instead crept into his favourite place. Right at the top of the stairwell, there was a dark alcove where the cleaning lady kept her supplies. He'd discovered it ten years earlier when they'd moved in. For a boy of eleven it had held fantastic possibilities. If you moved the cover of the air vent there was a little square snapshot of the living room in the apartment above his. Nancy's apartment.

Tonight, Hart had seen Nancy go into the apartment block with Jimmy Royal. Hart knew for a fact that they weren't serious. Jimmy's hair was already thinning and his job as a schoolteacher left him pale and blubbery.

'Hart, what are you doing up there? We need to get to church.'

Hart ignored his mother's calls and set about removing the cover of the vent so he could see what Nancy and Jimmy were doing.

The first time Hart had found the alcove was a few months after they'd moved to the city from the poultry farm. He'd been charged with looking after the coop and though he'd hated it at first, after a while it became comforting to him, a little piece of home. That day he'd been tired and wanted to read his copy of *Tales from the Crypt* in peace. He'd made his way into the little alcove and pulled the red curtain across so no one would see the beam from his torch. He'd been disturbed because he had heard someone crying in the apartment below the alcove. The sound was louder near the vent. Hart had pulled the cover off and had a perfect view through the air shaft, though he couldn't be seen. He'd noticed with surprise that his mother had been in there with Mr Peach.

'I can't believe it. I can't believe he's dead. They just called from the prison. He wasn't a great husband but he was my man.'

Hart remembered he didn't understand why she had said such awful lies to Mr Peach or why she had put her head on his shoulder.

'My God, what a mess. I knew things were tough for a while but I never expected this.'

Hart had peered down as her sobs lessened a little and she'd straightened up as though she'd sensed he was there.

'I've been fretting over what would happen if Hart saw something in the news about his father.'

Hart had flinched at his name. Hadn't been able to connect any of this with himself. Mr Peach had said nothing at all, just let her continue.

'It's worse than I expected. Oh God. Worse. Don't think I can bear to go to the funeral. I mean, what a mess. How do they even get knives in there? Don't they search them at all?' Hart recalled his mother fairly shaking Mr Peach then, her voice angry and sad at the same time. She'd left the apartment and Hart had been scared that she'd come and find him. But she never had. No one ever had in all those years.

Hart knew that Mr Peach would be having his nap now before the service. He always had one at this time. Looked like Jimmy knew it too. Hart'd like to see him try it on with Nancy. That would be something. There was a click as the living room door opened and Nancy entered from the kitchen. Streak-of-piss Jimmy followed her in and sat in Mr Peach's armchair.

'Nancy baby, come over to the tree and sit awhile. There's something I want to say.' Jimmy's face shone pink under the tree, the fairy lights mottling his face as his hands twisted nervously at a velvet box he'd brought out of his pocket. Nancy ignored this request and walked to the drinks cabinet.

'Jimmy, it's Christmas Eve, why so serious? Let's have a little drink. You want one? I'll get you one.'

'Oh, don't worry about that now, Nana, there's plenty of time.'

'And we're out of soda, there's only a dribble. Guess I could mix them strong but then I don't know if you'll be able to drive home.'

'I thought we'd take a walk later, after your dad gets up from his nap.'

'Jimmy, don't be silly. We've got to take Daddy to church. We'll have this one quickly and I'll get him up.'

'Nancy! Sit down!'

She replaced the glasses and looked over. Jimmy seldom raised his voice but when he did it was ridiculous. Like when Hart had hit Jimmy in the face for calling him a coward. It had turned into a stupid fist fight. Jimmy had been the coward then. Jimmy leaned forward and his face caught a yellow gleam from the tree. Nancy abandoned the drinks and came over, kissing the bright spot on Jimmy's cheek, but still she didn't sit down.

'Nana, you make me so happy, I want to do something to make you happy too.'

Jimmy went down on one knee and Hart couldn't hear what he was saying but he could imagine. Nancy had a bright false smile and accepted his ring. Her hand drooped then as though it was heavy. Hart couldn't believe the bastard had the nerve. They went over to the sofa and Nancy let Jimmy touch her breasts through the blouse for a little while. He looked so guilty, like he thought it was hurting her.

Hart flinched, hearing his mom moving about downstairs.

'Hart, have you finished with those chickens already? I thought I heard a cat out there last night. You make sure they're in secure,' she shouted up, and he put the cover back in place and went down to take her to church.

'Hart, don't. I can walk fine but you have to let me go at my own pace. Come on now, the reverend is looking over.' All through the service Hart had been annoyed with his mother. She was ugly now but didn't have the decency to admit it. She still acted all coquettish with the reverend, though she had to hobble on a stick like a woman twice her age. He felt sick when he thought of the beautiful redhead she used to be.

'Listen, Mom, I've got to talk to Lori. She's waiting for me and I said I'd see her home. I'll put you in a cab and see you back at the apartment later.'

'Hart, it's Christmas Eve.' She looked helplessly over at him and he knew what was in parenthesis under her breath. It was her last Christmas Eve. He didn't even particularly want to spend any time with Lori, but she'd been keen and he was willing, he guessed. It would certainly take the edge off the church service and all these old women.

'Wait there. I'll be ten minutes.' Hart shoved his mother down on to a stone bench, didn't wait to pull her shawl round her. She had no choice but to wait. He went to find Lori Culver, could see her yellow cape spreading biliously into the frosty night.

'Hart. Are you ready to go?'

'Sorry I haven't got time to take you back now. My mother's mind is wandering again. I'd better go back with her.'

'You bastard. Who is it?'

'Don't be like that, Lori. I've got ten minutes. We could go into the side chapel, get down on our knees maybe?'

'Oh, don't be clever, Hart, it doesn't suit you.' Lori tossed her tangled red hair like a cut-rate heroine and flipped Hart the bird. He smiled, mouthed Merry Christmas and quickly reached into his pocket to withdraw a sprig of mistletoe. He kissed Lori hard on the mouth and then turned away, walked back to his mother.

'Come on, get in the car. I need a drink. Don't know why you have to stay so long here talking to these old crones.'

'Just take me home, Hart. A drink sounds about right.'

Hart drove home recklessly, violence on his mind.

'That dirty bastard Peach. He'd better not try coming over tomorrow,' Hart said when they were back in the living room.

'Watch your mouth, Hart. He's been good to us. He's been very good to me. Not like some.'

'Not like some, no.' The words hung ugly between them as Hart went to the drinks cabinet. Whiskey for him. Nothing for her. Wouldn't say another word, Christmas Eve or no.

'Hart, I'm sorry. I'm sorry to ruin Christmas for you. I just can't bear going to church with my teeth like this and being dragged round on your arm like some old lady. I'm sorry I'm no fun. I'll make it up to you, baby boy.'

She fell back then, against the stack of cushions he'd put on the sofa to stop her getting sore.

'You don't need to be sorry. I don't remember having a normal Christmas before. Why should we start now?'

He took the bottle and poured another and one for her. He walked over and she leaned forward, took the glass in both hands and raised it to her lips. A little dribbled out and Hart leaned in to kiss her on the cheek. Cool as water he tongued the spilled liquor and then got up, wiped his mouth with the back of his hand and sipped slowly from his own glass. He strolled over to the window and looked back out over the snow.

'Fucking Jimmy.'

'What d'you say, Hart?'

'Jimmy. I saw him go upstairs with Nancy. They've got champagne.'

'Well, they've been courting some time now. I guess it's only natural.'

'What? What's natural?"

'Marriage. Mr Peach told me that Jimmy's bought one of those new houses. It's very pretty, by all accounts.'

'Mom, now why would I want to know what Jimmy's been doing? Anyway, it's not serious between them. It won't pan out, you'll see. You're just a gossipy old woman.'

She laughed then, a sound so surprising that he turned around. She held out her glass. By the time he had fixed her second drink, Hart heard music go on in the apartment upstairs and his mother was fast asleep.

'Some fucking Christmas,' he swore and downed both whiskeys. Time was, he thought, when it was him up in the Peaches' apartment. Not Jimmy. Ten years ago they'd been up in that apartment every Saturday night. They'd pulled the curtains shut at five every week whether it was dark or not and let the pale green light from the television fill the room. Hart's favourite show had been *Tales From Tomorrow*. He especially loved the ones where they had scientists and doctors doing mad experiments. He'd thought he'd be happy if Nancy would let him do one on her. God, it had all started because that boy at school, Larry, had showed him an old photo album that he said came from his grandmother's house. The pictures were of ghostly figures with thick white lines around their bodies.

'Ectoplasm,' Larry had told him. 'It's hard and it's painful like being born backwards.'

Hart had thought it must be strange being dead.

One of the nights, they'd sat watching TV and his mom had been in a bitch mood. She'd been sitting in the kitchen with Mr Peach and Hart had been starving for his dinner. The smell of burned cheese and cigarette smoke coming from the kitchen made him feel nauseous, though, and he'd wanted to get outside. That's when he'd had the idea. Nancy had been sitting curled up in her white dress on the sofa looking like a scoop of vanilla cream. The woman in one of the photos had had a white dress. He remembered how difficult Nancy had been to convince.

'Nancy, do you want to come and help me with something important? I need an assistant.'

'What are you doing, Hart? What is it?'

'It's kind of an experiment. I need a girl to do it properly.'

'Why? What do you mean? An experiment like they did on TV?'

'Kind of like that, yes.'

'But they sawed the lady in half. I don't want to be sawed in half and I don't want to get my dress dirty.'

'Don't be an idiot, Nancy. It's nothing like that. I guess I could ask stinky Marie from downstairs to be my assistant if you're too chicken.'

'Okay, Hart.'

Hart had been so excited that he'd run up the stairs ahead, not waiting for Nancy's little legs to catch up.

'First you need to lie down very still with the chickens.'

'Ew, no, Hart, I don't want to. I told you I can't get my dress dirty.'

'You don't want to die, do you, Nancy? Because that's what might happen if we don't get rid of the ectoplasm.'

Nancy had a little tear running down her face but she said nothing and lay down in the straw as the chickens pecked all around her. Hart took one of the pictures from his pocket and looked at the woman in the white dress. He thought it looked quite easy to get Nancy's legs to the same kind of angles and bent down slowly to her. Hart closed his dirty fingers around Nancy's ankle, just above the frill lace on her socks. Slowly he pulled the sock off and Nancy giggled. He pulled the other one off and tickled her feet. At last she seemed to be relaxing. Her hot little feet felt good in Hart's hand and he held them for just a little while. Then Nancy kicked, scattering straw and dislodging Hart's hands.

'When's the experiment, Hart? I don't want to die! I don't want to die.'

That's when Mr Peach had appeared with his mom.

'Daddy Daddy Daddy!' Nancy had screamed. Mr Peach had bent down to pick her up and swept her through the sky, blowing raspberries on her belly until she started giggling.

'Well, Nana baby, how about some strawberry lemonade, I know for a fact no one who drinks it can die. Hey, how about that?' Nancy had stopped her snivelling and Mr Peach had turned away from Hart, addressing his mom.

'I'd like it if you took your son home now, please.'

'How dare you talk to me like that? It's not Hart's fault, it's all this television you let her watch.'

Mr Peach continued as though Hart wasn't there.

'There's something wrong with that boy. He does everything he's told but does it so you know it's a game to him. Does it damn slowly as well. Takes his sweet time. Not normal for a kid his age to be sitting out on the roof doing nothing, frowning for no good reason. Messing with a little girl like that.'

'Well, if he's so awful why does Nancy trail after him all day long?'

'Well, please don't concern yourself any longer with that, it certainly won't happen again.'

'What do you mean?'

'I don't want him near her. If he's anything like his father, well. You can see what's happened here.'

And then Hart had walked over and punched Mr Peach on the nose. Hard enough so that his knuckles were covered in blood and snot as he climbed down the fire escape and back into his own apartment. He'd never expected to still be living there now at the age of twenty-one. Alone on Christmas Eve with two whiskeys and the music going on upstairs. His drunken mother asleep in her chair. Maybe she would wake up again, maybe she wouldn't.

By God, thought Hart, Nancy was plain. No one had expected Hart to come to the New Year's dance with all that he'd been through in the last week since his mother passed away on Christmas morning. But it was as though Nancy had made the effort, just in case. Where the other girls got away with a shoulder strap biting in, or gloves of two slightly different shades, she was immaculate. Hart looked past her for the right kind of girl. He caught Sarah's eye and she blew him a kiss but he wanted someone a little more feral tonight. Plump shoulders were good, or hair that hadn't been brushed through. The kind of girl whose neck you could kiss and sink right down into in front of everyone. Shit. Nancy was looking over. He knew she couldn't help it. But what an ugly show. He smiled and walked over to her. His grey boots were still new enough to creak on the polished wood.

'Hart, darling. But it's so wonderful to see you. We were all so sorry to hear of your loss.' Hart said nothing, looked at Nancy for a long time. Long enough that she started to embarrass herself by going on about his poor dead mother, how his mother would have loved this. And all the while she twirled Jimmy's mean little diamond right under his nose, as though something so despicable could make him feel jealous. God, but she was transparent.

The band was slowing down and there was some commotion

while couples left the floor to refill their drinks or sit awhile in dark corners. Hart didn't take his eyes off Nancy while she turned her head to search for Jimmy across the floor. Her spangly green dress looked cheaper under the lights than when she had been dancing.

'Meet me outside before the last dance, Nancy. I think Jimmy's well enough occupied for now.'

Nancy tightened her shoulders and refused to look behind her to where Jimmy was dancing with her friend Jane. Hart could see she was very drunk.

'Jimmy's not like that, Hart. He's not like. Well, some.'

'Not like me?'

'He's good to me.'

Hart turned away. Then when he was outside, she came to him at last. He led her to where it was quiet and told her what she wanted to hear.

'I think you're beautiful, Nancy. You know it's not serious with me and Sarah. She's just a whore.'

They kissed for a long time, Hart pushing her up against a wall.

'Hart.' She slurred her mouth so close to his ear he could feel the grease of her lipstick. 'Hart, I love you.' He shivered. He did shiver then.

'Nancy. You're drunk, Go back to Jimmy and let him take you home.'

'Oh God, Hart. Oh God, I'm really, oh God. I'm. I'll come up to the coop tomorrow and we can have some fun.'

She swayed a little and he had no choice but to hold her hair away from her face while she vomited behind the cars.

It was a fiercely cold March that year. Hart and Nancy couldn't get up to the coop as often as before and finally they decided to risk meeting in the new house where Jimmy was doing some decorating. There was a smell of fresh paint when Hart arrived one afternoon. Nancy showed him in quickly, keeping her eyes down as though she didn't even want to think about who might see them together in the middle of the day when Jimmy was at work.

'So, how're the big wedding plans?' Hart looked around the mint-coloured living room in distaste as he said it. Nancy turned her back on him and began to place white sheets on all the furniture.

'Don't tell me Jimmy has been coming home from work and doing all this himself?'

'It's more than I would expect from you, Hart.'

'Yeah but you expect something a bit different from me, don't you, Nance?'

Hart walked over to the couch and put his hands around her waist from behind. She continued to smooth the vinyl covers and acted like Hart wasn't there at all. But she didn't seem to mind when he pulled her down on to the rug. Funny thing was that all the way through she sighed very softly, like she was working out the housekeeping and it didn't add up. As they lay still afterwards Hart cold see the scarred, lumpen surface of the green walls.

'Fucking Jimmy couldn't even do a good paint job.'

'What?' Nancy replied, pushing him off her. 'I can't do this here again, Hart. It's not right.'

Hart thought she was probably on to something. Last thing he wanted was to be distracted by Jimmy's walls. At least the chickens were something wholesome to look at.

For a few days after that Hart didn't hear from Nancy. When she rang and asked him to go to a movie he hadn't expected they would actually go to see one. Now they were sitting in the dark as close together as if they were in love.

Nancy drew a gold lighter from her purse and started flicking it on and off. Then she let the flame linger, staring hard at it. It was as though she were separating the colours with her eyes – gold, violet, hot white. Hart leaned in towards her, cigarette in mouth, and snatched a light. Nancy lit her own cigarette and replaced the lighter in her purse, snapping it shut.

'Hey, Nancy, do you want something sweet?' Hart let his free hand wander, settling in her lap. He gave her thigh a squeeze.

'Thank you, no.' Nancy recrossed her legs, deftly shifting Hart's hand from her thigh. Amused, he stuck it in his pocket and continued to smoke as the feature began.

'Nancy?' he started.

Nancy pressed a finger to her lips and told Hart to shush. On screen a woman was wandering around a room full of caged birds. Her hair was stiff with lacquer and she held a pencil in her capable hands. Hart lit a second cigarette and sat back. Nancy watched him as the thick, unfiltered tip went in and out of his mouth. She felt queasy. The smell of smoke seemed to thicken around them and the light from the projector was bright. Nancy dipped forward in her seat and hung her head down between her knees. Hart stubbed out his cigarette and began to smooth her hair.

'Hart, I told Jimmy and he doesn't mind. You understand, he doesn't mind.' She sat up slowly, hair trailing across her face where Hart's hands had been. She took out her mirror and began to straighten her face. The screen was darker now, filled with black birds. Their thin cries were loud.

'Hart.' She made the shape of his name but the word melted almost into silence. Hart put his arm around her and the woman beside Nancy gave her a sly smile. Nancy pushed him away.

'I'm going to have a baby, Hart. I told Jimmy and he doesn't mind.' She whispered as loud as she dared in Hart's ear, wanting him to understand what she was saying. He said nothing.

'Jimmy doesn't mind about it but I do. It's not right because he's made such a sweet home for us and he's done all the work himself. And of course my father loves him.'

Hart thought of the green walls Jimmy had picked for the building over the road from Hart's. It was smaller and more garish than any of the others, a seasick little house that he expected Nancy to live in. He laughed.

'So I'm going to leave and think about what to do. Jimmy's very kind but I can't do it.' She was so angry she stopped whispering.

'And you! You can tell them why if they ask.' Nancy got up and pushed her way past the people who were not even pretending to watch the film any longer. She escaped the smoky picture-house. Hart did not follow, neither did he light a cigarette. He knew from the way she said it that she wasn't going to come back here any more. He wouldn't see her again. Hart watched the birds in amazement for more than an hour. They had the whole sky and yet they chose to hurl themselves through glass and bleed to death. He couldn't see why they would do it. It seemed to Hart a funny kind of film. And then, at last, he saw the dead man, his eyes ragged holes full of blood. He laughed at the lunacy of it, the sacrifice the birds had made. But he respected them, those crazy birds, he liked their style. Still laughing he left the film early and made his way home.

When he returned, Hart sat awhile in his chair. He didn't bother with bed just yet. The sky was fretting to snow again and he knew he should have brought the chickens in before he went out. He felt ashamed he'd been so eager to see Nancy that he hadn't been as careful as he should have been. He hated the corn-yellow stink of hens in the apartment but in winter needs must. He realised he hadn't taken his overcoat off yet and thought to look in on the chickens, to see how they were faring.

The fire escape was treacherous with ice and he thought too

late he should have worn gloves. It was colder than it had been earlier. Much too cold for him to think properly. He reached the roof and opened the coop. Hart looked at the soft brown heads of the chickens as they bent to eat their corn. He wanted to get near to the smell of them that reminded him of home. He leant down to breathe it in slowly. He felt like he was going to cry.

Hart turned away and went to the little shed. He got a handful of cleaning rags and returned to the coop. It would have to be a good heat for what he wanted. The kind of heat that turned bone to ash. It was hard to set the fire but he worked for a long time pressing the flame from his lighter to the fluid on the rags.

It was peaceful, thought Hart, up on the roof. He sat down, cross-legged like a little boy, and thought about the time his father had taught him to shoot a gun. They'd still been on the farm then, before his dad had gone to prison for the last time. He'd told Hart to throw away his toy gun and his spurs and be a real cowboy. He'd taken Hart out to the back field and helped him hold the pistol. His father's strong, tanned hands had held Hart's small white ones and between them they squeezed and squeezed the trigger, firing at tin cans lined up. Hart couldn't get the hang of it, his arms hurt, and his shoulder was tense. He didn't see the need for it, anyway. But his dad was amazing at shooting things, he was just such a natural. The smell of it had followed Hart all his life, the sweet, clean smell of gunpowder calmed his nerves and reminded him of his daddy. Hart remembered that when they'd finished shooting, his father had given him a slow salute, like when they played soldiers with his cousins in the summertime.

Now, the chickens had started to burn and a different smell drifted out, a thick, meaty stink that wasn't unpleasant. Soon the smoke was too much and he had to shut his eyes. He curled up and was peaceful. But even in the dark behind his eyelids Hart could see how beautiful the sky was with the lines of the city muted by grey smoke and in the centre the half-toppled coop made a flaming arc over all. He felt as though a scattering of chicken feathers as soft and deep as snow were covering him and keeping him warm. At last he was alone.

The Birds
Daphne du Maurier

On December the third the wind changed overnight and it was winter. Until then the autumn had been mellow, soft. The leaves had lingered on the trees, golden red, and the hedgerows were still green. The earth was rich where the plough had turned it.

Nat Hocken, because of a war-time disability, had a pension and did not work full-time at the farm. He worked three days a week, and they gave him the lighter jobs: hedging, thatching, repairs to the farm buildings.

Although he was married, with children, his was a solitary disposition; he liked best to work alone. It pleased him when he was given a bank to build up, or a gate to mend at the far end of the peninsula, where the sea surrounded the farm land on either side. Then, at midday, he would pause and eat the pasty that his wife had baked for him, and sitting on the cliff's edge would watch the birds. Autumn was best for this, better than spring. In spring the birds flew inland, purposeful, intent; they knew where they were bound, the rhythm and ritual of their life brooked no delay. In autumn those that had not migrated overseas but remained to pass the winter were caught up in the same driving urge, but because migration was denied them followed a pattern of their own. Great flocks of them came to the peninsula, restless, uneasy, spending themselves in motion; now wheeling, circling in the sky, now settling to feed on the rich new-turned soil, but even when they fed it was as though they did so without hunger, without desire. Restlessness drove them to the skies again.

Black and white, jackdaw and gull, mingled in strange partnership, seeking some sort of liberation, never satisfied, never still. Flocks of starlings, rustling like silk, flew to fresh pasture, driven by the same necessity of movement, and the smaller birds, the finches and the larks, scattered from tree to hedge as if compelled.

Nat watched them, and he watched the sea-birds too. Down in the bay they waited for the tide. They had more patience.

Oyster-catchers, redshank, sanderling, and curlew watched by the water's edge; as the slow sea sucked at the shore and then withdrew, leaving the strip of seaweed bare and the shingle churned, the sea-birds raced and ran upon the beaches. Then that same impulse to flight seized upon them too. Crying, whistling, calling, they skimmed the placid sea and left the shore. Make haste, make speed, hurry and begone; yet where, and to what purpose? The restless urge of autumn, unsatisfying, sad, had put a spell upon them and they must flock, and wheel, and cry; they must spill themselves of motion before winter came.

Perhaps, thought Nat, munching his pasty by the cliff's edge, a message comes to the birds in autumn, like a warning. Winter is coming. Many of them perish. And like people who, apprehensive of death before their time, drive themselves to work or folly, the birds do likewise.

The birds had been more restless than ever this fall of the year, the agitation more marked because the days were still. As the tractor traced its path up and down the western hills, the figure of the farmer silhouetted on the driving-seat, the whole machine and the man upon it would be lost momentarily in the great cloud of wheeling, crying birds. There were many more than usual, Nat was sure of this. Always, in autumn, they followed the plough, but not in great flocks like these, nor with such clamour.

Nat remarked upon it, when hedging was finished for the day. 'Yes,' said the farmer, 'there are more birds about than usual; I've noticed it too. And daring, some of them, taking no notice of the tractor. One or two gulls came so close to my head this afternoon I thought they'd knock my cap off! As it was, I could scarcely see what I was doing, when they were overhead and I had the sun in my eyes. I have a notion the weather will change. It will be a hard winter. That's why the birds are restless.'

Nat, tramping home across the fields and down the lane to his cottage, saw the birds still flocking over the western hills, in the last glow of the sun. No wind, and the grey sea calm and full. Campion in bloom yet in the hedges, and the air mild. The farmer was right, though, and it was that night the weather turned. Nat's bedroom faced east. He woke just after two and heard the wind in the chimney. Not the storm and bluster of a sou'westerly gale, bringing the rain, but east wind, cold and dry. It sounded hollow in the chimney, and a loose slate rattled on the roof. Nat listened, and he could hear the sea roaring in the bay. Even the air in the small bedroom had turned chill: a draught came under the skirting of the door, blowing upon the bed. Nat drew the blanket round him, leant closer to the back of his sleeping wife, and stayed wakeful, watchful, aware of misgiving without cause.

Then he heard the tapping on the window. There was no creeper on the cottage walls to break loose and scratch upon the pane. He listened, and the tapping continued until, irritated by the sound, Nat got out of bed and went to the window. He opened it, and as he did so something brushed his hand, jabbing at his knuckles, grazing the skin. Then he saw the flutter of the wings and it was gone, over the roof, behind the cottage.

It was a bird, what kind of bird he could not tell. The wind must have driven it to shelter on the sill.

He shut the window and went back to bed, but feeling his knuckles wet put his mouth to the scratch. The bird had drawn blood. Frightened, he supposed, and bewildered, the bird, seeking shelter, had stabbed at him in the darkness. Once more he settled himself to sleep.

Presently the tapping came again, this time more forceful, more insistent, and now his wife woke at the sound, and turning in the bed said to him, 'See to the window, Nat, it's rattling.'

'I've already seen to it,' he told her, 'there's some bird there, trying to get in. Can't you hear the wind? It's blowing from the east, driving the birds to shelter.'

'Send them away,' she said, 'I can't sleep with that noise.'

He went to the window for the second time, and now when he opened it there was not one bird upon the sill but half a dozen; they flew straight into his face, attacking him.

He shouted, striking out at them with his arms, scattering them; like the first one, they flew over the roof and disappeared. Quickly he let the window fall and latched it.

'Did you hear that?' he said. 'They went for me. Tried to peck my eyes.' He stood by the window, peering into the darkness, and could see nothing. His wife, heavy with sleep, murmured from the bed.

'I'm not making it up,' he said, angry at her suggestion. 'I tell you the birds were on the sill, trying to get into the room.'

Suddenly a frightened cry came from the room across the passage where the children slept.

'It's Jill,' said his wife, roused at the sound, sitting up in bed. 'Go to her, see what's the matter.'

Nat lit the candle, but when he opened the bedroom door to cross the passage the draught blew out the flame.

There came a second cry of terror, this time from both children, and stumbling into their room he felt the beating of wings about him in the darkness. The window was wide open.

Through it came the birds, hitting first the ceiling and the walls, then swerving in mid-flight, turning to the children in their beds.

'It's all right, I'm here,' shouted Nat, and the children flung themselves, screaming, upon him, while in the darkness the birds rose and dived and came for him again.

'What is it, Nat, what's happened?' his wife called from the further bedroom, and swiftly he pushed the children through the door to the passage and shut it upon them, so that he was alone now, in their bedroom, with the birds.

He seized a blanket from the nearest bed, and using it as a weapon flung it to right and left about him in the air. He felt the thud of bodies, heard the fluttering of wings, but they were not yet defeated, for again and again they returned to the assault, jabbing his hands, his head, the little stabbing beaks sharp as a pointed fork. The blanket became a weapon of defence; he wound it about his head, and then in greater darkness beat at the birds with his bare hands. He dared not stumble to the door and open it, lest in doing so the birds should follow him.

How long he fought with them in the darkness he could not tell, but at last the beating of the wings about him lessened and then withdrew, and through the density of the blanket he was aware of light. He waited, listened; there was no sound except the fretful crying of one of the children from the bedroom beyond. The fluttering, the whirring of the wings had ceased.

He took the blanket from his head and stared about him. The cold grey morning light exposed the room. Dawn, and the open window, had called the living birds; the dead lay on the floor. Nat gazed at the little corpses, shocked and horrified. They were all small birds, none of any size; there must have been fifty of them lying there upon the floor. There were robins, finches, sparrows, blue tits, larks and bramblings, birds that by nature's law kept to their own flock and their own territory, and now, joining one with another in their urge for battle, had destroyed themselves against the bedroom walls, or in the strife had been destroyed by him. Some had lost feathers in the fight, others had blood, his blood, upon their beaks.

Sickened, Nat went to the window and stared out across his patch of garden to the fields.

It was bitter cold, and the ground had all the hard black look of frost. Not white frost, to shine in the morning sun, but the black frost that the east wind brings. The sea, fiercer now with the turning tide, white-capped and steep, broke harshly in the bay. Of the birds there was no sign. Not a sparrow chattered in the hedge beyond the garden gate, no early missel-thrush or blackbird pecked on the grass for worms. There was no sound at all but the east wind and the sea.

Nat shut the window and the door of the small bedroom, and went back across the passage to his own. His wife sat up in bed, one child asleep beside her, the smaller in her arms, his face bandaged. The curtains were tightly drawn across the window, the candles lit. Her face looked garish in the yellow light. She shook her head for silence.

'He's sleeping now,' she whispered, 'but only just. Something must have cut him, there was blood at the corner of his eyes. Jill said it was the birds. She said she woke up, and the birds were in the room.'

His wife looked up at Nat, searching his face for confirmation. She looked terrified, bewildered, and he did not want her to know that he was also shaken, dazed almost, by the events of the past few hours.

'There are birds in there,' he said, 'dead birds, nearly fifty of them. Robins, wrens, all the little birds from hereabouts. It's as though a madness seized them, with the east wind.' He sat down on the bed beside his wife, and held her hand. 'It's the weather,' he said, 'it must be that, it's the hard weather. They aren't the birds, maybe, from here around. They've been driven down, from up country.'

'But Nat,' whispered his wife, 'it's only this night that the weather turned. There's been no snow to drive them. And they can't be hungry yet. There's food for them, out there, in the fields.'

'It's the weather,' repeated Nat. 'I tell you, it's the weather.'

His face too was drawn and tired, like hers. They stared at one another for a while without speaking.

'I'll go downstairs and make a cup of tea,' he said.

The sight of the kitchen reassured him. The cups and saucers, neatly stacked upon the dresser, the table and chairs, his wife's roll of knitting on her basket chair, the children's toys in a corner cupboard.

He knelt down, raked out the old embers and relit the fire. The glowing sticks brought normality, the steaming kettle and the brown teapot comfort and security. He drank his tea, carried a cup up to his wife. Then he washed in the scullery, and, putting on his boots, opened the back door.

The sky was hard and leaden, and the brown hills that had gleamed in the sun the day before looked dark and bare. The east wind, like a razor, stripped the trees, and the leaves, crackling and dry, shivered and scattered with the wind's blast. Nat stubbed the earth with his boot. It was frozen hard. He had never known a change so swift and sudden. Black winter had descended in a single night.

The children were awake now. Jill was chattering upstairs and young Johnny crying once again. Nat heard his wife's voice, soothing, comforting. Presently they came down. He had breakfast ready for them, and the routine of the day began.

'Did you drive away the birds?' asked Jill, restored to calm because of the kitchen fire, because of day, because of breakfast.

'Yes, they've all gone now,' said Nat. 'It was the east wind brought them in. They were frightened and lost, they wanted shelter.'

'They tried to peck us,' said Jill. 'They went for Johnny's eyes.'

'Fright made them do that,' said Nat. 'They didn't know where they were, in the dark bedroom.'

'I hope they won't come again,' said Jill. 'Perhaps if we put bread for them outside the window they will eat that and fly away.'

She finished her breakfast and then went for her coat and hood, her school books and her satchel. Nat said nothing, but his wife looked at him across the table. A silent message passed between them.

'I'll walk with her to the bus,' he said, 'I don't go to the farm today.'

And while the child was washing in the scullery he said to his wife, 'Keep all the windows closed, and the doors too. Just to be on the safe side. I'll go to the farm. Find out if they heard anything in the night.' Then he walked with his small daughter up the lane. She seemed to have forgotten her experience of the night before. She danced ahead of him, chasing the leaves, her face whipped with the cold and rosy under the pixie hood.

'Is it going to snow, Dad?' she said. 'It's cold enough.'

He glanced up at the bleak sky, felt the wind tear at his shoulders.

'No,' he said, 'it's not going to snow. This is a black winter, not a white one.'

All the while he searched the hedgerows for the birds, glanced over the top of them to the fields beyond, looked to the small wood above the farm where the rooks and jackdaws gathered. He saw none.

The other children waited by the bus-stop, muffled, hooded like Jill, the faces white and pinched with cold.

Jill ran to them, waving. 'My Dad says it won't snow,' she called, 'it's going to be a black winter.'

She said nothing of the birds. She began to push and struggle with another little girl. The bus came ambling up the hill. Nat saw her on to it, then turned and walked back towards the farm. It was not his day for work, but he wanted to satisfy himself that all was well. Jim, the cowman, was clattering in the yard.

'Boss around?' asked Nat.

'Gone to market,' said Jim. 'It's Tuesday, isn't it?'

He clumped off round the corner of a shed. He had no time for Nat. Nat was said to be superior. Read books, and the like. Nat had forgotten it was Tuesday. This showed how the events of the preceding night had shaken him. He went to the back door of the farm-house and heard Mrs Trigg singing in the kitchen, the wireless making a background to her song.

'Are you there, missus?' called out Nat.

She came to the door, beaming, broad, a good-tempered woman.

'Hullo, Mr Hocken,' she said. 'Can you tell me where this cold is coming from? Is it Russia? I've never seen such a change. And it's going on, the wireless says. Something to do with the Arctic Circle.'

'We didn't turn on the wireless this morning,' said Nat. 'Fact is, we had trouble in the night.'

'Kiddies poorly?'

'No…' He hardly knew how to explain it. Now, in daylight, the battle of the birds would sound absurd.

He tried to tell Mrs Trigg what had happened, but he could see from her eyes that she thought his story was the result of a nightmare.

'Sure they were real birds,' she said, smiling, 'with proper feathers and all? Not the funny-shaped kind, that the men see after closing hours on a Saturday night?'

'Mrs Trigg,' he said, 'there are fifty dead birds, robins, wrens, and such, lying low on the floor of the children's bedroom. They went for me; they tried to go for young Johnny's eyes.'

Mrs Trigg stared at him doubtfully.

'Well there, now,' she answered, 'I suppose the weather brought them. Once in the bedroom, they wouldn't know where they were to. Foreign birds maybe, from that Arctic Circle.'

'No,' said Nat, 'they were the birds you see about here every day.'

'Funny thing,' said Mrs Trigg, 'no explaining it, really. You ought to write up and ask the *Guardian*. They'd have some answer for it. Well, I must be getting on.'

She nodded, smiled, and went back into the kitchen.

Nat, dissatisfied, turned to the farm-gate. Had it not been for those corpses on the bedroom floor, which he must now collect and bury somewhere, he would have considered the tale exaggeration too.

Jim was standing by the gate.

'Had any trouble with the birds?' asked Nat.

'Birds? What birds?'

'We got them up our place last night. Scores of them, came in the children's bedroom. Quite savage they were.'

'Oh?' It took time for anything to penetrate Jim's head.

'Never heard of birds acting savage,' he said at length. 'They get tame, like, sometimes. I've seen them come to the windows for crumbs.'

'These birds last night weren't tame.'

'No? Cold maybe. Hungry. You put out some crumbs.'

Jim was no more interested than Mrs Trigg had been. It was, Nat thought, like air-raids in the war. No one down this end of the country knew what the Plymouth folk had seen and suffered. You had to endure something yourself before it touched you.

He walked back along the lane and crossed the stile to his

cottage. He found his wife in the kitchen with young Johnny.

'See anyone?' she asked.

'Mrs Trigg and Jim,' he answered. 'I don't think they believed me. Anyway, nothing wrong up there.'

'You might take the birds away,' she said. 'I daren't go into the room to make the beds until you do. I'm scared.'

'Nothing to scare you now,' said Nat. 'They're dead, aren't they?'

He went up with a sack and dropped the stiff bodies into it, one by one. Yes, there were fifty of them, all told. Just the ordinary common birds of the hedgerow, nothing as large even as a thrush. It must have been fright that made them act the way they did. Blue tits, wrens, it was incredible to think of the power of their small beaks, jabbing at his face and hands the night before. He took the sack out into the garden and was faced now with a fresh problem. The ground was too hard to dig. It was frozen solid, yet no snow had fallen, nothing had happened in the past hours but the coming of the east wind. It was unnatural, queer. The weather prophets must be right. The change was something connected with the Arctic Circle.

The wind seemed to cut him to the bone as he stood there, uncertainly, holding the sack. He could see the white-capped seas breaking down under in the bay. He decided to take the birds to the shore and bury them.

When he reached the beach below the headland he could scarcely stand, the force of the east wind was so strong. It hurt to draw breath, and his bare hands were blue. Never had he known such cold, not in all the bad winters he could remember. It was low tide. He crunched his way over the shingle to the softer sand and then, his back to the wind, ground a pit in the sand with his heel. He meant to drop the birds into it, but as he opened up the sack the force of the wind carried them, lifted them, as though in flight again, and they were blown away from him along the beach, tossed like feathers, spread and scattered, the bodies of the fifty frozen birds. There was something ugly in the sight. He did not like it. The dead birds were swept away from him by the wind.

'The tide will take them when it turns,' he said to himself.

He looked out to sea and watched the crested breakers, combing green. They rose stiffly, curled, and broke again, and because it was ebb tide the roar was distant, more remote, lacking the sound and thunder of the flood.

Then he saw them. The gulls. Out there, riding the seas.

What he had thought at first to be the white caps of the waves were gulls. Hundreds, thousands, tens of thousands... They rose and fell in the trough of the seas, heads to the wind, like a mighty fleet at anchor, waiting on the tide. To eastward, and to the west, the gulls were there. They stretched as far as his eye could reach, in close formation, line upon line. Had the sea been still they would have covered the bay like a white cloud, head to head, body packed to body. Only the east wind, whipping the sea to breakers, hid them from the shore.

Nat turned, and leaving the beach climbed the steep path home. Someone should know of this. Someone should be told. Something was happening, because of the east wind and the weather, that he did not understand. He wondered if he should go to the call-box by the bus-stop and ring up the police. Yet what could they do? What could anyone do? Tens and thousands of gulls riding the sea there, in the bay, because of storm, because of hunger. The police would think him mad, or drunk, or take the statement from him with great calm. 'Thank you. Yes, the matter has already been reported. The hard weather is driving the birds inland in great numbers.' Nat looked about him. Still no sign of any other bird. Perhaps the cold had sent them all from up country? As he drew near to the cottage his wife came to meet him, at the door. She called to him, excited. 'Nat,' she said, 'it's on the wireless. They've just read out a special news bulletin. I've written it down.'

'What's on the wireless?' he said.

'About the birds,' she said. 'It's not only here, it's everywhere. In London, all over the country. Something has happened to the birds.'

Together they went into the kitchen. He read the piece of paper lying on the table.

'Statement from the Home Office at eleven a.m. today. Reports from all over the country are coming in hourly about the vast quantity of birds flocking above towns, villages, and outlying districts, causing obstruction and damage and even attacking individuals. It is thought that the Arctic air stream, at present covering the British Isles, is causing birds to migrate south in immense numbers, and that intense hunger may drive these birds to attack human beings. Householders are warned to see to their windows, doors, and chimneys, and to take reasonable precautions for the safety of their children. A further statement will be issued later.'

A kind of excitement seized Nat; he looked at his wife in triumph.

'There you are,' he said, 'let's hope they'll hear that at the farm. Mrs Trigg will know it wasn't any story. It's true. All over the country. I've been telling myself all morning there's something wrong. And just now, down on the beach, I looked out to sea and there are gulls, thousands of them, tens of thousands, you couldn't put a pin between their heads, and they're all out there, riding on the sea, waiting.'

'What are they waiting for, Nat?' she asked.

He stared at her, then looked down again at the piece of paper.

'I don't know,' he said slowly. 'It says here the birds are hungry.'

He went over to the drawer where he kept his hammer and tools.

'What are you going to do, Nat?'

'See to the windows and the chimneys too, like they tell you.'

'You think they would break in, with the windows shut? Those sparrows and robins and such? Why, how could they?'

He did not answer. He was not thinking of the robins and the sparrows. He was thinking of the gulls...

He went upstairs and worked there the rest of the morning, boarding the windows of the bedrooms, filling up the chimney bases. Good job it was his free day and he was not working at the farm. It reminded him of the old days, at the beginning of the war. He was not married then, and he had made all the blackout boards for his mother's house in Plymouth. Made the shelter too. Not that it had been of any use, when the moment came. He wondered if they would take these precautions up at the farm. He doubted it. Too easy-going, Harry Trigg and his missus. Maybe they'd laugh at the whole thing. Go off to a dance or a whist drive.

'Dinner's ready.' She called him, from the kitchen.

'All right. Coming down.'

He was pleased with his handiwork. The frames fitted nicely over the little panes and at the base of the chimneys.

When dinner was over and his wife was washing up, Nat switched on the one o'clock news. The same announcement was repeated, the one which she had taken down during the morning, but the news bulletin enlarged upon it. 'The flocks of birds have caused dislocation in all areas,' read the announcer, 'and in London the sky was so dense at ten o'clock this morning that it seemed as if the city was covered by a vast black cloud.

'The birds settled on roof-tops, on window ledges and on chimneys. The species included blackbird, thrush, the common

224

house-sparrow, and, as might be expected in the metropolis, a vast quantity of pigeons and starlings, and that frequenter of the London river, the black-headed gull. The sight has been so unusual that traffic came to a standstill in many thoroughfares, work was abandoned in shops and offices, and the streets and pavements were crowded with people standing about to watch the birds.'

Various incidents were recounted, the suspected reason of cold and hunger stated again, and warnings to householders repeated. The announcer's voice was smooth and suave. Nat had the impression that this man, in particular, treated the whole business as he would an elaborate joke. There would be others like him, hundreds of them, who did not know what it was to struggle in darkness with a flock of birds. There would be parties tonight in London, like the ones they gave on election nights. People standing about, shouting and laughing, getting drunk. 'Come and watch the birds!'

Nat switched off the wireless. He got up and started work on the kitchen windows. His wife watched him, young Johnny at her heels.

'What, boards for down here too?' she said. 'Why, I'll have to light up before three o'clock. I see no call for boards down here.'

'Better be sure than sorry,' answered Nat. 'I'm not going to take any chances.'

'What they ought to do,' she said, 'is to call the army out and shoot the birds. That would soon scare them off.'

'Let them try,' said Nat. 'How'd they set about it?'

'They have the army to the docks,' she answered, 'when the dockers strike. The soldiers go down and unload the ships.'

'Yes,' said Nat, 'and the population of London is eight million or more. Think of all the buildings, all the flats, and houses. Do you think they've enough soldiers to go round shooting birds from every roof?'

'I don't know. But something should be done. They ought to do something.'

Nat thought to himself that 'they' were no doubt considering the problem at that very moment, but whatever 'they' decided to do in London and the big cities would not help the people here, three hundred miles away. Each householder must look after his own.

'How are we off for food?' he said.

'Now, Nat, whatever next?'

'Never mind. What have you got in the larder?'

'It's shopping day tomorrow, you know that. I don't keep uncooked food hanging about, it goes off. Butcher doesn't call till the day after. But I can bring back something when I go in tomorrow.'

Nat did not want to scare her. He thought it possible that she might not go to town tomorrow. He looked in the larder for himself, and in the cupboard where she kept her tins. They would do, for a couple of days. Bread was low.

'What about the baker?'

'He comes tomorrow too.'

He saw she had flour. If the baker did not call she had enough to bake one loaf.

'We'd be better off in the old days,' he said, 'when the women baked twice a week, and had pilchards salted, and there was food for a family to last a siege, if need be.'

'I've tried the children with tinned fish, they don't like it,' she said.

Nat went on hammering the boards across the kitchen windows. Candles. They were low in candles too. That must be another thing she meant to buy tomorrow. Well, it could not be helped. They must go early to bed tonight. That was, if...

He got up and went out of the back door and stood in the garden, looking down towards the sea. There had been no sun all day, and now, at barely three o'clock, a kind of darkness had already come, the sky sullen, heavy, colourless like salt. He could hear the vicious sea drumming on the rocks. He walked down the path, half-way to the beach. And then he stopped. He could see the tide had turned. The rock that had shown in midmorning was now covered, but it was not the sea that held his eyes. The gulls had risen. They were circling, hundreds of them, thousands of them, lifting their wings against the wind. It was the gulls that made the darkening of the sky. And they were silent. They made not a sound. They just went on soaring and circling, rising, falling, trying their strength against the wind.

Nat turned. He ran up the path, back to the cottage.

'I'm going for Jill,' he said. 'I'll wait for her, at the bus-stop.'

'What's the matter?' asked his wife. 'You've gone quite white.'

'Keep Johnny inside,' he said. 'Keep the door shut. Light up now, and draw the curtains.'

'It's only just gone three,' she said.

'Never mind. Do what I tell you.'

He looked inside the toolshed, outside the back door. Nothing there of much use. A spade was too heavy, and a fork no good. He took the hoe. It was the only possible tool, and light enough to carry.

He started walking up the lane to the bus-stop, and now and again glanced back over his shoulder.

The gulls had risen higher now, their circles were broader, wider, they were spreading out in huge formation across the sky.

He hurried on; although he knew the bus would not come to the top of the hill before four o'clock he had to hurry. He passed no one on the way. He was glad of this. No time to stop and chatter.

At the top of the hill he waited. He was much too soon. There was half an hour still to go. The east wind came whipping across the fields from the higher ground. He stamped his feet and blew upon his hands. In the distance he could see the clay hills, white and clean, against the heavy pallor of the sky. Something black rose from behind them, like a smudge at first, then widening, becoming deeper, and the smudge became a cloud, and the cloud divided again into five other clouds, spreading north, east, south and west, and they were not clouds at all; they were birds. He watched them travel across the sky, and as one section passed overhead, within two or three hundred feet of him, he knew, from their speed, they were bound inland, up country, they had no business with the people here on the peninsula. They were rooks, crows, jackdaws, magpies, jays, all birds that usually preyed upon the smaller species; but this afternoon they were bound on some other mission.

'They've been given the towns,' thought Nat, 'they know what they have to do. We don't matter so much here. The gulls will serve for us. The others go to the towns.'

He went to the call-box, stepped inside and lifted the receiver. The exchange would do. They would pass the message on.

'I'm speaking from Highway,' he said, 'by the bus-stop. I want to report large formations of birds travelling up country. The gulls are also forming in the bay.'

'All right,' answered the voice, laconic, weary.

'You'll be sure and pass this message on to the proper quarter?'

'Yes ... yes...' Impatient now, fed-up. The buzzing note resumed.

'She's another,' thought Nat, 'she doesn't care. Maybe she's had to answer calls all day. She hopes to go to the pictures tonight. She'll squeeze some fellow's hand, and point up at the sky, and "Look at all them birds!" She doesn't care.'

The bus came lumbering up the hill. Jill climbed out and three or four other children. The bus went on towards the town.

'What's the hoe for, Dad?'

They crowded around him, laughing, pointing.

'I just brought it along,' he said. 'Come on now, let's get home. It's cold, no hanging about. Here, you. I'll watch you across the fields, see how fast you can run.'

He was speaking to Jill's companions who came from different families, living in the council houses. A short cut would take them to the cottages.

'We want to play a bit in the lane,' said one of them.

'No, you don't. You go off home, or I'll tell your mammy.'

They whispered to one another, round-eyed, then scuttled off across the fields. Jill stared at her father, her mouth sullen.

'We always play in the lane,' she said.

'Not tonight, you don't,' he said. 'Come on now, no dawdling.'

He could see the gulls now, circling the fields, coming in towards the land. Still silent. Still no sound.

'Look, Dad, look over there, look at all the gulls.'

'Yes. Hurry, now.'

'Where are they flying to? Where are they going?'

'Up country, I dare say. Where it's warmer.'

He seized her hand and dragged her after him along the lane.

'Don't go so fast. I can't keep up.'

The gulls were copying the rooks and crows. They were spreading out in formation across the sky. They headed, in bands of thousands, to the four compass points.

'Dad, what is it? What are the gulls doing?'

They were not intent upon their flight, as the crows, as the jackdaws had been. They still circled overhead. Nor did they fly so high. It was as though they waited upon some signal. As though some decision had yet to be given. The order was not clear.

'Do you want me to carry you, Jill? Here, come pick-a-back.'

This way he might put on speed; but he was wrong. Jill was heavy. She kept slipping. And she was crying too. His sense of urgency, of fear, had communicated itself to the child.

'I wish the gulls would go away. I don't like them. They're coming closer to the lane.'

He put her down again. He started running, swinging Jill after him. As they went past the farm turning he saw the farmer backing his car out of the garage. Nat called to him.

'Can you give us a lift?' he said.

'What's that?'

Mr Trigg turned in the driving seat and stared at them. Then a smile came to his cheerful, rubicund face.

'It looks as though we're in for some fun,' he said. 'Have you seen the gulls? Jim and I are going to take a crack at them. Everyone's gone bird crazy, talking of nothing else. I hear you were troubled in the night. Want a gun?'

Nat shook his head.

The small car was packed. There was just room for Jill, if she crouched on top of petrol tins on the back seat.

'I don't want a gun,' said Nat, 'but I'd be obliged if you'd run Jill home. She's scared of the birds.'

He spoke briefly. He did not want to talk in front of Jill.

'OK,' said the farmer, 'I'll take her home. Why don't you stop behind and join the shooting match? We'll make the feathers fly.'

Jill climbed in, and turning the car the driver sped up the lane. Nat followed after. Trigg must be crazy. What use was a gun against a sky of birds?

Now Nat was not responsible for Jill he had time to look about him. The birds were circling still, above the fields. Mostly herring gull, but the black-backed gull amongst them. Usually they kept apart. Now they were united. Some bond had brought them together. It was the black-backed gull that attacked the smaller birds, and even new-born lambs, so he'd heard. He'd never seen it done. He remembered this now, though, looking above him in the sky. They were coming in towards the farm. They were circling lower in the sky, and the black-backed gulls were to the front, the black-backed gulls were leading. The farm, then, was their target. They were making for the farm.

Nat increased his pace towards his own cottage. He saw the farmer's car turn and come back along the lane. It drew up beside him with a jerk.

'The kid has run inside,' said the farmer. 'Your wife was watching for her. Well, what do you make of it? They're saying in town the Russians have done it. The Russians have poisoned the birds.'

'How could they do that?' asked Nat.

'Don't ask me. You know how stories get around. Will you join my shooting match?'

'No, I'll get along home. The wife will be worried else.'

'My missus says if you could eat gull, there'd be some sense in it,' said Trigg, 'we'd have roast gull, baked gull, and pickle 'em into the bargain. You wait until I let off a few barrels into the brutes. That'll scare 'em.'

'Have you boarded your windows?' asked Nat.

'No. Lot of nonsense. They like to scare you on the wireless. I've had more to do today than to go round boarding up my windows.'

'I'd board them now, if I were you.'

'Garn. You're windy. Like to come to our place to sleep?'

'No, thanks all the same.'

'All right. See you in the morning. Give you a gull breakfast.'

The farmer grinned and turned his car to the farm entrance.

Nat hurried on. Past the little wood, past the old barn, and then across the stile to the remaining field.

As he jumped the stile he heard the whirr of wings. A black-backed gull dived down at him from the sky, missed, swerved in flight, and rose to dive again. In a moment it was joined by others, six, seven, a dozen, black-backed and herring mixed. Nat dropped his hoe. The hoe was useless. Covering his head with his arms he ran towards the cottage. They kept coming at him from the air, silent save for the beating wings. The terrible, fluttering wings. He could feel the blood on his hands, his wrists, his neck. Each stab of a swooping beak tore his flesh. If only he could keep them from his eyes. Nothing else mattered. He must keep them from his eyes. They had not learnt yet how to cling to a shoulder, how to rip clothing, how to dive in mass upon the head, upon the body. But with each dive, with each attack, they became bolder. And they had no thought for themselves. When they dived low and missed, they crashed, bruised and broken, on the ground. As Nat ran he stumbled, kicking their spent bodies in front of him.

He found the door, he hammered upon it with his bleeding hands. Because of the boarded windows no light shone. Everything was dark.

'Let me in,' he shouted, 'it's Nat. Let me in.'

He shouted loud to make himself heard above the whirr of the gulls' wings.

Then he saw the gannet, poised for the dive, above him in the sky. The gulls circled, retired, soared, one with another, against the wind. Only the gannet remained. One single gannet, above him in the sky. The wings folded suddenly to its body. It dropped, like a stone. Nat screamed, and the door opened. He stumbled across the threshold, and his wife threw her weight against the door.

They heard the thud of the gannet as it fell.

His wife dressed his wounds. They were not deep. The backs of his hands had suffered most, and his wrists. Had he not worn a cap they would have reached his head. As to the gannet ... the gannet could have split his skull.

The children were crying, of course. They had seen the blood on their father's hands.

'It's all right now,' he told them. 'I'm not hurt. Just a few scratches. You play with Johnny, Jill. Mammy will wash these cuts.'

He half shut the door to the scullery, so that they could not see. His wife was ashen. She began running water from the sink.

'I saw them overhead,' she whispered. 'They began collecting just as Jill ran in with Mr Trigg. I shut the door fast, and it jammed. That's why I couldn't open it at once, when you came.'

'Thank God they waited for me,' he said. 'Jill would have fallen at once. One bird alone would have done it.'

Furtively, so as not to alarm the children, they whispered together, as she bandaged his hands and the back of his neck.

'They're flying inland,' he said, 'thousands of them. Rooks, crows, all the bigger birds. I saw them from the bus-stop. They're making for the towns.'

'But what can they do, Nat?'

'They'll attack. Go for everyone out in the streets. Then they'll try the windows, the chimneys.'

'Why don't the authorities do something? Why don't they get the army, get machine-guns, anything?'

'There's been no time. Nobody's prepared. We'll hear what they have to say on the six o'clock news.'

Nat went back into the kitchen, followed by his wife. Johnny was playing quietly on the floor. Only Jill looked anxious.

'I can hear the birds,' she said. 'Listen, Dad.'

Nat listened. Muffled sounds came from the windows, from the door. Wings brushing the surface, sliding, scraping, seeking a way of entry. The sound of many bodies, pressed together, shuffling on the sills. Now and again came a thud, a crash, as some bird dived and fell. 'Some of them will kill themselves that way,' he thought, 'but not enough. Never enough.'

'All right,' he said aloud, 'I've got boards over the windows, Jill. The birds can't get in.'

He went and examined all the windows. His work had been thorough. Every gap was closed. He would make extra certain, however. He found wedges, pieces of old tin, strips of wood and metal, and fastened them at the sides to reinforce the boards. His hammering helped to deafen the sound of the birds, the shuffling, the tapping, and more ominous – he did not want his wife or the children to hear it – the splinter of cracked glass.

'Turn on the wireless,' he said, 'let's have the wireless.'

This would drown the sound also. He went upstairs to the bedrooms and reinforced the windows there. Now he could hear the birds on the roof, the scraping of claws, a sliding, jostling sound.

He decided they must sleep in the kitchen, keep up the fire, bring down the mattresses and lay them out on the floor. He was afraid of the bedroom chimneys. The boards he had placed at the chimney bases might give way. In the kitchen they would be safe, because of the fire. He would have to make a joke of it. Pretend to the children they were playing at camp. If the worst happened, and the birds forced an entry down the bedroom chimneys, it would be hours, days perhaps, before they could break down the doors. The birds would be imprisoned in the bedrooms. They could do no harm there. Crowded together, they would stifle and die.

He began to bring the mattresses downstairs. At sight of them his wife's eyes widened in apprehension. She thought the birds had already broken in upstairs.

'All right,' he said cheerfully, 'we'll all sleep together in the kitchen tonight. More cosy here by the fire. Then we shan't be worried by those silly old birds tapping at the windows.'

He made the children help him rearrange the furniture, and he took the precaution of moving the dresser, with his wife's help, across the window. It fitted well. It was an added safeguard.

The mattresses could now be lain, one beside the other, against the wall where the dresser had stood.

'We're safe enough now,' he thought, 'we're snug and tight, like an air-raid shelter. We can hold out. It's just the food that worries me. Food, and coal for the fire. We've enough for two or three days, not more. By that time...'

No use thinking ahead as far as that. And they'd be giving directions on the wireless. People would be told what to do. And now, in the midst of many problems, he realized that it was dance music only coming over the air. Not *Children's Hour*, as it should have been. He glanced at the dial. Yes, they were on the Home Service all right. Dance records. He switched to the Light programme. He knew the reason. The usual programmes had been abandoned. This only happened at exceptional times. Elections, and such. He tried to remember if it had happened in the war, during the heavy raids on London. But of course. The BBC was not stationed in London during the war. The programmes were broadcast from other, temporary quarters. 'We're better off here,' he thought, 'we're better off here in the kitchen, with the windows and the doors boarded, than they are up in the towns. Thank God we're not in the towns.'

At six o'clock the records ceased. The time signal was given. No matter if it scared the children, he must hear the news. There was a pause after the pips. Then the announcer spoke. His voice was solemn, grave. Quite different from midday.

'This is London,' he said. 'A National Emergency was proclaimed at four o'clock this afternoon. Measures are being taken to safeguard the lives and property of the population, but it must be understood that these are not easy to effect immediately, owing to the unforeseen and unparalleled nature of the present crisis. Every householder must take precautions to his own building, and where several people live together, as in flats and apartments, they must unite to do the utmost they can to prevent entry. It is absolutely imperative that every individual stays indoors tonight, and that no one at all remains on the streets, or roads, or anywhere without doors. The birds, in vast numbers, are attacking anyone on sight, and have already begun an assault upon buildings; but these, with due care, should be impenetrable.

The population is asked to remain calm, and not to panic. Owing to the exceptional nature of the emergency, there will be no further transmission from any broadcasting station until seven a.m. tomorrow.'

They played the National Anthem. Nothing more happened. Nat switched off the set. He looked at his wife. She stared back at him.

'What's it mean?' said Jill. 'What did the news say?'

'There won't be any more programmes tonight,' said Nat. 'There's been a breakdown at the BBC.'

'Is it the birds?' asked Jill. 'Have the birds done it?'

'No,' said Nat, 'it's just that everyone's very busy, and then of course they have to get rid of the birds, messing everything up, in the towns. Well, we can manage without the wireless for one evening.'

'I wish we had a gramophone,' said Jill, 'that would be better than nothing.'

She had her face turned to the dresser, backed against the windows. Try as they did to ignore it, they were all aware of the shuffling, the stabbing, the persistent beating and sweeping of wings.

'We'll have supper early,' suggested Nat, 'something for a treat. Ask Mammy. Toasted cheese, eh? Something we all like?'

He winked and nodded at his wife. He wanted the look of dread, of apprehension, to go from Jill's face.

He helped with the supper, whistling, singing, making as much clatter as he could, and it seemed to him that the shuffling and the tapping were not so intense as they had been at first. Presently he went up to the bedrooms and listened, and he no longer heard the jostling for place upon the roof.

'They've got reasoning powers,' he thought, 'they know it's hard to break in here. They'll try elsewhere. They won't waste their time with us.'

Supper passed without incident, and then, when they were clearing away, they heard a new sound, droning, familiar, a sound they all knew and understood.

His wife looked up at him, her face alight. 'It's planes,' she said, 'they're sending out planes after the birds. That's what I said they ought to do, all along. That will get them. Isn't that gun-fire? Can't you hear guns?'

It might be gun-fire, out at sea. Nat could not tell. Big naval guns might have an effect upon the gulls out at sea, but the gulls were inland now. The guns couldn't shell the shore, because of the population.

'It's good, isn't it,' said his wife, 'to hear the planes?'

And Jill, catching her enthusiasm, jumped up and down with Johnny. 'The planes will get the birds. The planes will shoot them.'

Just then they heard a crash about two miles distant, followed by a second, then a third. The droning became more distant, passed away out to sea.

'What was that?' asked his wife. 'Were they dropping bombs on the birds?'

'I don't know,' answered Nat, 'I don't think so.'

He did not want to tell her that the sound they had heard was the crashing of aircraft. It was, he had no doubt, a venture on the part of the authorities to send out reconnaissance forces, but they might have known the venture was suicidal. What could aircraft do against birds that flung themselves to death against propeller and fuselage, but hurtle to the ground themselves? This was being tried now, he supposed, over the whole country. And at a cost. Someone high up had lost his head.

'Where have the planes gone, Dad?' asked Jill.

'Back to base,' he said. 'Come on, now, time to tuck down for bed.'

It kept his wife occupied, undressing the children before the fire, seeing to the bedding, one thing and another, while he went round the cottage again, making sure that nothing had worked loose. There was no further drone of aircraft, and the naval guns had ceased. 'Waste of life and effort,' Nat said to himself. 'We can't destroy enough of them that way. Cost too heavy. There's always gas. Maybe they'll try spraying with gas, mustard gas. We'll be warned first, of course, if they do. There's one thing, the best brains of the country will be on to it tonight.'

Somehow the thought reassured him. He had a picture of scientists, naturalists, technicians, and all those chaps they called the back-room boys, summoned to a council; they'd be working on the problem now. This was not a job for the government, for the chiefs-of-staff – they would merely carry out the orders of the scientists.

'They'll have to be ruthless,' he thought. 'Where the trouble's worst they'll have to risk more lives, if they use gas. All the livestock, too, and the soil all contaminated. As long as everyone doesn't panic. That's the trouble. People panicking, losing their heads. The BBC was right to warn us of that.'

Upstairs in the bedrooms all was quiet. No further scraping and stabbing at the windows. A lull in battle. Forces regrouping. Wasn't that what they called it, in the old war-time bulletins? The wind hadn't dropped, though. He could still hear it, roaring in the chimneys. And the sea breaking down on the shore. Then he remembered the tide. The tide would be on the turn. Maybe the lull in battle was because of the tide. There was some law the birds obeyed, and it was all to do with the east wind and the tide.

He glanced at his watch. Nearly eight o'clock. It must have gone high water an hour ago. That explained the lull: the birds attacked with the flood tide. It might not work that way inland, up country, but it seemed as if it was so this way on the coast. He reckoned the time limit in his head. They had six hours to go, without attack. When the tide turned again, around one-twenty in the morning, the birds would come back...

There were two things he could do. The first to rest, with his wife and the children, and all of them snatch what sleep they could, until the small hours. The second to go out, see how they were faring at the farm, see if the telephone was still working there, so that they might get news from the exchange.

He called softly to his wife, who had just settled the children. She came half-way up the stairs and he whispered to her.

'You're not to go,' she said at once, 'you're not to go and leave me alone with the children. I can't stand it.'

Her voice rose hysterically. He hushed her, calmed her.

'All right,' he said, 'all right. I'll wait till morning. And we'll get the wireless bulletin then too, at seven. But in the morning, when the tide ebbs again, I'll try for the farm, and they may let us have bread and potatoes, and milk too.'

His mind was busy again, planning against emergency. They would not have milked, of course, this evening. The cows would be standing by the gate, waiting in the yard, with the household inside, battened behind boards, as they were here at the cottage. That is, if they had time to take precautions. He thought of the farmer, Trigg, smiling at him from the car. There would have been no shooting party, not tonight.

The children were asleep. His wife, still clothed, was sitting on her mattress. She watched him, her eyes nervous.

'What are you going to do?' she whispered.

He shook his head for silence. Softly, stealthily, he opened the back door and looked outside.

It was pitch dark. The wind was blowing harder than ever, coming in steady gusts, icy, from the sea. He kicked at the step outside the door. It was heaped with birds. There were dead birds everywhere. Under the windows, against the walls. These were the suicides, the divers, the ones with broken necks. Wherever he looked he saw dead birds. No trace of the living. The living had flown seaward with the turn of the tide. The gulls would be riding the seas now, as they had done in the forenoon.

In the far distance, on the hill where the tractor had been two days before, something was burning. One of the aircraft that had crashed; the fire, fanned by the wind, had set light to a stack.

He looked at the bodies of the birds, and he had a notion that if he heaped them, one upon the other, on the window sills they would make added protection for the next attack. Not much, perhaps, but something. The bodies would have to be clawed at, pecked, and dragged aside, before the living birds gained purchase on the sills and attacked the panes. He set to work in the darkness. It was queer; he hated touching them. The bodies were still warm and bloody. The blood matted their feathers. He felt his stomach turn, but he went on with his work. He noticed, grimly, that every window-pane was shattered. Only the boards had kept the birds from breaking in. He stuffed the cracked panes with the bleeding bodies of the birds.

When he had finished he went back into the cottage. He barricaded the kitchen door, made it doubly secure. He took off his bandages, sticky with the birds' blood, not with his own cuts, and put on fresh plaster.

His wife had made him cocoa and he drank it thirstily. He was very tired.

'All right,' he said, smiling, 'don't worry. We'll get through.'

He lay down on his mattress and closed his eyes. He slept at once. He dreamt uneasily, because through his dreams there ran a thread of something forgotten. Some piece of work, neglected, that he should have done. Some precaution that he had known well but had not taken, and he could not put a name to it in his dreams. It was connected in some way with the burning aircraft and the stack upon the hill. He went on sleeping, though; he did not awake. It was his wife shaking his shoulder that awoke him finally.

'They've begun,' she sobbed, 'they've started this last hour, I can't listen to it any longer, alone. There's something smelling bad too, something burning.'

Then he remembered. He had forgotten to make up the fire. It was smouldering, nearly out. He got up swiftly and lit the lamp. The hammering had started at the windows and the doors, but it was not that he minded now. It was the smell of singed feathers. The smell filled the kitchen. He knew at once what it was. The birds were coming down the chimney, squeezing their way down to the kitchen range.

He got sticks and paper and put them on the embers, then reached for the can of paraffin.

'Stand back,' he shouted to his wife, 'we've got to risk this.'

He threw the paraffin on to the fire. The flame roared up the pipe, and down upon the fire fell the scorched, blackened bodies of the birds.

The children woke, crying. 'What is it?' said Jill. 'What's happened?'

Nat had no time to answer. He was raking the bodies from the chimney, clawing them out on to the floor. The flames still roared, and the danger of the chimney catching fire was one he had to take. The flames would send away the living birds from the chimney top. The lower joint was the difficulty, though. This was choked with the smouldering helpless bodies of the birds caught by fire. He scarcely heeded the attack on the windows and the door: let them beat their wings, break their beaks, lose their lives, in the attempt to force an entry into his home. They would not break in. He thanked God he had one of the old cottages, with small windows, stout walls. Not like the new council houses. Heaven help them up the lane, in the new council houses.

'Stop crying,' he called to the children. 'There's nothing to be afraid of, stop crying.'

He went on raking at the burning, smouldering bodies as they fell into the fire.

'This'll fetch them,' he said to himself, 'the draught and the flames together. We're all right, as long as the chimney doesn't catch. I ought to be shot for this. It's all my fault. Last thing I should have made up the fire. I knew there was something.'

Amid the scratching and tearing at the window boards came the sudden homely striking of the kitchen clock. Three a.m. A little more than four hours yet to go. He could not be sure of the exact time of high water. He reckoned it would not turn much before half past seven, twenty to eight.

'Light up the primus,' he said to his wife. 'Make us some tea, and the kids some cocoa. No use sitting around doing nothing.'

That was the line. Keep her busy, and the children too. Move about, eat, drink; always best to be on the go.

He waited by the range. The flames were dying. But no more blackened bodies fell from the chimney. He thrust his poker up as far as it could go and found nothing. It was clear. The chimney was clear. He wiped the sweat from his forehead.

'Come on now, Jill,' he said, 'bring me some more sticks. We'll have a good fire going directly.' She wouldn't come near him, though. She was staring at the heaped singed bodies of the birds.

'Never mind them,' he said, 'we'll put those in the passage when I've got the fire steady?'

The danger of the chimney was over. It could not happen again, not if the fire was kept burning day and night.

'I'll have to get more fuel from the farm tomorrow,' he thought. 'This will never last. I'll manage, though. I can do all that with the ebb tide. It can be worked, fetching what we need, when the tide's turned. We've just got to adapt ourselves, that's all.'

They drank tea and cocoa and ate slices of bread and Bovril. Only half a loaf left, Nat noticed. Never mind though, they'd get by.

'Stop it,' said young Johnny, pointing to the windows with his spoon, 'stop it, you old birds.'

'That's right,' said Nat, smiling, 'we don't want the old beggars, do we? Had enough of 'em.'

They began to cheer when they heard the thud of the suicide birds.

'There's another, Dad,' cried Jill, 'he's done for.'

'He's had it,' said Nat, 'there he goes, the blighter.'

This was the way to face up to it. This was the spirit. If they could keep this up, hang on like this until seven, when the first news bulletin came through, they would not have done too badly.

'Give us a fag,' he said to his wife. 'A bit of a smoke will clear away the smell of the scorched feathers.'

'There's only two left in the packet,' she said. 'I was going to buy you some from the Co-op.'

'I'll have one,' he said, 't'other will keep for a rainy day.'

No sense trying to make the children rest. There was no rest to be got while the tapping and the scratching went on at the windows. He sat with one arm round his wife and the other round Jill, with Johnny on his mother's lap and the blankets heaped about them on the mattress.

'You can't help admiring the beggars,' he said, 'they've got persistence. You'd think they'd tire of the game, but not a bit of it.'

Admiration was hard to sustain. The tapping went on and on and a new rasping note struck Nat's ear, as though a sharper beak than any hitherto had come to take over from its fellows. He tried to remember the names of birds, he tried to think which species would go for this particular job. It was not the tap of the woodpecker. That would be light and frequent. This was more serious, because if it continued long the wood would splinter as the glass had done. Then he remembered the hawks. Could the hawks have taken over from the gulls? Were there buzzards now upon the sills, using talons as well as beaks? Hawks, buzzards, kestrels, falcons — he had forgotten the birds of prey. He had forgotten the gripping power of the birds of prey. Three hours to go, and while they waited the sound of the splintering wood, the talons tearing at the wood.

Nat looked about him, seeing what furniture he could destroy to fortify the door. The windows were safe, because of the dresser. He was not certain of the door. He went upstairs, but when he reached the landing he paused and listened. There was a soft patter on the floor of the children's bedroom. The birds had broken through… He put his ear to the door. No mistake. He could hear the rustle of wings, and the light patter as they searched the floor. The other bedroom was still clear. He went into it and began bringing out the furniture, to pile at the head of the stairs should the door of the children's bedroom go. It was a preparation. It might never be needed. He could not stack the furniture against the door, because it opened inward. The only possible thing was to have it at the top of the stairs.

'Come down, Nat, what are you doing?' called his wife.

'I won't be long,' he shouted. 'Just making everything ship-shape up here.'

He did not want her to come; he did not want her to hear the pattering of the feet in the children's bedroom, the brushing of those wings against the door.

At five-thirty he suggested breakfast, bacon and fried bread, if only to stop the growing look of panic in his wife's eyes and to calm the fretful children. She did not know about the birds upstairs. The bedroom, luckily, was not over the kitchen. Had it been so she could not have failed to hear the sound of them, up there, tapping the board. And the silly, senseless thud of the suicide birds, the death-and-glory boys, who flew into the bedroom, smashing their heads against the walls. He knew them of old, the herring gulls. They had no brains. The black-backs were different, they knew what they were doing. So did the buzzards, the hawks…

He found himself watching the clock, gazing at the hands that went so slowly round the dial. If his theory was not correct, if the attack did not cease with the turn of the tide, he knew they were beaten. They could not continue through the long day without air, without rest, without more fuel, without… his mind raced. He knew there were so many things they needed to withstand siege. They were not fully prepared. They were not ready. It might be that it would be safer in the towns after all. If he could get a message through, on the farm telephone, to his cousin, only a short journey by train up country, they might be able to hire a car. That would be quicker – hire a car between tides…

His wife's voice, calling his name, drove away the sudden, desperate desire for sleep.

'What is it? What now?' he said sharply.

'The wireless,' said his wife. 'I've been watching the clock. It's nearly seven.'

'Don't twist the knob,' he said, impatient for the first time, 'it's on the Home where it is. They'll speak from the Home.'

They waited. The kitchen clock struck seven. There was no sound. No chimes, no music. They waited until a quarter past, switching to the Light. The result was the same. No news bulletin came through.

'We've heard wrong,' he said, 'they won't be broadcasting until eight o'clock.'

They left it switched on, and Nat thought of the battery, wondered how much power was left in it. It was generally recharged when his wife went shopping in the town. If the battery failed they would not hear the instructions.

'It's getting light,' whispered his wife, 'I can't see it, but I can feel it. And the birds aren't hammering so loud.'

She was right. The rasping, tearing sound grew fainter every moment. So did the shuffling, the jostling for place upon the step, upon the sills. The tide was on the turn. By eight there was no sound at all. Only the wind. The children, lulled at last by the stillness, fell asleep. At half past eight Nat switched the wireless off.

'What are you doing? We'll miss the news,' said his wife.

'There isn't going to be any news,' said Nat. 'We've got to depend upon ourselves.'

He went to the door and slowly pulled away the barricades. He drew the bolts, and kicking the bodies from the step outside the door breathed the cold air. He had six working hours before him, and he knew he must reserve his strength for the right things, not waste it in any way. Food, and light, and fuel; these were the necessary things. If he could get them in sufficiency, they could endure another night.

He stepped into the garden, and as he did so he saw the living birds. The gulls had gone to ride the sea, as they had done before; they sought sea food, and the buoyancy of the tide, before they returned to the attack. Not so the land birds. They waited and watched. Nat saw them, on the hedgerows, on the soil, crowded in the trees, outside in the field, line upon line of birds, all still, doing nothing.

He went to the end of his small garden. The birds did not move. They went on watching him.

'I've got to get food,' said Nat to himself, 'I've got to go to the farm to find food.'

He went back to the cottage. He saw to the windows and the doors. He went upstairs and opened the children's bedroom. It was empty, except for the dead birds on the floor. The living were out there, in the garden, in the fields. He went downstairs.

'I'm going to the farm,' he said.

His wife clung to him. She had seen the living birds from the open door.

'Take us with you,' she begged, 'we can't stay here alone. I'd rather die than stay here alone.'

He considered the matter. He nodded.

'Come on, then,' he said, 'bring baskets, and Johnny's pram. We can load up the pram.'

They dressed against the biting wind, wore gloves and scarves.

His wife put Johnny in the pram. Nat took Jill's hand.

'The birds,' she whimpered, 'they're all out there, in the fields.'

'They won't hurt us,' he said, 'not in the light.'

They started walking across the field towards the stile, and the birds did not move. They waited, their heads turned to the wind.

When they reached the turning to the farm, Nat stopped and told his wife to wait in the shelter of the hedge with the two children.

'But I want to see Mrs Trigg,' she protested. 'There are lots of things we can borrow, if they went to market yesterday; not only bread, and...'

'Wait here,' Nat interrupted. 'I'll be back in a moment.'

The cows were lowing, moving restlessly in the yard, and he could see a gap in the fence where the sheep had knocked their way through, to roam unchecked in the front garden before the farm-house. No smoke came from the chimneys. He was filled with misgiving. He did not want his wife or the children to go down to the farm.

'Don't jib now,' said Nat, harshly, 'do what I say.'

She withdrew with the pram into the hedge, screening herself and the children from the wind.

He went down alone to the farm. He pushed his way through the herd of bellowing cows, which turned this way and that, distressed, their udders full. He saw the car standing by the gate, not put away in the garage. The windows of the farm-house were smashed. There were many dead gulls lying in the yard and around the house. The living birds perched on the group of trees behind the farm and on the roof of the house. They were quite still. They watched him.

Jim's body lay in the yard ... what was left of it. When the birds had finished, the cows had trampled him. His gun was beside him. The door of the house was shut and bolted, but as the windows were smashed it was easy to lift them and climb through. Trigg's body was close to the telephone. He must have been trying to get through to the exchange when the birds came for him. The receiver was hanging loose, the instrument torn from the wall. No sign of Mrs Trigg. She would be upstairs. Was it any use going up? Sickened, Nat knew what he would find.

'Thank God,' he said to himself, 'there were no children.'

He forced himself to climb the stairs, but half-way he turned and descended again. He could see her legs, protruding from the open bedroom door. Beside her were the bodies of the black-backed gulls, and an umbrella, broken.

'It's no use,' thought Nat, 'doing anything. I've only got five hours, less than that. The Triggs would understand. I must load up with what I can find.'

He tramped back to his wife and children.

'I'm going to fill up the car with stuff,' he said. 'I'll put coal in it, and paraffin for the primus. We'll take it home and return for a fresh load.'

'What about the Triggs?' asked his wife.

'They must have gone to friends,' he said.

'Shall I come and help you, then?'

'No; there's a mess down there. Cows and sheep all over the place. Wait, I'll get the car. You can sit in it.'

Clumsily he backed the car out of the yard and into the lane. His wife and the children could not see Jim's body from there.

'Stay here,' he said, 'never mind the pram. The pram can be fetched later. I'm going to load the car.'

Her eyes watched his all the time. He believed she understood, otherwise she would have suggested helping him to find the bread and groceries.

They made three journeys altogether, backwards and forwards between their cottage and the farm, before he was satisfied they had everything they needed. It was surprising, once he started thinking, how many things were necessary. Almost the most important of all was planking for the windows. He had to go round searching for timber. He wanted to renew the boards on all the windows at the cottage. Candles, paraffin, nails, tinned stuff; the list was endless. Besides all that, he milked three of the cows. The rest, poor brutes, would have to go on bellowing.

On the final journey he drove the car to the bus-stop, got out, and went to the telephone box. He waited a few minutes, jangling the receiver. No good, though. The line was dead. He climbed on to a bank and looked over the countryside, but there was no sign of life at all, nothing in the fields but the waiting, watching birds. Some of them slept – he could see the beaks tucked into the feathers.

'You'd think they'd be feeding,' he said to himself, 'not just standing in that way.'

Then he remembered. They were gorged with food. They had eaten their fill during the night. That was why they did not move this morning…

No smoke came from the chimneys of the council houses. He thought of the children who had run across the fields the night before.

'I should have known,' he thought, 'I ought to have taken them home with me.'

He lifted his face to the sky. It was colourless and grey. The bare trees on the landscape looked bent and blackened by the east wind. The cold did not affect the living birds, waiting out there in the fields.

'This is the time they ought to get them,' said Nat, 'they're a sitting target now. They must be doing this all over the country. Why don't our aircraft take off now and spray them with mustard gas? What are all our chaps doing? They must know, they must see for themselves.'

He went back to the car and got into the driver's seat.

'Go quickly past that second gate,' whispered his wife. 'The postman's lying there. I don't want Jill to see.'

He accelerated. The little Morris bumped and rattled along the lane. The children shrieked with laughter.

'Up-a-down, up-a-down,' shouted young Johnny.

It was a quarter to one by the time they reached the cottage. Only an hour to go.

'Better have cold dinner,' said Nat. 'Hot up something for

yourself and the children, some of that soup. I've no time to eat now. I've got to unload all this stuff.'

He got everything inside the cottage. It could be sorted later. Give them all something to do during the long hours ahead. First he must see to the windows and the doors.

He went round the cottage methodically, testing every window, every door. He climbed on to the roof also, and fixed boards across every chimney, except the kitchen. The cold was so intense he could hardly bear it, but the job had to be done. Now and again he would look up, searching the sky for aircraft. None came. As he worked he cursed the inefficiency of the authorities.

'It's always the same,' he muttered, 'they always let us down. Muddle, muddle, from the start. No plan, no real organisation. And we don't matter, down here. That's what it is. The people up country have priority. They're using gas up there, no doubt, and all the aircraft. We've got to wait and take what comes.'

He paused, his work on the bedroom chimney finished, and looked out to sea. Something was moving out there. Something grey and white amongst the breakers.

'Good old Navy,' he said, 'they never let us down. They're coming down channel, they're turning in the bay.'

He waited, straining his eyes, watering in the wind, towards the sea. He was wrong, though. It was not ships. The Navy was not there. The gulls were rising from the sea. The massed flocks in the fields, with ruffled feathers, rose in formation from the ground, and wing to wing soared upwards to the sky.

The tide had turned again.

Nat climbed down the ladder and went inside the kitchen. The family were at dinner. It was a little after two. He bolted the door, put up the barricade, and lit the lamp.

'It's night-time,' said young Johnny.

His wife had switched on the wireless once again, but no sound came from it.

251

'I've been all round the dial,' she said, 'foreign stations, and that lot. I can't get anything.'

'Maybe they have the same trouble,' he said, 'maybe it's the same right through Europe.'

She poured out a plateful of the Triggs' soup, cut him a large slice of the Triggs' bread, and spread their dripping upon it.

They ate in silence. A piece of the dripping ran down young Johnny's chin and fell on to the table.

'Manners, Johnny,' said Jill, 'you should learn to wipe your mouth.'

The tapping began at the windows, at the door. The rustling, the jostling, the pushing for position on the sills. The first thud of the suicide gulls upon the step.

'Won't America do something?' said his wife. 'They've always been our allies, haven't they? Surely America will do something?'

Nat did not answer. The boards were strong against the windows, and on the chimneys too. The cottage was filled with stores, with fuel, with all they needed for the next few days. When he had finished dinner he would put the stuff away, stack it neatly, get everything shipshape, handy-like. His wife could help him, and the children too. They'd tire themselves out, between now and a quarter to nine, when the tide would ebb; then he'd tuck them down on their mattresses, see that they slept good and sound until three in the morning.

He had a new scheme for the windows, which was to fix barbed wire in front of the boards. He had brought a great roll of it from the farm. The nuisance was, he'd have to work at this in the dark, when the lull came between nine and three. Pity he had not thought of it before. Still, as long as the wife slept, and the kids, that was the main thing.

The smaller birds were at the window now. He recognized the light tap-tapping of their beaks, and the soft brush of their wings. The hawks ignored the windows. They concentrated their attack upon the door. Nat listened to the tearing sound of splintering wood, and wondered how many million years of memory were stored in those little brains, behind the stabbing beaks, the piercing eyes, now giving them this instinct to destroy mankind with all the deft precision of machines.

'I'll smoke that last fag,' he said to his wife. 'Stupid of me, it was the one thing I forgot to bring back from the farm.'

He reached for it, switched on the silent wireless. He threw the empty packet on the fire, and watched it burn.

Biographical Notes

Born in Bath in 1984, Socrates Adams-Florou lives in Manchester and works as a bookseller. His first novel, *Everything's Fine*, is due to be published by Transmission Print in October 2011. He has had short stories published in *Shoestring* and *Word Soup: Year One* and online at *Metazen*. He blogs at *Chicken and Pies*.

Born in Nottinghamshire in 1971, Stephen Bacon lives in South Yorkshire with his wife and two sons. He has published numerous short stories in a variety of magazines and anthologies, including, most recently, *Where the Heart Is* (ed Gary Fry), *The Sixth Black Book of Horror* (ed Charles Black), *Dark Horizons*, and the last three editions of DF Lewis's *Nemonymous* project.

Bill Broady is the author of two novels, *Swimmer* (2001) and *Eternity is Temporary* (2006), and a short story collection, *In This Block There Lives a Slag* (2002). He is currently writing his third novel, *The Night-Soil Men*. With Jane Metcalfe he edited Redbeck Press's *You Are Here: The Redbeck Anthology of Contemporary Short Stories* (2006).

Neil Campbell was born in Audenshaw, Manchester, in 1973. His poems and stories have appeared in a number of small press magazines; he was a founder-editor of *Lamport Court* (2003-8). Currently studying for a PhD in short story writing at Northumbria University, he is the author of two short story collections published by Salt, *Broken Doll* and *Pictures From Hopper*, as well as two poetry chapbooks, *Birds* (Knives Forks and Spoons Press) and *Bugsworth Diary* (forthcoming from the same publisher).

Born and brought up in Switzerland, Regi Claire now lives with writer Ron Butlin in Edinburgh and is the author of *Fighting It* (2009; shortlisted for the Saltire Book of the Year Award, longlisted for the Edge Hill Short Story Prize), *The Beauty Room* (2002; longlisted for the Allen Lane/MIND Book of the Year Award) and *Inside~Outside* (1998; shortlisted for the Saltire First Book of the Year Award).

Daphne du Maurier was born in London in 1907 but lived most of her life in Cornwall, where her surroundings inspired her most celebrated novels, *Jamaica Inn*, *Frenchman's Creek* and *Rebecca*. Her short story 'The Birds', which appeared in her 1952 collection *The Apple Tree*, was the third of her works to be adapted for film by Alfred Hitchcock. The author of dozens of novels, short story collections and works of non-fiction, she died in 1989.

Tom Fletcher was born in Worcester in 1984, but has spent most of his life in west Cumbria. He now lives with his wife in Manchester. He writes a blog, *The Endist*, and is the author of two novels, *The Leaping* (2010) and *The Thing on the Shore* (2011), as well as a number of short stories.

Adèle Geras was born in Jerusalem in 1944. Since becoming a full-time writer in 1976, she has published more than ninety books for children and young adults as well as four novels for adults – *Facing the Light*, *Hester's Story*, *Made in Heaven* and

255

A Hidden Life. Having lived in Manchester for forty years, she and her husband Norman Geras recently moved to Cambridge.

Bruce Gilbert was co-founder of Wire, and responsible for much of the band's guitar work and many of its lyrics. Alongside Wire, he has worked on numerous solo projects and has collaborated with many other artists. In 2004, he left Wire to concentrate on other projects. 'Sliding Off the World' was included as a spoken-word piece set to music on the compilation CD *Touch 25* (Touch). It appears here in print for the first time.

Born in Pennsylvania in 1925, Russell Hoban has lived in London since 1969. He is the author of sixteen novels, including *Riddley Walker*, *Amaryllis Night and Day* and *Angelica Lost and Found*, and numerous children's books. His 1975 novel *Turtle Diary* was made into a film with a screenplay by Harold Pinter and starring Glenda Jackson and Ben Kingsley. 'The Raven' is taken from *The Moment Under the Moment*, a 1992 collection comprising stories, a libretto, essays and sketches.

Laura Ellen Joyce was born in Birmingham in 1981. She has published stories and poetry in *Succour* and has contributed stories to Interact Reading Service, a charity that provides reading therapy for stroke patients. She won the Anchor Press Top 100 Award for Poetry in 1999 and now works as a creative literacy tutor and disability support worker in Manchester. Her first novel, *The Museum of Atheism*, is forthcoming from Salt Publishing's new crime imprint.

Anna Kavan was born Helen Emily Woods in Cannes in 1901. She wrote almost two dozen novels and short story collections, including *Asylum Piece*, *Eagles' Nest*, *Ice* and *I Am Lazarus*, from which 'The Gannets' is taken; *Sleep Has*

His House (1948) is a unique blend of memoir, experimental fiction and dream diary. She worked as a secretary for literary journal *Horizon*, to which she contributed numerous stories and reviews. She died in 1968.

Michael Kelly lives in Pickering, Ontario. He is the author of two short story collections, *Scratching the Surface* and *Undertow and Other Laments*, as well as co-author of the novel *Ouroboros*. His short fiction has appeared in a number of books and magazines and he has edited three anthologies, *Songs From Dead Singers*, *Apparitions* and *Chilling Tales*. His small press, Undertow Publications, is behind a new journal, *Shadows & Tall Trees*, published each October.

Deborah Kermode was born in Reading shortly after her twin brother. The family moved around – Manchester, the US, Bristol – before settling in north London, where she has remained. She worked in film and TV, producing music videos then working on documentaries, and for the last ten years has been a freelance copywriter. During that time she has written two and a half novels and two short stories. 'The Candling' is her first published short story.

Joel Lane is the author of two novels, *From Blue to Black* and *The Blue Mask*; three short story collections, *The Earth Wire*, *The Lost District* and *The Terrible Changes*; a novella, *The Witnesses Are Gone*; and three volumes of poetry, *The Edge of the Screen*, *Trouble in the Heartland* and *The Autumn Myth*. He has edited two anthologies of short stories, *Birmingham Noir* (with Steve Bishop) and *Beneath the Ground*. Born in Exeter in 1963, he lives in Birmingham.

Adam Marek was born in 1974. His stories have appeared

in *Prospect*, *New Writing 15*, *Parenthesis* and elsewhere. He lives in Bedfordshire with his wife and sons. His collection, *Instruction Manual for Swallowing*, was long-listed for the Frank O'Connor Prize, and in 2010 he was shortlisted for the *Sunday Times* EFG Private Bank Prize. In January 2011 he was awarded an Arts Foundation Fellowship in Short Story Writing, whereupon he left his editorial job at the RSPB to write full time.

Claire Massey's fiction, poetry and articles have appeared in *Cabinet des Fées*, *Enchanted Conversation*, *Flax*, *Rainy City Stories*, *Magpie Magazine*, *Brittle Star* and *The Best British Short Stories 2011*. She was founder-editor of online magazine *New Fairy Tales* and has recently started up a new online project, *Paraxis*, at paraxis.org, with Andy Hedgecock. She lives in Lancashire with her two young sons.

Angelica Michelis is a Senior Lecturer in English at Manchester Metropolitan University. She is the author of *Women, Poets and Other Mysteries: Feminist Theory and 20th Century British and American Women's Poetry* and co-editor (with Antony Rowland) of *Choosing Tough Words: The Poetry of Carol Ann Duffy*. Forthcoming is *Eating Theory: A Theory of Eating*, a monograph for Manchester University Press. Her research specialisms include the Gothic and the relationship between art, writing and gender.

Alison Moore was born in Manchester in 1971. Since 2000, her short stories have been published in various magazines and anthologies including *The Best British Short Stories 2011*. She was awarded first prize in the Novella category of The New Writer Prose and Poetry Prizes 2009, and has been shortlisted for the Bridport Prize, the Fish Prize and the

Manchester Fiction Prize. She lives in Leicestershire with her husband and young son.

Originally from California, GA Pickin came to Britain as a student and settled in the UK permanently in 1976. Now living in Stranraer, she sings and plays guitar and concertina in a band, Luce Women, specialising in traditional music. Her short stories have appeared in a number of anthologies, including *New Scottish Writing 1997*, from which 'Flight of Fancy' was taken. A new story, 'Remains', has been published as a chapbook by Nightjar Press.

Geeta Roopnarine is a visual artist born in Trinidad and Tobago and now living in Greece. She has participated in eleven group shows and has had one solo exhibition. In addition, she has provided illustrations for three collections of poetry. 'Corbeaux Bay' is her first published short story and she is currently at work on her first novel.

David Rose was born in 1949 and lives in Middlesex. A co-founder of literary magazine *Main Street Journal*, his short fiction has appeared in a range of magazines and anthologies, as well as a mini-collection, *Stripe*, and a chapbook, *Being a Greek*, both from Black Bile Press of Ottawa. His first novel, *Vault*, was published in 2011 and is due to be followed by a short story collection, *Posthumous Stories*.

Nicholas Royle was born in 1957 and lives in Seaford, East Sussex. He has written numerous books on literature, including *Telepathy and Literature*, *The Uncanny*, and *Veering*. Previous short stories appeared in *Succour* and *Neonlit: Time Out Book of New Writing Volume 2*. His first novel, *Quilt*, was published in 2010.

RB Russell is the author of two collections of short stories – *Putting the Pieces in Place* (Ex Occidente Press) and *Literary Remains* (PS Publishing) – and a novella, *Bloody Baudelaire* (Ex Occidente Press). Born in Sussex in 1966 and now living in the Yorkshire Dales, he runs Tartarus Press with his wife, Rosalie Parker.

Jack Trevor Story was born in 1917. He was the author of many novels, including *The Trouble With Harry* (filmed by Alfred Hitchcock) and *Live Now, Pay Later*, and of a regular column in the *Guardian* newspaper in the 1970s. He also wrote numerous film scripts, radio plays, episodes of TV drama series, short stories and a run of crime novellas for the Sexton Blake Library. He died in 1991.

Elizabeth Stott was born in Kent and now lives in Cumbria with her husband and occasional children. After taking a degree in physics, she worked in industry. She started writing when her children were young and has published fiction and poetry in various places; a short collection of stories, *Familiar Possessions* (Northern Lights), appeared in 2002. She has two novels in preparation.

Emma Jane Unsworth's short fiction has been published by Comma, *Prospect*, Redbeck Press and Channel 4 Books. She has worked as a journalist in Manchester for many years and currently writes a fortnightly column for the *Big Issue in the North*. Her first novel, *Hungry, the Stars and Everything*, was published by the Hidden Gem Press in 2011.

Mark Valentine's short stories have been collected most recently in *The Nightfarers* (Ex Occidente Press) and *The Mascarons of the Late Empire & Other Studies* (Ex Occidente Press), and his series of tales about an occult detective was recently assembled as *The Collected Connoisseur* (Tartarus Press, with John Howard). He lives in North Yorkshire with his wife Jo and their cat Percy.

Marc Werner was born in London in 1968. His stories have appeared in *The Time Out Book of Paris Short Stories* and *The Time Out Book of London Short Stories Volume 2*. His story in *'68: New Stories From Children of the Revolution* was reprinted in *Best British Crime 8*. He has published art criticism in *Art Review*. Living in London, he works as a journalist and photographer and is writing a novel and more short stories.

Born in 1970, Juliet West grew up in Worthing. She worked as a journalist before taking an MA in Creative Writing at Chichester University. She has won prizes for poetry and short stories, including the HE Bates Prize 2009, and her short stories have appeared online and in the *New Writer* magazine. She lives in West Sussex and is currently working part-time as a copywriter.

Conrad Williams was born in Warrington in 1969. He is the author of seven novels, including *Head Injuries*, *One* and *Loss of Separation*, four novellas (*Nearly People*, *Game*, *The Scalding Rooms* and *Rain*) and a collection of short stories, *Use Once Then Destroy*. He has won the August Derleth Award for Best Novel and the International Horror Guild Award for Best Novel. He lives in Manchester with his wife and three sons.

Acknowledgements

'Dead Bird', copyright © Socrates Adams-Florou 2011

'Husks', copyright © Stephen Bacon 2011

'The Brids', copyright © Bill Broady 2011

'Barren Clough', copyright © Neil Campbell 2011

'When the Red, Red Robin', copyright © Regi Claire 2011

'The Birds', copyright © Daphne du Maurier 1952, was first published in *The Apple Tree*, and is reprinted by kind permission of the author's estate

'Huginn and Muninn', copyright © Tom Fletcher 2011

'Tsipporah', copyright © Adèle Geras 1994, was first published in *The Kingfisher Book of Scary Stories*, and is reprinted by kind permission of the author

'Sliding Off the World', copyright © Bruce Gilbert 2006, was included as a spoken-word piece set to music on the CD *Touch 25* (Touch) and is printed here by kind permision of the author and Mike Harding of Touch www.touchmusic.org.uk

'The Raven', copyright © Russell Hoban 1992, was first published in *The Moment Under the Moment*, and is reprinted by kind permission of the author

Two Ravens Press is the most remote literary publisher in the UK, operating from a working croft by the sea, right at the end of the most westerly road on the Isle of Lewis in the Outer Hebrides. Our approach to publishing is as radical as our location: Two Ravens Press is run by two writers with a passion for language and for books that are non-formulaic and that take risks. We publish cutting-edge and innovative contemporary fiction, nonfiction and poetry.

Visit our website for comprehensive information on all of our books and authors – and for much more:

- browse all Two Ravens Press books (print books and e-books too) by category or by author, and purchase them online at an average 20% discount on retail price, post & packing-free (in the UK, and for a small fee overseas)

- there is a separate page for each book, including summaries, extracts and reviews, and a page for each of our authors, including interviews, biographies and photographs.

www.tworavenspress.com